The Gaia Effect

By Claire Buss

 New Generation Publishing

For Kevin

Chapter One

CORPCHAT: Corporation's 150th Anniversary Lottery winners receive Collection today - what would you choose? Join the virtual conversation in social hub beta throughout the day.

The light-alarm filled the square bedroom with a warm yellow glow that grew brighter and brighter. Kira Jenkins snuggled deeper into the sheets, reluctant to move. Suddenly she sat up, brown eyes wide open, her short brown hair sticking out at odd angles.

'It's today, it's today,' she squealed, turning to shake her husband. 'Jed. Wake up! It's today!'

Jed grunted, still half asleep. 'Synth-caf?' he asked as he opened one pale grey eye.

Ten minutes later they were both air washed and dressed in standard Corporation tunic and trousers, dark blue for Jed and a mix of forest green and cream for his wife. They stood in the tiny kitchen area of their open plan living space, glancing at each other in excitement as they tried to do normal things like eat breakfast and drink their stimulants. Kira fished out her handheld from her tunic pocket.

'Hey hon, look - we made top sweep.'

She held the touchscreen up for Jed to see, then began flicking through her dailies and saw one from her friend Ruth.

MADSR: Luck K, you'll be a great Mum - so proud xx

Kira saved the message. Her friends, Ruth and Martha, firmly supported the unusual choice she'd made to parent naturally. Most of their family and work colleagues thought it was peculiar. Putting the handheld back in her pocket, Kira picked up her cup and held it in both hands, sipping the hot drink looking up at her husband over the

1

rim.

'You're not likely to get pulled into work tomorrow afternoon, are you?'

'No, should be fine love.' Jed picked up his breakfast bowl. 'Who's coming again?'

Kira rolled her eyes at him in mock exasperation as she ticked the guests off her fingers.

'Our parents, your sister, Pete obviously, Martha and Ruth and her latest fledgling, some of my work colleagues, some of yours – oh, and your cousins. Did you know they're studying at The Academy?'

Jed nodded, his mouth full of food. Before he could speak the vidcom on the wall in the lounge area chimed. Kira walked over and touched the illuminated panel to accept the call.

'Hi Mum.'

'Oh my goodness.' Jean Bishop's smiling round face and twinkly brown eyes appeared on screen. 'I'm so excited for you. Are you ready? Do you think she'll have brown hair like you or will she be darker like Jed. Oh it' s so exciting. Did you think about getting the neural jack like I told you? I don't know why you want to be so natural, it's not normal honey. Did I tell you about that girl over on Fifth? Terrible time she had, just terrible and that was all because she didn't want the NanNan....'

Jed watched in amusement as his wife tried to get a word in edgeways. He kissed her on the cheek, motioning that he had to leave for work but she stopped him by waving at the vidcom link. It was flashing blue. Another call was coming through, this time audio only.

Jed answered the call on his ear comm, the implanted chip that allowed the user to receive and make audio calls. 'Hello?'

'Oh good, I got you before work. Your father and I have been talking, Jeddidah, and we agree it's not the right time. Don't you think you should wait? Early Collection never goes well. You recently became the youngest detective on Force and raising children is hard work - do you really think you should be splitting your focus now? At least choose the early years option, it really is a wonderful time saver...'

Jed rolled his eyes at Kira as he left, taking the call with him. He walked down the corridor to the lift, descended four floors into the foyer of their apartment building and out through the double doors, murmuring in all the right places until he reached the public skimmer stop.

'Mother, I have to go to work now. We will send an update out later I promise.'

Jed grinned to himself as he cut her off mid-sentence – parents. The grin slipped, soon that would be him.

MADSR: Bridget Mahoney reads excerpts from 21st century top literature.
Tonight @ Community Hub Four. No virtuality!
This is a sit in event hosted by HistoryNow - click to register.

Sitting on the floor and not bothering to look up, Ruth Maddocks called out through the thick mane of light brown hair hanging round her face.

'Dina? Share my latest. I need to sweep it.'

A younger woman sat on the teacher's chair. She was pixie like – petite with short cropped blonde hair and baby blue eyes. With a small sigh Dina Grey picked up her hand-held and began scrolling.

'The one about boycotting the 150th Anniversary celebrations?'

'No – but do that one too,' Ruth said, trying to tuck her unruly hair out of the way and looking up at her PhD student. 'Bridget's lit reading – she thinks that because it's not virtual more people will come.'

Dina kept scrolling, looking for the right sweep.

'Who knows - they might.'

'Are you going?' Ruth arched her eyebrow at Dina.

'Well.. no... I...you see.' Dina started making excuses before she realised Ruth was teasing. 'I'm going to work on my thesis tonight.'

'Dina,' Ruth let out a heavy sigh, 'You can have fun you know. You should come outside with us tonight.'

'Outside?'

Ruth stood up and went to the open door. She poked her head out and looked up and down the corridor to make sure no-one was about before keying the classroom door shut and walking back to Dina with a mischievous glint in her brown eyes.

'We're going to the beach.'

'Beyond the forcefield? Is that allowed?'

Ruth coloured slightly and chose not to answer, instead she began to pack her bag.

'What about the radiation levels?' Dina asked in concern as she gathered her own notes.

'I've being going out of the city for years and I'm okay.' Ruth said, spreading her arms out, bangles clattering. 'There is no toxicity – people need to get a life.'

Dina shrugged, tucking her hair behind her ear.

'Shouldn't you be teaching me good Corporation values?'

'Just because I teach history at Academy, doesn't make me an old Corp fossil you know.' Ruth retorted and started to shut down all her classroom connections.

'I know, I'm sorry.' Dina said in a small voice. She went to the door and re-opened it.

'Relax.' Ruth picked up her bag and followed Dina out of the classroom. 'Are you still coming to the party tomorrow?'

'If it's okay?'

'Yeah sure. I've told K you wanna ask questions.'

'I do.' Dina nodded, relieved at the change of topic. 'Do you think she'll have time?'

The two women continued chatting down the corridor, Dina worrying and Ruth reassuring.

Jed passed through security, looking up at the silver star shaped shield depicting the scales of justice and the sword of truth crested high up on the wall. The office was buzzing as he walked towards his desk.

'What's going on?' Jed nodded a greeting to his partner, Pete Barnes.

'We've got a top priority case meeting with the Chief.' Pete replied as he stood. 'Lucky us.'

Jed followed his partner into the Chief's office, surprised to see a Corporation Medical Agent standing by the side of the Chief's desk. Usually you only saw them at autopsy.

'Sit down Detectives.' The Chief's gruff voice sounded strained.

The two men sat down in chairs opposite the desk as the Chief, a short man with thining grey hair and a thick moustache looked worried and shuffled his notes, unwilling to begin.

'Usual disclaimers, no interviews, no family involvement – this is highly classified. We find this bastard and we deal out justice.'

The Chief gestured for the Corporation Medical Agent to address Jenkins and Barnes. Wearing standard black Corporation uniform, the young man held up a touchscreen and began to read.

'At three forty-five this morning a young woman was brought to Corporation Medical by her parents. It appears she was attacked, whilst out walking, by an unknown male assailant and was violated sexually.'

The two detectives both leaned forward, intent on the details of the attack.

'The Corporation frowns severely upon such activity and wants to promote a clear message of harsh action. It has been approved that the assailant be terminated.'

Pete sat back in his chair and raised his hand to ask a question but the Corporation Medical Agent ignored him and continued to read.

'Corporation will be recirculating the 'Why Walk?' Campaign throughout media sweeps.' He paused to pick up two info jacks from the Chief's desk and leaning forward, handed one to Pete, the other to Jed. 'Here are your info jacks with all the case details so far. Corporation is confident Force will catch this offender.'

With a nod towards the detectives the agent turned, shook hands with the Chief and left the now silent room. Pete bounced the jack in his hand before looking up at his boss.

'Whose the Vic, Chief?'

The Chief shuffled his papers again.

'At this time it's classified.' He stroked his moustache, avoiding the gaze of the two detectives.

'How are we supposed to work the case if we don't know whose been attacked?'

'Review what you've been given.' replied the Chief. 'Get an ID on the perp. That's your first priority. Dismissed.'

As they left the office Pete looked at Jed.

'Jenks, you believe this frag?'

Jed shook his head as they returned to their desks to plug in the info jacks. They were non-neural and slotted into the side of their consoles. Once loaded, there wasn't much information. The only real addition were hours and hours and hours of Drone TV covering the approximate area where the attack happened. Jed programmed the ident system to look for two people in the park at the same time and sat back to wait for the results.

ANTIC: In celebration of the relaunch of the Why Walk? Campaign, Anti-Corp are holding a peaceful stroll through City Forty-Two. Stretch your legs and your rights, sign up now!

'I see AC are already on the Why Walk? bandwagon.' Pete remarked, checking the sweeps on his handheld as Jed stood up to leave.

'They don't miss a trick do they?' Jed bent down slightly to check his console. 'The matrix is still running Pete but I've got to go – you okay handling this for now?'

Pete gave his partner a mock salute as he continued to scroll the dailies.

Jed shoved his jacket on, trying to clear his head. It was such an odd case and it bothered him that he didn't know who the victim was. But he had other important things to think about right now. Hurrying past security Jed nodded at the guard on the desk. He had to make it to Collection on time so he decided against taking the public skimmer.

City Forty-Two had a square layout with forcefield generators at each corner. Corporation buildings filled the bulk of the west side with Archive and Academy in the centre and residential flats beyond. The far east of the city was officially abandoned however some people did live there, the ones who couldn't or wouldn't conform to Corporation rule. Force Headquarters were located in the Upper North West, sectors First and Second, looking out over the city - set apart from Corporation yet protecting the citizens.

Checking his wristplant, Jed figured he could make it on time if he cut through Third, the advantage of using his own feet rather than following a skimmer rail. As he set off down the pavement a beautiful woman, with skin that glowed blue, brushed his hand as she walked past him. He jerked it away in surprise. Looking back over his shoulder Jed realised she had stopped and was staring straight at him with eyes sparkling like a thousand stars. He began apologising when a bee, an actual bee, zoomed across his face, taking his attention away.

'Did you see that?' Jed asked, turning back, but the woman had gone. Jed blinked in confusion. Must have been a new kind of advert he thought. The Corporation was always thinking up new ways to insinuate itself into your subconscious. But why a bee? The wristplant beeped a reminder for his appointment. Jed jogged through Third, checking the sweeps as he went – nothing about a bee. As he approached Fourth Sector and the blue-tinged, smart-glass fronted skyscraper - known as Collection Towers, Jed could see Kira waiting for him inside the large open plan lobby.

PEBAR: Good luck Jenks

CORP: 150th Anniversary Celebrations continue with VR parade at 4pm – just jack in to join in, bring a friend and experience all the excitement inside your home. Remember the fallen, relive the final victory and rejoice with the founding of Corporation.

'Hi, sorry hon.' Jed hugged his wife. 'I got here quick as I could.'

'It's fine, they haven't called us yet.'

They stood to one side of the front desk while Kira rummaged in her bag for the necessary paperwork. Behind the reception desk a woman with immaculate black hair and wearing a crisp black Corp Medical uniform, waved them forward.

'Here for Collection?'

Kira and Jed nodded.

'Okay, I need your credentials. That means photo, biometric and employment plus evidence of good credits for increased living costs, as well as your references.'

The woman held out her hand, fingers grasping at the empty air whilst Jed found his ident and chip and passed it to Kira, her paperwork already in her hand. The woman scanned each item individually, pressed a few buttons on the screen in front of her, and sniffed.

'Lottery winners – the Jenkins?' Again they nodded. 'I need proof of entry. This isn't enough.'

Kira looked at Jed, biting the corner of her lower lip.

'I didn't bring it,' she said in a small voice.

Jed grinned and took out the winning card from his

back pocket.

They hadn't even entered the Anniversary Lottery, thinking it was too small a chance to actually win. Someone had pushed the card through their door on the eve of the Anniversary celebrations. Jed thought it was Kira's mother, but despite being asked numerous times, she was not admitting it. The woman behind the desk swiped the card and passed it back.

'Your references are Miss Martha Hamble and Mr Pete Barnes. Neither one related to either of you, correct?'

They nodded.

'Hmm, seems to be in order. Do you want standard manuals, neural jacks or the full package which...' The woman looked down. 'You're not covered for so it'll be extra.'

'Standard,' Kira said, a touch defiantly. Both of them wanted to try the less popular natural route. They could always change their minds later, and besides, this was how their ancestors had done it. Kira had been researching the archives, something her position as junior city archivist allowed. It had been a different world back then but the way women had looked after their babies personally had resonated deep within her.

The woman sniffed again.

'Suit yourself. I'm guessing you want the VR experience? Nine months of pregnancy in nine minutes?' Not waiting for a reply she went on. 'We're all out so you'll have to contact your local agent.'

'Its fine' Kira murmured, secretly relieved.

'Top floor.'

And with that the woman dismissed them from her desk.

Listening to the quiet hum of machinery, Kira could feel the pitter patter of butterfly wings in her stomach and her mouth felt dry. Jed cleared his throat and squeezed his wife's hand. Finally the elevator stopped and the doors slid open onto a pristine white corridor. The door at the end

9

was marked Collections. As the young couple walked towards the door, Jed couldn't get the bee he'd seen out of his mind.

'Hey, guess what?' he said.

Kira looked up at him.

'I saw a bee on the way here. Can you believe that? That's gotta be a good sign right? I mean, I never thought I'd see a *live* one.'

Kira shrugged, too nervous to speak and Jed softly kissed the top of her head as they stopped in front of an illuminated wall panel.

'*Name*' it chimed.

'Kira & Jed Jenkins.'

The door swooshed open.

The square white room was empty, devoid of any decoration and lit with harsh, bright white strips. The couple glanced at each other, was this the right place? Another chime sounded, and a soft blue light illuminated a small recess towards the back of the room. As they walked towards it, they became aware of other niches where multiple choice screens hung ready. This was the hard part of Collection, not knowing what your choices would be and trying hard not to hope – any choice could be life changing. Anything at all. They sat on the thin bench provided, looking up at the screen which read 'Baby Jenkins multiple choice, tap when ready.'

Jed turned to look at Kira, 'Ready?'

She couldn't speak, she could only nod. Together they tapped.

Choice 1
Blue eyes & greater academic aptitude
OR
Brown eyes & improved reaction times

Choice 2*
Predisposition to cancer

OR

Predisposition to heart disease

note – Corp Medical reminds you that genetic predisposition has yet to be eradicated however consequences can be neutralised provided you maintain regular health checks.

Choice 3
Boy, assigned name Kai
OR
Girl, assigned name Grace

'Three choices, what do you think?' Kira whispered to Jed.

'I don't mind hon, what do you want?' Jed knew his wife had been thinking about this moment for a long time and he wanted her to be happy. She fidgeted on the bench next to him. Kira had been hoping for the girl/boy choice – not everyone had it. She had been so desperate for a girl she had even prepped the nursery cube for one, despite being told she was silly to have such hope.

'I'd like girl, blue and heart.'

'As you wish.'

He pressed the screen. It blanked then read .... *Processing........Please Wait.*

Jed's ear comm pinged. It was Force Control.

'Jenkins. You're wanted in a security level six briefing, a hover is on its way to pick you up. Be ready in sixty seconds.'

'I've got to go in.' He stood slowly, not wanting to leave.

Kira looked at him in dismay, how could he leave when they were so close to Collection. She was about to protest when there was a hum from the screen in front of them. It slid upwards and a small hatch opened. Inside was their collection. A baby girl, freshly grown in the lab womb and ready to be taken home.

Chapter Two

Martha Hamble lay still, her head facing the door. She felt nothing. Numb. Oblivious to the young nurse bustling around, checking her vitals and updating the med log. Unaware of her clothes tagged in an evidence bag on the floor. Not seeing her father through the slim window in the door gesturing angrily outside. Her eyes were unfocused and a tear rolled down her cheek.

The door banged open making her flinch. A tall, broad shouldered man stepped through the doorway, his bald head narrowly missing the top of the door frame.

'Out,' barked Martha's father at the frightened nurse, who immediately put down the med log and swiftly left the room. Roger Hamble breathed heavily through his bulbous nose as he placed a bag of clothes on the floor, by the end of the hospital bed. Unable to look at his daughter he addressed the wall above her head.

'I've made sure your file is redacted. This doesn't go any further. As soon as you're fit to leave you'll come home and we'll forget this ugly mess.'

When Martha didn't respond he nodded. 'Good. I have a meeting at Force HQ.'

He moved forward half a step, hesitated and nodded again before leaving. Martha watched the door close before touching her ear comm.

'Kira,' she whispered.

'You can't just leave. How am I supposed to get back by myself?'

Anger had flushed Kira's cheeks as she stared at Jed who shrugged helplessly.

'It's not my call. I've no choice. You know I'd rather...' he trailed off looking at the sleeping baby in Kira's arms.

'It's not fair,' Kira said softly, gazing down at the perfect bundle. 'You haven't even held her yet.'

'I will, we're a family now.'

Jed kissed them both and with a last look back he was gone. Kira took a moment to compose her thoughts.

'Right,' she said. 'We can do this Grace.'

Bending slightly she picked up the user manual care pack and her bag. Luckily everything else was being delivered, all she had to do was get back to the apartment. But she didn't have the stroller and couldn't use a public skimmer. She had no way of getting home with the baby. They had planned to all walk back together but Kira was feeling too nervous to walk by herself. What if Grace was too hot or too cold or started crying or wanted feeding or she fell out of Kira's arms or .... her ear comm pinged.

'Kira?'

'Martha? Is that you?'

There was a long pause.

'Yes, I ..'

'Hon, I can't talk right now.'

'NO, wait! May I come over? Please? It's .... I ...something happened.' Her voice broke and she was unable to continue.

'What happened?' Kira asked, brow furrowed in concerned.

'I....I just...'

'Yes. Yes. Come over. Use your fob if I'm not there. I won't be far behind you.'

Kira cancelled the call and gently stroked the cheek of the peaceful, sleeping baby in her arms.

'I wonder what that's all about,' she pondered aloud before making her outgoing call.

'I need a hover lift from Corp Medical to

13

Apartment Forty-Seven, Upper North please. Mother and child. No luggage.'

As she began to walk towards the door, thinking about the long corridor and elevator journey down to the large foyer below, Kira felt suddenly small and extremely isolated. She paused before pressing the elevator's call button not knowing if she could do this alone.

'Let's just get home,' she thought. 'And then we can figure this out.'

Kira pressed the button and made sure she had a tight hold of her new baby.

ANON45: Images of Detective Jed Jenkins leaving wife alone at Collection

JMBISH: Congratulations to KJ42 & JENKS. Can't wait to meet my granddaughter.

INJEN: In honour of my new niece, here are Corp Tech's latest baby-tech deals.

The starter pack was waiting when they got in. Kira gently placed the still sleeping Grace in her cube then stood by her for a moment, unwilling to leave the baby alone. Eventually she began looking through the pack with high hopes. They were soon dashed - despite their request for the least invasive option, there seemed to be a lot of gadgets.

The WBW strip (What Baby Wants) which told you whether the baby was hungry, tired or needed a nappy change. The self feeding hover bottle that could be programmed for regular feeds and didn't require holding. Mother scent stickers for Kira to rub on her body and then place around the baby and, worst of all, the baby neural jack. Filled with nursery rhymes and early years education.

'As if I'm going to shove that into a newborn,' thought Kira. She closed the box and pushed it to one side. Her Academy dissertation had been on how much childcare had changed since The Event. She wished it had been taken more seriously when she presented her findings. Using technology to program a baby just didn't feel right. Kira was sure that the touch of one person to another was a far more fulfilling experience. She stroked Grace's soft and wispy fair hair and smiled. If this was motherhood it was very easy so far. Kira started checking her sweeps on her handheld while she waited for Martha.

MSCHILD: *We are submitting our 27th request for Collection.*
Support our cause and sweep it out across the city.

Martha ignored the nurse flapping round her as she dressed in the spare clothes her father had left. If she could just get out of here she'd feel so much better. But not home, not yet. She needed the one person who understood her completely. She needed to talk about what had happened. She scrubbed her eyes angrily, tears threatening to spill down her face as she turned to face the nurse.

'I'm leaving. My personal locater will inform Force where to find me. You can't keep me here against my will.'

She pushed past the young women trying to keep her in her room.

MED4AC: *Hamble seen at Med Centre – No Comment status issued.*

Pete glanced across the hover car at his partner.

'I'm sorry Jenks, if it were up to me...'

'It's alright, it's not your fault.' Jed looked out the window as they passed the gleaming blue Collection Towers. 'I don't like leaving Kira on her own and I didn't even get to hold the baby. I mean, it's Collection Day!' Jed hit the front of the hover car in anger. 'Do you even know what we're being pulled in for?'

Pete shook his head.

'Sync me, probably just some tech-head sticking

his nose in.' Pete began fiddling with the onboard sweep feed. After a few moments, he cleared his throat. 'Speaking of Corpers, is your sister coming to the baby homecoming?'

Jed knew Pete liked his sister Ingrid, although he wasn't sure why, she hadn't expressed any interest in Pete. All she cared about was her career at Corp Tech and climbing the career ladder as quickly as possible. She didn't talk to Jed often and was absolutely horrified to learn that he and Kira were planning to follow the long out of fashion natural approach to raising their baby.

'Yep. Don't get too excited though.'

'Why not?' Pete turned slightly to look at Jed.

'Unless you're the latest piece of Tech to hit the market I doubt she'll show much interest.'

'Don't you worry about that Jenks, I have a plan,' Pete said.

They landed at Force HQ and walked through the hover bay. Security waved them onwards to meeting room one.

The Chief stopped talking mid sentence and Roger Hamble looked up as the two detectives entered the room.

'Good,' Hamble nodded. 'You're here. Sorry to pull you away Jenkins, big day and all but I've got..well.. this needs to be sorted and sorted out quick.' He nodded again.

Pete and Jed looked at each other in confusion.

'Sit down detectives,' the Chief said. 'As of now, you two are the only ones cleared to work the rape case.'

Pete perched on the edge of his chair.

'Do we know who the victim is yet Sir?'

'The rape victim was, er..' The Chief cleared his throat and looked up at Mr Hamble who was now pacing by the door.

'The victim was Martha Hamble.'

Jed frowned in surprise. He knew Martha. She was Kira's best friend. He had wondered this morning when working through the rape case details why the victim was nameless, now he understood. The daughter of the Marketing Director of fragging Corporation. And not just an assigned daughter, she was an actual made to order. Obvious when you met her - red hair and green eyes were only available to those with the right connections, couple that with the creamy skin and freckles and it literally set her apart from everyone else. Babies weren't grown like that for Collection. It was extremely rare to grow your own these days but when you were on the Board, strings could be pulled. He was going to have to think of something to tell Kira before she got herself involved.

Hamble cleared his throat.

'Her medical file has been redacted, I want nothing on official record,' he said, not looking at either detective. 'You do your job and you find the bastard, and that's the end of it. Keep in contact, I want regular updates and I want a fast resolution Jenkins. I'm counting on you. See this through and Corporation will look after you.' He glanced at Pete. 'Both of you.'

Mr Hamble checked his wristplant, nodded and left the meeting room.

The detectives stared at the Chief who was frowning.

'I don't need to tell you the firestorm we'll be in if anything, and I mean *anything*, goes wrong on this case.' The Chief jabbed his finger at each man. 'Barnes, Jenkins – you get to the bottom of this if it kills you and you do it fast. You have full unit resources but nothing leaves HQ and you're not to bring anyone else in unless I authorise it, you hear? Get to work.'

Before either detective had chance to react, the Chief got up and walked out of the room.

'Frag. You know her right? She's one of Kira's friends isn't she? What, I mean, how do you process … are you good?'

Jed nodded tightly.

'Face it Pete, this just got personal and I want to close this case fast.'

17

They began to set themselves up in the meeting room moving furniture and setting up the internal monitors. Pete called up the case file and checked the progress made on the Drone TV. About half the footage had been screened, no leads. Both detectives sat down and focused on the monitors in front of them, determined to be the one who caught sight of the perpetrator.

***ANTIC:** Security lock down at Force – do you know what's happening? Upload now and keep the sweeps active, we need your input.*

The door chimed and Kira called out 'Open'. Grace stirred and whimpered.

'Shhhh my darling,' Kira whispered, bending over the baby cube as Martha came in.   Looking up with a smile to greet her friend Kira began frowning instead.

'Oh sweetie! What happened?'

Martha's face was streaked with dried tears, eyes red and puffy. She looked broken. Kira moved forward to hug her friend and Martha jerked back with a small cry. In her cube Grace started making snuffling noises, moving her head from side to side, small whimpers escaping as she grew more distressed.

'Oh, oh oh look at that.' Martha caught sight of the baby. 'Oh no. It was today, today was Collection. Oh I am so so sorry. I will leave you alone.'

Kira grabbed her friends hand and despite Martha's stiffening, held on and drew her forward, guiding her to sit on the couch.

'Sit. Breathe. I'll make us all some drinks.'

Martha just looked blankly at her friend. Kira raised her voice slightly, 'I'm going to get Grace's bottle and make us some synth-caf – okay?'

Martha looked towards the kitchen and seemed to realise what she was going to do. Kira squeezed Martha's hand, threw a slightly panicked look at the baby cube then hurried over to the kitchen area.

Grace cried louder and louder, sharp shrill wails that seemed to pierce Kira's heart.

'Where is it? Where is it?' she muttered to herself.

Kira opened two cupboards before remembering she'd put the baby formula in with the mugs and glasses. She flipped the drinks machine on and grabbed mugs, a bottle and the formula. When she opened the fridge she saw the pre-made bottles.

'Idiot.'

Scooping a bottle up, Kira flicked on the auto-warmer button whilst choosing the strong synth-caf option for herself and Martha.

Martha was fluttering her hands, looking worriedly at the crying baby in the cube next to her and half rose out of her seat.

'Should I do something?' she asked.

'No, no I got it. It's her first feed. Loud isn't she?' Kira's voice trembled as her hands shook to finish as quickly as possible. She could feel her scalp prickling as she got hotter.

'I'm coming, I'm coming,' Kira called. Everything binged at once so she took Martha her synth-caf and picked up her red-faced baby.

'Shhhh shhhh.' Kira began to bob the baby up and down as she went back to the kitchen for the milk.

'Here, here, here. It's here.' She put the bottle near Grace's face and the loud wailing cut off suddenly. Both women exhaled.

'Phew – that was intense. Poor little thing, I got you, I got you. You were hungry weren't you, it's okay, it's okay.'

Kira sat down with Martha. Both women watched the tiny baby drink hungrily. After a few moments Kira looked up at her friend.

'What happened honey?'

Martha's hands began shaking, sloshing the synth-caf. She gasped as the hot liquid spilled. Quickly she put the mug down on the floor beside her and scrubbed her hands on her trousers, wiping them dry. Martha tried to marshal her thoughts and without looking at her friend began speaking in a low monotone.

'I was walking home from work, through the park on fourth. It's so tranquil and I imagine what the trees will look like when, if, they ever grow back. It was a normal day at work. The same routine. I did...there was a bee. I wondered if I was imagining things. But it was definitely there. You do believe me Kira?' Martha begged, peering up at her friend with a note of desperation in her voice, eyebrows drawn together, eyes pleading for a positive response.

Kira nodded. She was sure Jed had mentioned a bee at Collection.

'I'm not sure what happened.. there was a sound.. a man... he grabbed me...' Martha started to breathe quicker and quicker, tears rolled down her face. 'I can't Kira, I just...please don't force me.'

'Shhhhh, shhhh it's alright Ma, it's alright.' Kira didn't know what to say, she looked down at Grace, who had stopped feeding and was once again blissfully asleep. 'Just let me put her down.'

Martha had drawn her legs up to meet her body and was hugging her knees, rocking backwards and forwards saying 'No, no, no, no, no' under her breath. Kira didn't know what to do but she couldn't leave her friend in such a state so she touched her ear comm.

'Forty-seven? I need a cocoon for visitor M2 please.'

The apartment lights took on a soft glow as a sedation patch appeared on the arm of the couch next to Martha, who continued to rock. The patch attached itself to Martha's arm and a sedative was released. Martha's movements slowed until she was still and her breathing returned to normal, then became deeper and calmer.

Kira reluctantly placed the baby back in her cube. She had wanted to enjoy their first moments together, but she felt tense and uneasy, sick with worry as she pulled the cocoon fabric from the top of the couch over her friend. Nothing was turning out the way she thought it would today, and she needed to clear her head before she rang Jed.

She walked over to the small altar in the corner of the room and a sense of calm came over her. She lit a candle, sat down and took a couple of cleansing breaths. Kira imagined herself surrounded by a ball of blue light. With each breath she took in she drew energy from the earth far beneath her, and with each exhale she visualised all her stress and anxiety leaving the top of her head. When she felt completely calm, Kira thought hard about the light around her and attempted to extend the protective energy from herself to her new daughter and her best friend. Kira was beginning to feel in control of herself again when the door chimed.

'IGA,' an efficient voice announced.

'Frag it,' thought Kira, they weren't supposed to come till tomorrow. She got up and went to the door. As she opened it, Jed and Pete walked up the corridor and stopped behind the officious looking woman.

'Timing,' muttered Jed as the three of them entered the apartment.

Chapter Three

'What are you two doing here?' Kira whispered as Jed and
Pete followed the Infant Growth Assessor lady into the
apartment and closed the door behind them. Pete pursed
his lips and Jed frowned as they both saw the activated
cocoon. The IGA ignored it and pulled out a touchscreen.

'Later,' Jed murmured.

'Good afternoon, I'm your IGA,' announced the
woman. 'Who are the parents?'

'We are.' Jed pointed at his wife and put on his best
smile as he ushered the IGA into the kitchen area and
offered her a beverage. Pete looked at the cocoon again.
Kira nibbled her fingernails, turning towards the cube
when Grace began to cry. She teetered, not knowing
whether to go to her or speak with the IGA. In the end the
plaintive noise decided her, and she scooped the baby up,
rocking Grace gently, and humming as she walked over to
the others.

'I'm here to carry out an infant suitability assessment not
drink synth-caf, but I suppose one would be nice. It's not
often we get time to indulge while at work. I'm surprised
you even have the drinks machine given your requests.'

Jed and Kira looked at each other in confusion.

'Requests?' Kira asked.

'Ah, sorry, we thought you'd be non-conformers
you see, because of the no technology request. I mean

almost all parents have a NanNan these days and we just thought... well, you know.' The IGA coloured slightly as she sipped her synth-caf. 'No offence.'

'None taken,' Kira said smiling. 'We're not pure naturals but we wanted to try the natural approach with the baby. After my studies I was curious....'

The IGA interrupted.

'Oh I see, hobbyists then. Well each to their own. I'll leave the paperwork for the NanNan as well as our latest brochure and then when you want to order, everything will be there for you.'

'If,' whispered Kira under her breath.

The agent frowned as she walked around the lounge area.

'What's that?' she asked, pointing at the lit candle in the corner of the room.

'Oh. Mm, that's mine. I was just meditating before you arrived.'

'Meditating?'

'Yes. You never heard of it?'

'No. I mean not in real life.' The IGA patted her neat bun. 'I read history at Higher Academy you know, I remember some of the strange customs.' She moved closer peering at the candle on the small table. 'So what do you do with it?'

'Well,' Kira had followed the IGA into the lounge and she sat down with Grace. 'I believe in balance, so sometimes when I feel stressed or out of sorts I like to try and focus my energy on releasing the things that made me *feel* out of balance. It's easier to think of it in terms of light and colour, moving from dark to bright,' Kira paused, searching for something else to say. 'Controlled breathing helps....'

The IGA interrupted again and pointed at the small blue statue.

'And who is that?'

'That's Gaia. She is the spirit of the Earth, dedicated to keeping the life force of the planet in balance.

She can be used as a focus point.' Kira could see the IGA was looking troubled. 'I work in the Archives so I have approved access.'

'Ah, well I guess that makes sense. Not sure how I would write this up anyway. Probably best not to mention it to anyone. I expect it's quite a personal thing and let's face it we don't tell everyone about everything we do behind closed doors do we?'

The IGA glanced at the cocoon before turning to look at Kira and smiling, not realising how offensive she sounded. Kira agreed, in disbelief yet relief that the topic would be dropped. The IGA finished her drink and fished out her paperwork.

'Right, here's my checklist. Neural jack's in use?'

'No'.

'Nan-Nan installed – no. Scent patches activated?'

'No'.

'Cube ordered?'

'Yes.'

'Type?'

'Standard sleeping, able to move around our apartment.'

'Hmm,' the IGA looked down her list. 'I don't think there's much point in me going through the rest of the options. They are all classified as high-tech and you've clearly decided against that kind of help. I don't think there's anything else I can do for you today.'

'Don't you want to look at the baby?' Kira queried.

'Do you mind a health probe?'

'Is it non-invasive?'

'It can be.'

'Alright then.'

Kira watched suspiciously while the IGA brought out a handheld, pressed some buttons and then directed the scan towards Grace laying in her cube. Several bleeps later the IGA handed Kira a readout.

'It's all good. Remember to visit your local Med Centre if you have any queries. Do you have a medical handheld?'

Kira shook her head.

'Well, you might want to look into that otherwise how will you know if the baby is okay? Contact your local Agent, they'll have what you need. I'd recommend a health check at six weeks but obviously get in touch beforehand if you have any worries. Babies are tough little things.'

The IGA gathered her things. After a cheery goodbye she left the apartment.

IGANN: Outdated practices on the rise – who do you know who is being retro?
Share your updates and sweep it out to City Forty-Two.

'Well that was a waste of time.' Kira lifted her daughter out of the cube and turned to look at Jed. 'Are you ready to meet Grace?'

She placed their daughter into Jed's arms. He held her away from him until he realised she wasn't going to cry, then he smiled and brought her closer to him. Kira touched his arm, kissing him on the cheek before walking away to the bedroom.

'My daughter,' Jed said. 'Wow. So tiny.'

He gently stroked her cheek and touched her tiny hand. When she curled her fingers round his, his breath caught.

'Pete, look, look - she's holding my finger.'

Pete grinned.

'She's so perfect. I'm a Dad.' It suddenly seemed like a huge responsibility. 'Woah. I'm a Dad.'

'You okay Jenks?'

'Yeah, yeah. Do you want to hold her?'

'You sure?'

'Course.' Jed transferred the sleeping baby into Pete's arms. His heart swelled in his chest as he watched his friend hold his tiny daughter. After a few moments the two men looked at each other and Pete cleared his throat meaningfully.

'Huh? Oh yeah.' Jed called through to the nearby bedroom. 'Kira, what is Martha doing here?'

Jed glanced back at Pete standing awkwardly with his daughter.

'She called me earlier, in pieces, asking if she could come round. I wasn't going to tell her no. What's going on?' Kira replied as she returned to the kitchen with a bundle of cloth in her hands. Jed sidestepped his wife's question.

'Why is she cocooned?'

'She was trying to tell me what happened to her. She was so upset, she wouldn't let me touch her. She started hyperventilating.' Kira gestured towards her cocooned friend. 'I didn't know what else to do – I know we installed the apartment protection system to combat any aggressive behaviour but I figure this way she'd get some rest and maybe feel better. I was just about to call you when the IGA arrived.' She turned to look at her husband. 'What the frag is going on Jed?'

She unwrapped the cloth and tied it around her body, watching Jed and Pete, waiting for an answer. Pete half shrugged.

'We can't Kira, it's classified.' He frowned. 'What are you doing?'

Kira looked confused for a moment then realised what he was talking about.

'It's a baby wrap. I discovered them in Archive. Don't distract me Pete. What do you mean it's classified? What does that mean? Is she in danger? Am *I* in danger?' She took half a step towards Grace.

'No, you're not in danger hon,' Jed said. 'It's just...out of our hands. I'm sorry, I know she's your friend but I can't break case confidentiality.'

Kira huffed a little and took the baby from Pete, placing Grace inside the fabric wrap, close to her body.

'I'm sorry hon.' Jed tried to placate his wife. 'We needed to speak to Martha and when we checked her locator expecting her to be at the med centre, it flashed up here.'

Kira glared at him.

'I have to finish organising the baby homecoming.'

She pushed past him and stormed straight through to the bedroom.

Jed sighed then looked at his partner.

'Have you got your holo-recorder, Pete?'

'Here? Now?'

'How else are we going to get her into questioning without everyone seeing?'

Pete looked at the cocoon then motioned for Jed to lead the way over to the couch.

'Forty-seven? Retract cocoon please. Administer revival.'

'Affirmative.'

'Pretty techy for you isn't it, Jenks?'

'Mum - Ingrid talked her into getting them for the whole family because she gets serious discount. Not that we had much choice. We came home one day and it had already been installed.'

While Jed was talking the cocoon disengaged, slid up and over the sleeping Martha and returned to a recess at the top of the couch.

After a few moments Martha began to stir. She looked around.

'Wha…Where is Kira? Why are you here? What's going on?'

'It's alright Martha, may I call you Martha? We just want to talk to you about what happened.' Pete tried to sound as non-threatening as possible.

'Oh.'

Jed moved to sit next to Martha on the couch but she shrank back with a small gasp so he veered to one side and sat in the armchair.

'Your father made sure we'd get the case,' Jed said. 'No-one else in Force has any details. Nor will they. But we need to take your statement.' He paused. 'I understand

27

how uncomfortable it might be to talk about.'

Martha looked at him. 'I doubt that.'

'We've found the footage of the attack.'

Martha didn't react, she continued to stare at Jed.

'All we need is your statement and we're one step closer to closing the case.'

Martha didn't respond.

Pete placed the holo on the table in front of the couch and activated the recorder.

'Force Case G7753. Detective Jenkins speaking, also present is Detective Barnes. The date is 15th April 2215. Interview being held with Miss Martha Hamble. Could you please state your name for the record.'

There was a long silence.

'Martha Evelyn Hamble.'

Kira could hear Jed's voice from the bedroom and although she couldn't make out the exact words he sounded firm and in control, interviewing Martha. The homecoming party was pre-organised, all Kira had to do was access the social file and hit confirm. Everyone knew it was tomorrow but at least this way the parentals would be happy with the officialness. Nothing to do now but relax with her new family yet Martha's distressed arrival had stopped that from happening.

Should she go through to the lounge and interrupt a Force matter? Her friend had after all come to confide in her. Kira looked down at the innocent, sleeping baby peeping out through the folds of the baby wrap and a wave of protectiveness swept over her. Martha had come to Kira for help not the Force. She couldn't leave Martha out there by herself. Kira came into the lounge. Jed and Pete looked at her, but neither man spoke. Kira sat next to Martha, found her hand and squeezed it tight.

'Mrs Kira Jenkins and child have entered the room,' Jed said.

'Tell us in your own words what happened Martha.'

28

Pete tried to sound encouraging.

Martha bit her lower lip and swallowed, shifting in her seat. It wasn't until Kira squeezed her hand again that she managed to find the words. In a hushed voice, she began to speak.

'I was walking home from work. It was such a beautiful day yesterday, I could imagine birds singing. I was feeling so happy.' Martha paused then looked up at Kira. 'I knew you had Collection. I was so pleased for you.' She shook her head. 'There was a woman. She was blue. And a bee. There was definitely a bee. I think. Why would I have imagined that?' she said half to herself.

Jed stared at Martha. It can't have been the same person. It was a new ad by Corp. A coincidence, surely. Martha stopped talking and looked down at her hands.

'Go on,' Pete said. Martha looked up at him, her eyes full of tears.

'He hit me. I fell. I don't remember ... my head.' She touched the side of her head. 'Hurt. I couldn't see. But there was someone on top of me and he, and he, he was..' She started sobbing.

'He was…..in me. I never. I had not….I didn't want to. I tried to push him but I had no strength. He was smothering me and I had no strength.'

She trailed off.

'I was powerless.'

Her shoulders shook as she cried.

Kira looked at Jed horrified, then tried to hug her friend as best as she could but Grace in the baby wrap made her bulky and Kira was frightened of squashing the baby.

Jed motioned for Pete to stop the recorder.

'Kira,' he said. 'You can't breathe a word of this to anyone.'

Kira scowled at him.

'And who exactly am I going to tell?'

Pete spoke to Jed.

'Her statement matches the footage. We've got the

29

medical files - why don't we leave it as is Jenks. There's no conflicting evidence. Once facial re-cog comes back we've got him.'

Jed nodded in agreement and the two men stood, Pete packing away the holo recorder.

'You head home Pete,' Jed said. 'I've got re-cog on my ear comm, I'll let you know when it pings through.'

'No problem. I'll upload the interview and wait to hear.'

They clasped forearms and Pete left. After the door closed Jed sagged slightly, his head planted for a brief moment against the wall.

Kira and Martha were speaking softly on the couch together. Martha stood and headed through a door on the other side of the lounge.

'Is she okay?' Jed asked.

'She's going to shower. I told her she could use our water credit, we've stockpiled a bit and I think she needs to feel clean.'

'Yeah sure. We've got the physical evidence.' Jed caught his wife's hand and held it tight. 'I'm so sorry this happened.'

'You will catch him won't you?'

'We will do whatever it takes to catch him, I promise.'

'And then what happens?'

'It's a termination. You'll probably never hear it on the sweeps. Martha being who she is.'

Grace began to stir inside the baby wrap, making small noises as if she was searching for something.

'I guess she wants feeding again,' Kira said. 'Do you want to do it?'

Jed smiled. 'More than anything.' He made himself comfortable on the couch but before Kira could pass Grace over he suddenly sat bolt upright.

'What's wrong?'

'Oh no, don't worry it's not a bad thing. I just

remembered something, I promised Mother I'd send out an update and I haven't had time to put anything together yet.'

'Oh, I've already prepared one.' Feeling rather pleased with herself she brought it up on the portable touchscreen for Jed to read through. He read it and handed it back with a grin as he took Grace.

'It's great hon, thank you. Get it sent out and we can finally start being a real family.'

JENHUB: So excited to have Grace, she's the most beautiful baby I've ever seen.

CORP: Latest Collection a success - baby Grace Jenkins joins Detective Jed Jenkins and Junior Archivist Kira Jenkins, the youngest family unit so far.

INJEN: Latest model NanNan beta test's are extremely favourable. Click through for details on how to pre-order.

A few hours later Jed was scrolling through his dailies, looking at who had read their update, which was in fact everyone they knew. There were several comments from people expressing their congratulations and excitement about meeting Grace at the party tomorrow. Ingrid's response had been typically impersonal, with the usual new tech links inserted at the bottom. Kira's close friend, Ruth, had been the complete opposite, gushing with congratulations and enthusiastic support for their choice of parenting style.

There was one post from someone he didn't recognise - Dina something or other - expressing her sincere delight at coming to the party. She must be a new friend of Kira's, Jed thought. His jaw cracked as he yawned. Checking his wristplant Jed realised if he didn't go to sleep soon he'd probably end up going without. Re-cog should be through in a couple of hours and with it Pete and Jed could arrest the bastard behind Martha's attack.

Chapter Four

Kira stared at the sleeping baby in the crib next to her. She was frightened that if she closed her eyes Grace might need her and she'd miss it. Or even that someone would come in and take her - which was ridiculous seeing as the apartment was locked. But Kira couldn't shake the feeling that something awful was going to happen.

The evening had been extremely subdued. Martha had seemed calmer after her shower, even holding Grace for a time, though she hadn't eaten much. None of them had. Kira and Jed hadn't felt like talking either. They hadn't even celebrated the first day of their new family. Today would be difficult too. With all their guests descending for the homecoming, not only would Kira have to defend her natural parenting style but she had to make sure no-one found out about Martha, especially Ruth. Ruth might sweep it and use the attack as a soap box to complain about Corporation, not thinking about how upsetting that would be for Martha.

Kira turned over and watched Jed as he slept. He looked so peaceful, as if nothing bad could touch him. Then his ear comm began to ping. Kira elbowed him in the ribs. Jed groaned and touched his ear.

'This is facial re-cog with results for Detective Jenkins. Please activate verbal confirmation.'

'Confirmation activated.'

'Positive match for Michael Greenwood. Apartment Six, Lower 7th. Information uploaded to file.'

The call ended and Jed sat up, touching his comm again.

'Lower 7th.'

Kira shushed him pointing at Grace. Jed continued in a quieter tone.

'I need a security lock-down on Apartment Six. No entry or exit except for Detectives Jenkins and Barnes.' He ended the call and looked at Kira, grim-faced.

32

'We've got him. I've gotta go.'

He quickly got dressed and nodded towards Grace.

'She slept well.'

'She woke up twice for a feed. You slept right through.'

Jed looked a little sheepish.

'Don't worry. You'll be getting your share of night shifts.' Kira grinned at him.

Jed kissed his wife, turned to leave then came back and kissed his baby.

'Will you be alright, you know, with Martha?' He jerked his head in the direction of the guest room.

'We'll be fine. I won't say anything to anyone. You won't be late home will you?'

'I'll do my best hon. This is a big deal, you know what Mr Hamble is like.'

'I know. See you later. Love you.'

'Love you.'

Jed left the room quietly. Kira checked the time. Three thirty am. She could doze for a bit. She looked over at Grace, and scooped the baby out of the cube, laying her gently in the bed. Then she curled her body around the tiny shape, closed her eyes, and tried to sleep.

ANTIC: Rare snake sighted but not caught – did it slither to freedom?

CORP: We remind citizens that animal sightings MUST be reported for immediate containment. Wildlife from outside the city will contain harmful contaminants – don't risk contact. Stay safe, stay inside.

The skimmer hummed as Jed went through the Upper Community Hub, deserted now but with benches for people to meet, sit and chat, play areas for the children and during the day vendors hawked food and other knick knacks. The streets were empty and apartment blocks dark as he went to pick up his partner. Pete lived in the last apartment block in the Upper sector, the one designed for individual dwelling. As Jed drew close he saw Pete standing on the corner bleary eyed.

'We got him then?' Pete asked climbing into the skimmer.

'Yep'.

'Where are we going?'

'Apartment Six, Lower 7th – one of the student blocks.'

'Lock-down?'

'Yep.'

Pete grunted. 'Where are we going to question him? Is HQ secure?'

'Should be,' Jed said. 'We can use meeting room one. You still got your holo?'

'Yep.'

The two men spent the rest of the journey in silence, engrossed in their own thoughts.

It was all quiet on Lower 7th, every apartment window dark. The lock-down was still in place and the detectives found apartment six easily. Jed touched the security plate on the side of the door.

'Access request for Detectives Jenkins and Barnes.'

'Confirmed.'

The door slid open. Both men entered. Jed motioned for Pete to go left as he went right. Armed with stunners, they separated to explore the apartment.

Michael Greenwood tossed and turned, dreaming of footsteps. He sat up as the door to his bedroom banged open and a Force Detective aimed a stunner right at him.

'Frag!' Greenwood yelled, arms up. 'Don't shoot!'

'Be quiet,' Jed snapped. 'Michael Greenwood, you are bound by Force Law. Anything you say may be used as evidence against you. At this time you do not have the right to a Defender. You will be escorted for immediate questioning. You may dress but any act of aggression will be dealt with. Do you understand?'

Greenwood nodded.

'What did I do?'

Jed motioned Greenwood towards a pile of clothes on the floor. He slid out of bed, glancing nervously at the armed stunners following his every move and put on the green tunic and trousers he had discarded earlier that night. Within minutes the detectives had bundled their suspect into the waiting skimmer and were traveling in silence to HQ. Greenwood looked at each of the detectives in turn, and then down at his magno-bound hands.

'But I haven't done anything,' he said.

HQ was dark except for a pool of light where the night guard sat on reception. He greeted them sleepily. 'Detectives.'

Jed and Pete took Greenwood into the meeting room, magno-binding him to an interrogation desk. He started to speak, but stopped at the fierce look on Jed's face and dropped his gaze to his bound hands. Jed turned to Pete.

'I need a truth patch, a lie catcher and your holo.'

Pete gathered the various items from the corner of the room where all their equipment was piled. He connected the lie catcher into Greenwood's info jack port at the back of his head and stuck the truth patch to his arm. The lie catcher was designed to pick up on unusual brain wave activity, whilst the truth patch released chemicals that made most people eager to share whatever information they knew. Occasionally the truth patch had no effect. There were other, less accepted, methods of gathering intel – usually left as a last resort.

Greenwood swallowed nervously and watched as Pete took a seat behind the lie catcher readout and Jed sat down in front of him, beginning the holo recorder.

'Force Case G7753. Detective Jenkins speaking, also present is Detective Barnes. The date is 16th April 2215. Mr Michael Greenwood is present for questioning.

In use for interrogation are standard issue lie catcher and Corp Tech truth patch, version four.' Jed looked at the prisoner. 'Please confirm your identity for the record.'

'Michael Greenwood.' He leaned forwards. 'Why am I here?'

'I remind you that you are still under caution. You have been bound by Force Law. Anything you say may be used as evidence against you. At this time you do not have the right to a Defender. Do you understand?'

Greenwood nodded, sat back in his chair then cleared his throat. 'Yes.'

'Where were you between four and six on the afternoon of April fourteenth?'

'Walking home? I think?' Greenwood looked confused.

There was a pause in the questioning as Pete watched the lie catcher trackers. 'Confirmed.'

'What route did you walk home?' Jed asked.

'Through the park in fourth,' Greenwood answered. 'It's beautiful.'

Jed looked at Pete.

'Confirmed.'

'Did you meet anyone?'

'I don't know....maybe,' Greenwood said, trying to remember. 'There was, I can't....'

'Think harder.'

'Yes, there was a lady, a blue lady.'

'Blue?'

Jed was hoping for more information but Greenwood only nodded.

'Confirmed,' Pete said, looking back at the screen, sounding surprised.

'And....' Greenwood continued. 'There was a bee.' He reached round to touch the side of his neck, and felt a slight bump. 'It stung me!'

'Hands down,' Jed barked.

'Med scan?' Pete said, already getting up and searching the pile of equipment in the corner.

'Interrogation calls for medical scan. Results uploaded to file.'

Pete brought back a handheld and scanned Greenwood. After a few moments the scanner beeped.

'Positive for bee venom,' Pete said slowly.

Jed and Pete looked at each other for a moment before Pete sat back down. Jed cleared his throat and turned back to the suspect.

'Did you see anyone else?'

'No, I … no. The next thing I remember is being at home.' Greenwood looked at each Detective in turn, his brow creased, eyes wide. 'Did something happen?'

'Cue the footage,' Jed said to Pete.

The vid-screen on the wall glowed briefly as Drone TV flickered into life. A young woman walks into view. Greenwood shook his head. The woman seemed familiar. The footage blanked out, then resumed. The woman continues walking past a man, walking past Greenwood himself. He leans forward, unsure as to what he will see himself do next.

The screen blanks out again. When the footage continues the man on the screen is holding his neck, looking round as if trying to find someone. He spots the woman who is walking away from him. He moves quickly to catch up with her. He grabs her by the arm and spins her round. She loses her balance and falls, hitting the ground hard. She does not move.

Greenwood gasps.

'Keep watching,' Pete menaced.

The man on the screen has his back to the drone camera, yet despite this it becomes clear that he is undoing his trousers. Greenwood watched with increasing horror as the man sexually assaults the prone woman. When he has finished, the man gets up and walks away as if nothing unusual has happened.

'It might look like me but it wasn't me. I'd never do something like that.' Greenwood's face turned pale and tears formed in his eyes. 'You have to believe me. I couldn't... that poor woman...I didn't...'. He sniffed, licked his lips and looked up at the two detectives. 'Those footage blackouts. That's unusual right?' His voice got firmer. 'That sort of thing doesn't happen anymore. Obviously this is someone's idea of a sick joke, isn't it? The footage must have been tampered with – maybe it's Anti-Corp - I'm being set up, I would never.'

He trailed off as the two detectives looked at him dispassionately. He lowered his head, his words now no more than a disbelieving whisper.

'It wasn't me, it wasn't me.'

Pete turned the vid-screen off. After a brief pause Jed cleared his throat.

'Your DNA was identified and matched after the victim was taken to Medical and scanned. The footage corroborates your presence at the scene of the crime.'

'I didn't do this, I didn't.'

Pete watched the lie catcher readout, his brow furrowed. He leaned over to Jed and spoke to him in a hushed tone.

'According to this he thinks he's telling the truth but he can't be, can he? Drugs?'

'We'd better run the full spectrum,' Jed whispered back, then watched as Pete got the syringe from the med kit.

'End of interrogation. Drug analysis requested – full spectrum ordered. Results uploaded to file.'

Jed watched Greenwood as he sat behind the desk muttering to himself, head bowed and shoulders slumped. Something about this didn't feel right. Hamble had declared the culprit would be terminated, and Jed wanted to be one hundred percent sure that Michael Greenwood had knowingly committed this crime and wasn't an unwitting accomplice to someone or something else.

It must have something to do with the blue woman. Greenwood had seen her, Martha too. And the bee. Just like him, it had to mean something. Anti Corp could be trying out a new aggressive campaign to destablise Corporation. It didn't make sense. Even if they were, Anti-Corp would never advocate rape, and why didn't the blue woman affect him when he saw her? Why didn't the bee sting him? If indeed there even was a bee. Jed's head was beginning to ache.

Pete finished taking the blood samples.

'Where shall we put him?' he said.

Jed refocused.

'The isolation cell. No-one will go that way if we lock it down, and we need to keep this off the mainstream.'

'You take him, I'll get these samples over to analysis,' Pete said, agreeing with his partner. He looked at his watch. 'Should be done by nine.'

Greenwood flinched as Jed came over to him. He tried to protest his innocence again, desperately.

'I didn't do this. You have to believe me. I don't remember a thing, it wasn't me, I'd never...'

He was cut off mid-sentence as Jed administered a sedative. The dose was enough to stop the man from talking but not too much that he couldn't walk by himself. Jed released the magno-binders from the table and took the prisoner out of the room, guiding him through the corridor to isolation.

Jed wasn't convinced whether Greenwood was truly guilty or not but the evidence against him was strong. He was hoping the drug sweep would come back positive for something. At least that would make some sort of sense and it might be the only way to keep the man from death. Jed was appalled someone he knew had been raped in broad daylight by a random stranger, but the confusion and horror Greenwood had shown whilst watching the footage made it difficult for Jed to believe that he was putting on an act.

ANTIC: Early Force birds catch worm. Do you know more? Share & sweep.

Thunder rolled through the overcast sky as Martha lay on the bed listening to the rain pelting the window. The weather suited her mood. In fact if a lightening bolt were to somehow hit her right now she didn't think it would be a bad thing.

She could hear Kira and Grace moving about in the next room. Holding Grace had been a real comfort last night. She was so pure and innocent.

Holding the baby had washed away some of the badness Martha felt inside. The shower she had taken last night hadn't done anything to get rid of the dirty feeling. Her skin still crawled and she didn't think she would ever be able to bear the touch of any man ever again.

Why her? Why had that man, that nobody of a man, why had he attacked her?

Martha was used to hate mail, she was the daughter of the Marketing Director on the Board of Corporation - but she didn't think this was aimed at him. It wouldn't gain Anti Corp anything to have Mr Hamble's daughter raped. The only person she knew involved with Anti Corp was Ruth and she would never be part of an organisation who would condone sexual assault.

She could ask Ruth later, at the party - that would help set the mood. *'Hi Ruth – were you aware of an Anti-Corp plan to rape me?'*

A loud banging interrupted Martha's thoughts.

Kira held Grace awkwardly in one arm as she opened the front door and then stepped back as Roger Hamble came striding through.

'Kira,' he nodded as a way of greeting. 'Is my daughter here?'

'I am,' Martha said, appearing from the spare room but not looking at her father.

Kira closed the door as Mr Hamble strode over to where Martha stood in the middle of the lounge. Kira walked past them both and hovered by her bedroom door, unsure whether she should stay or go.

40

'Your mother and I were worried when you didn't come home. We spoke with Medical and they said you'd checked out. We thought something might have happened.'

He peered at his daughter under his bushy eyebrows.

'Something else you mean?' Martha said in a small voice.

Her father ran a hand through his thick hair.

'Yes, well, no need for all that. I've got something for you.' He fished in his jacket pocket and brought out a vial of clear liquid. 'A Nano tech memory wipe. Designed to remove painful events. Your mother thought it might be useful, you know, so you can put it behind you and get on with …. things.'

Martha glared at her father.

'You mean so she doesn't have to talk to me about it.'

'Now, now Martha, that's not fair. Your mother is delicate.'

'Not fair!' Martha shouted. 'Not fair! Can you even hear the words coming out of your mouth? I do not want your frag damn memory wipe and I do not want you pushing me back into my perfect daughter mold.' She took a step toward him. 'He *raped* me, Father. He raped me. He pushed me and hurt me and raped me. And there was nothing I could do about it.' Martha lurched forward into her father's arms, sobbing. 'I am so sorry Daddy.'

Hamble wrapped his arms around her and stroked her hair.

'There, there. It's alright. Shhhh,' he whispered, his gaze soft.

Kira hesitated a moment before slipping back into her bedroom.

While she waited Kira stared out of the window watching the rain as it continued to pour down.

'What has upset you so much today?' she said, to the darkening sky.

Grace began to snuffle in her arms, looking for milk and crying.

'Alright, alright baby. We'll get your bottle.'

Kira stood by the bedroom door, trying to hear whether the coast was clear or not so she could get to the kitchen. Grace's cry was traveling right through her, and Kira's anxiety level was beginning to rise. She poked her head out the door. Martha and her father were sat on the couch, talking.

Kira tiptoed towards the kitchen, an intruder in her own apartment. Once there, Kira took a bottle out of the fridge and activated the self-warmer, turning to go back to her bedroom, but Martha's father was now on his feet.

'Kira', he said nodding in her direction before letting himself out of the apartment. Once the door had shut behind him, Kira went over to where Martha sat with the memory wipe vial in her hands.

'You alright Ma?'

'Yes. No. I have no idea. I am so sorry Kira – have I ruined Grace's party?'

'No, don't be silly,' Kira replied. 'It's all pre-organised, you know what my mum is like.' She paused, not sure what to say. 'Are you sure you want to stay for it? Because I completely understand if you don't want to be around lots of people.'

'Of course I will be here,' Martha said. 'I think I would rather have something to do then be left alone right now. As long as you don't mind me being here?'

'Of course not,' Kira replied, smiling at her friend. 'You can help me figure out what to wear. Party set-up are arriving at ten and the first guest is due early afternoon. I expect the mothers will turn up anytime before that, so we'd better get this little one sorted out at least.'

Both women stood for a moment looking at the baby in Kira's arms before walking together towards Kira's bedroom discussing party dresses and checking the latest sweeps.

Jed returned to the meeting room where Pete was waiting.

'Hamble's on his way,' Pete said.

'Great.' Jed sighed and sat down.

'What's wrong Jenks?'

'This case. This whole thing is so odd. First we have a rape – a rape! I mean, when was the last time you remember hearing about one of those?'

Pete shrugged.

'Then there's this whole blue lady, bee thing. I mean I thought it was some kind of promotion for something or other but this guy saw it too and now he's facing termination for a crime he has no memory of committing. I mean, what the frag?'

'You saw a blue lady?'

'Yeah. On the way to Collection. I just thought it was, you know, advertising or something.'

Pete bit the side of his thumb.

'I saw her too Jenks. I mean, I think I did. I'm not sure. I didn't see a bee, though.' He paused for a moment. 'I saw a snake.'

' A snake!' Jed's eyes widened.

'Fragging thing slithered round the corner from my apartment and when I followed it I think I saw a blue lady turn into the alley. I checked it out but there was nothing there. Can you imagine how many credits I'd get for a live snake?'

Snakes were extremely rare but very, very occasionally they turned up in the city, attracted to the heat given off by the solar power hubs. They were worth a small fortune.

'What is going on, Pete?'

'No idea,' Pete said. 'You should be talking to Kira and her mates. Aren't they meant to be regularly communing with nature or something?'

Before Jed could answer the door opened and Mr Hamble entered. Both detectives stood and spoke as one, 'Sir.'

'Sit.'

Pete and Jed sat. Hamble remained standing by the door.

'You've got the bastard then?'

'Yes Sir,' Jed said. 'Although there seems to be some discrepancies in his statement.'

'Discrepancies? Did Drone TV positively identify him?'

'Yes Sir.'

'Did you get the DNA sample you needed from Corp Medical?'

'Yes Sir.'

'And it was a positive match?'

'Yes Sir but..'

'Then I don't see what the problem is. Get the damn statement completed and I'll order Termination to come and finish the job.'

'We've got the statement, Sir, but the lie catcher shows that whilst Greenwood committed the crime, he has absolutely no memory of doing so. We think a new drug might have affected him so we're just waiting for the labs to come back and..'

Hamble cut him off again.

'There's no new drug. I'm calling in Termination and that's the end of it. Good work men.'

He moved forward to shake Pete's hand, then Jeds.

'But Sir … '

'It's done Jenkins. You should be pleased. Go home, spend time with your new family. Nothing more important than family. I'll send my man over to seal the files.'

He nodded to himself then moved over to the far side of the room, and made the call for Termination.

Pete looked at Jed's worried face.

'Jenks,' he whispered. 'Greenwood is guilty. He committed the assault, we have the corroborating evidence.'

'I know. It just seems wrong.'

'Of course it does. It happened to someone you

know. To someone we know for frag sake. Hamble's right – go home, enjoy being a daddy. I'll stay, close the file and wait for the terminators.'

'You sure?'

'Course.' Pete smiled to himself. 'I can work on my amazing chat up lines for later.'

'Good luck with that.'

Pete's infatuation with Jed's sister Ingrid was a great source of amusement for himself and Kira. Ingrid was so Corp that sometimes they wondered whether she even realised Pete was a person and not an A.I. projection. She certainly had no idea that he near worshipped the ground she walked on. It would be interesting to see if she even turned up at the party at all.

Jed gathered his jacket and clapped his partner on the shoulder before following Hamble, who had finished his call, out of the room. He was waiting for Jed in the corridor.

'Martha is staying at yours.'

Jed wasn't sure whether it was a question or a statement and before he could comment Hamble continued.

'Bill me water and energy rates, you've got extra as it is and it's tight all round. We'll send some of her things over. I understand forty-eight's empty, so consider it an extension. Think of it as my gratitude for, well, you know.'

Hamble strode off leaving Jed staring after him in amazement. It had taken them months of waiting on housing to get their apartment and suddenly they'd been handed an extension. Glancing outside he noticed the bucketing rain. Turning the collar up on his jacket, Jed nodded to security and went to wait for a public skimmer home.

ANTIC: *Hamble seen leaving Force. Info lock down in place.*
Do you know more? Share & sweep.

Chapter Five

Kira flitted round the apartment in her new pink dress, carrying out last minute checks to make sure everything was perfect. She had thought about leaving Grace in her cube but she didn't want anyone and everyone picking her up and passing her around like a little toy doll. Instead the baby was snuggled into her wrap, close to her mummy. Kira paused for a moment looking down at the beautiful baby wondering to herself whether she'd earnt the right to call herself a mum.

'Is everything in order?' Martha broke Kira's reverie as she walked over from the kitchen looking demure in a perfectly tailored white tunic suit.

'I think so.' Kira looked around the apartment. 'We've got food, drink, music and the door barrier set up to our room when Grace is ready to snooze. I turned the sound proof on, didn't I?'

'Yes, you did.' Martha fiddled with the ornate titanium and sapphire ring on her finger. 'Will Ruth be coming?'

'Yep, and she's bringing a young graduate with her. Why – is that a problem?'

Martha shook her head and walked a few steps back over to the kitchen area before turning around again.

'I think I should take the memory wipe. Do you think I should?' Martha took a step towards her friend. 'I don't know what to do.'

Kira walked over to her friend, 'You have to do what you think is best, sweetie.' She put her arm round her.

'I can't bear to feel like this. I do not want to remember. I do not want to have to tell anybody about what happened.' Martha looked away. 'Yet if I do take it I

46

feel like I am giving in. I always thought I was stronger than that.'

'You are strong, Ma. Stronger than me,' Kira said, putting an arm round her friend, squeezing her shoulder. 'Stronger than anyone I've ever known. If taking the wipe will help then take it. At the end of the day you have to do what's best for you. Are you sure you can cope with the party?'

Martha didn't answer. She wiped her eyes and sniffed, pulling the memory wipe vial out of her pocket.

'I am going to take it Kira. When you were getting Grace ready, I sat in your meditation spot to try and clear my head. If I do not take this wipe I don't think I will ever stop feeling like this.' She paused, turning the vial up and down in her hand, tears in her eyes. 'I can't spend the rest of my life hoping no-one touches me, talks to me or asks me how I am.'

The two women shared a moment of quiet sympathy, broken only by the door pinging to announce visitors on their way.

'Look, I keyed the door barrier to accept you Ma, so if you need to escape the party you can,' Kira said.

'Thank you.' Martha unscrewed the vial and swallowed the liquid with a bitter grimace as Jed came rushing through the door.

'Everything alright?' he asked not waiting for a reply. 'I pinged the door to give you a bit of warning. Mother is downstairs so I need to ask you not to mention Martha's case - it's classified. We can't discuss it with anyone, okay?' He stared at the two women. 'Promise me?'

They nodded as Jed's mother – a tall, slender woman with elegantly coiffed silvery hair and creamy brown skin - swept into the apartment followed by a shorter, harassed looking yet smartly dressed black man carrying several bags and packages. Martha discreetly put the empty vial in her pocket.

'Darlings! How are you? The place looks,' Mrs

Jenkins paused. 'So quaint. You should have let us host darling, we have so much more space and our décor is so tasteful – especially since we had Pierre in to redecorate.' She waved an immaculately manicured hand around the apartment. 'Where is my gorgeous granddaughter? I simply have to see her. Where is she?'

Kira's mouth tightened.

'Right in front of you.'

Mrs Jenkins stared in horror at the wrap over Kira's party dress which did, Kira had to admit, mar the overall effect. She took the baby out of the wrap.

'This,' Kira smiled, 'is Grace.'

Jed leaned in and gave his daughter a soft kiss on the head. 'Back in a parse.'

Mr Jenkins, struggling to keep control of the packages, coughed. 'Gretchen, dear?'

'Oh for goodness sake Henry, anywhere, anywhere. Can't you see I'm busy?'

Martha came to the rescue helping Mr Jenkins find a place for the various bags and deftly taking his jacket. Mrs Jenkins, leaned over the baby.

'Such a darling, darling. But why are you wearing that … thing?' She looked around, a faint frown wrinkling her brow. 'Where is the NanNan?'

'We decided not to get one Gretchen,' Kira explained.

'I know that but …. Ingrid. Well, I won't say anymore. She's on her way. Must visit the powder room.' Mrs Jenkins glided off to the bathroom leaving a waft of floral perfume in her wake.

'One parent down, one to go,' Kira said under her breath.

When Jed reappeared a few more people had arrived. No sign of his sister yet, or Pete. No doubt Pete would somehow manage to time his arrival to coincide with Ingrid. He usually did. Sometimes Jed wished his sister would show an interest in Pete. He was sure that once it happened, his friend would move on and he would stop having to listen to Pete telling him about how perfect Ingrid was.

Jed walked through the sitting room, nodding and smiling at guests when Kira's parents arrived. Jean and Malcolm Bishop were warm hearted and generous. He loved spending time with them and joined his wife at the door in welcome.

'Mum, Dad. Good journey?'

'Hello lovely.' Jean kissed her son in law on the cheek. 'Yes it was a good run, wasn't it Malcolm. Not too bad now the skypass has reopened. We parked round the back, son, so as not to take up spaces. You doing alright love, you look a bit peaky. I bought some things, a bit of this, a bit of that. Just put it out on the counter dear.'

Kira tried to look in the containers as Jed carried some over to the kitchen.

'Is this her?' Jean asked, peering into the wrap. 'Oh honey, she's so tiny. Hard to believe you were ever that little. I remember going to collect you and being too scared to even pick you up, you were so small. I thought you would break the minute I touched you, I said to your father, I said Malcolm..' and she carried on chattering away.

Once Jean got going, there was little stopping her. She scooped Grace into her arms and settled down in a nearby chair, directing her husband with the odd word and nod to put the various cakes and other sweetments he was holding on the table.

'Mum,' Kira said slightly bemused. 'We catered.'

'Yes well, those caterers don't know everything, my dear. This celebration cake was passed down six generations, six you hear, so it's just the right sort of occasion to bring it out and share it with your friends. I'm sure no-one will mind. Did I tell you about Betty down the street? No? Well, you know she installed a 'feed-me' because she thought it would help her lose weight? Well, you'll never guess what happened. I said to your father, you'll never guess what happened..' and she was off again, hardly pausing for breath.

Kira shook her head and smiled at Jed, who had returned and was nodding and laughing in all the right places - he had hours and hours of time for her parents. She saw Martha chatting quietly with Jed's father. The door opened, and Ruth arrived resplendent in a red top and bright blue skirt that jingled slightly as she moved, completely overshadowing Dina who followed behind her, dressed in pale shades of grey. Kira leant down to retrieve a sleeping Grace from her mother. The baby was completely unaware the room was full of people who had gathered especially to meet her.

ACAD: Highest number of new PhD students enrolled. Support your future and get involved, register your interest for placement – VR interview opportunities available.

Dina looked around with interest at Kira's apartment. She wanted to use Mrs Jenkins as one of her research subjects for her own dissertation - Natural Vs NanNan: is technology a realistic substitute? - and was hoping she'd agree.

'K! Hi honey.' Ruth waved. 'Is this the little bundle? Oh isn't she adorable.' Ruth cooed over Grace before turning to introduce Dina. 'This is my PhD student Dina Grey, I told you about her didn't I?' She peered over Kira's shoulder, not waiting for a reply. 'Miserable weather, we almost drowned on the way. Oooh is that some of your mum's cake?' She drifted over to the kitchen, leaving Dina standing awkwardly on her own, not knowing what to say.

'Congratulations on Collection.'

'Thank you.' Kira studied Dina for a moment before taking pity on the young girl. 'I understand you want to interview me as part of your studies? Give me a couple of weeks to get used to having Grace and then we can plan some time to meet up. You can come to the Archives if you like.'

Dina smiled in relief at Kira.

'That would be amazing. Thank you so much.'

'No problem. Here, come and meet Jed's cousins, they've just finished studying at Academy too.'

Kira manoeuvred the girl towards a small group haphazardly sprawled in the corner of the room, congratulating herself on her hostess skills.

'Who needs auto-pairing,' she thought.

CORP: Bob Fellows dies, age 105, inventor of original NanNan - his work lives on. New model to be released soon. Pre-order the NanNan 3000 with your local Corporation Rep.

As Jed had expected, Pete and Ingrid arrived at the same time. It was clear they had however, travelled separately as Pete was chatting to Ingrid about the weather and the state of the skimmer way. Ingrid, looking immaculate in her standard issue pale green tunic suit, had obviously come straight from work and had a large grey Corp Tech box on levitate next to her.

'Jed,' she gestured curtly to her brother as he greeted them. 'This is for you – in honour of Bob Fellows. It's the next gen NanNan 3000. Beta test was highly favourable, but it's not on the market yet so make sure you fulfil the feedback requirements.'

She left Jed with the box, and moved through the apartment with purpose towards the wine, and her mother. Jed sighed. Kira would not be impressed. He moved the box over to the side of the doorway and hoped it wouldn't get in the way too much. People could always use it as a drinks table. Jed looked round for Pete, who was standing half way to the kitchen and staring longingly after Ingrid.

'Everything okay at HQ, Pete?' Jed spoke in a low tone.

'What?' Pete jumped slightly as he turned round. 'Yeah. Terminators arrived and have it scheduled for nine tonight.'

Jed checked his wristplant, it was almost six.

'I figured they didn't need me there twiddling my thumbs, so I went and got my secret weapon.'

'Secret weapon?'

'Watch this.'

Pete walked towards the kitchen rolling up his sleeve, revealing a silver coin shaped device attached to his forearm. Ingrid glanced over, noted the device and her whole demeanour changed. From where Jed was standing it looked as if she was praising Pete, asking him questions, even smiling at him.

INJEN: *Latest Force tech bio-monitor generating positive results in initial testing.*

Jed put two and two together. Pete had volunteered for the new equipment beta-test at HQ. Ingrid worked in tech development and lived for her career. If anything would work for Pete, this would. Jed grinned as he watched his friend top up his sisters wine glass and guide her to a free couch. Kira came up behind Jed, and leant into him.

'What are you looking so pleased about?'

Jed nodded towards Pete and Ingrid.

'That's not the only one,' she said, pointing out Dina and Ben - one of Jed's cousins - heads together, talking intently, oblivious to the room around them. 'It's almost as if we used pheromone spray.'

Jed laughed. 'How do you know I didn't?'

Kira swatted him playfully.

'How's Grace doing love?' Jed said, changing the subject.

Kira looked down at the little lady snuggled in her wrap.

'She is just fine. I expect she'll want a feed in a bit, and then I'll put her down.'

Jed gently stroked the top of his daughter's head.

Kira continued. 'She's been round to everyone, and they all said she is gorgeous. What was in Ingrid's box?'

'Oh, nothing important. We can open it tomorrow.'

CORPCHAT: *Today's hot topic – should Natural Parenting be banned now that NanNan technology is so advanced? New parents, the Jenkins went natural – what would you do? Share your opinion, spread the sweep.*

Kira settled herself on the couch to feed Grace. She was feeling tired at having to explain, for what felt like the hundredth time, their natural parenting choice to her guests as well as answering the same question over and over, - 'Why haven't you activated a NanNan?' But now, with her friends grouped round her, Kira didn't think she could feel any happier. Out of the corner of her eye, she watched a dishevelled Dina and Ben attempt to sneak back to the party from the bathroom. Kira chuckled to herself.

'Something amusing Kira?' Martha asked.

'The audacity of youth.'

'Hey,' protested Ruth. 'You don't have to be young to be audacious you know.'

'Is that a fact, Ruth?' Martha said, not altogether friendly. 'Why, what have you been up to lately?'

Ruth frowned at her tone, but carried on talking.

'Don't give me the lecture Ma. We sneaked out last night. It was awesome and the sunset over the beach was epic.'

'We?' Kira asked.

'Yes, we.' Ruth blushed slightly and began twirling a stray strand of hair around a finger. 'Just a guy, no-one you know. And before you ask, he is an Anti-Corp supporter and no, he is not a terrorist and yes, I am being careful.' She looked pointedly at Martha as she spoke, who raised her hands and shook her head.

'Don't look at me,' Martha said. 'Who you do in your spare time is up to you.'

There was a pause, then the three women started laughing.

'Oh, K. It was amazing,' Ruth continued. 'There

was something in the air, it felt so natural to be out there. I almost felt like,' she gestured towards the small blue figurine nestled in the corner of Kira's alter space, 'like Gaia was right there on that beach with us. Marshall reckons he saw a blue lady in the distance but I'm pretty sure that was either the drugs or the alcohol.' She laughed. 'Maybe both.'

Kira raised an eyebrow.

'What? I'm a grown up. It's all legit. I don't do dodgy anymore. Honest.'

'No, it's not that,' Kira clarified. 'The blue lady – did you see her?'

'No,' Ruth shook her head. 'I mean, it felt very spiritual but I had other things on my mind and some of that was trying to make sure we didn't get caught. Why do you ask?'

'Well, it's just a bit odd. These blue lady sightings.' Kira also glanced at the little blue figurine in the corner. 'Jed told me he saw a blue lady yesterday, on the way to Collection. And he saw a bee, or at least that what he says.'

Ruth thought back.

'Well there definitely wasn't a bee. Marshall only said he thought he saw a blue lady, and it was pretty dark out there. I was more interested in...other things.'

Dina had moved closer to them, listening in to their conversation, she tucked her hair behind her ear and coughed nervously.

'Umm, I've seen her too.' Dina blushed under the sudden scrutiny as the three women turned to look at her.

'I mean, I think I have.' Dina ducked her head slightly, and tucked her hair behind her ear again. 'It was a couple of days ago. I was sitting outside Academy waiting for Ruth to come out of class. I suddenly realised there was someone sitting next to me. I was surprised, I hadn't notice them arrive, and before I had time to look round properly, they'd already gone.'

Martha interrupted her.

'So how do you even know anyone was there? It

sounds like you never saw them in the first place.'

Dina spoke half to herself, half to Martha sounding frustrated.

'Maybe I'm just not explaining it very well.' Dina pushed her hair behind her ear again, and spoke up with more determination. 'I saw a blue lady, but when I looked she'd already gone. But I know I saw her. She touched my hand. That's how I knew someone was sitting next to me.'

Realising she'd spoken up so loudly, Dina shrank back a little, but Ruth leant over and patted her knee.

'I wondered why you seemed so off when I met you that day.' Ruth began tapping the table thoughtfully. 'You know, now that I think about it, I'm pretty sure it was a blue lady who brushed past me when Marshall and I were on our way out of the city.'

Martha snorted. 'You are just saying that because everyone else has seen her.'

Ruth glared at Martha.

'Have you seen her?'

'Actually, yes,' Martha countered. 'She brushed past me in the park when....' She stopped looking confused.

Kira filled the sudden silence.

'I think it's interesting that so many people have seen a blue lady. Do you think it's a new advert?' Kira wanted to divert the focus from Martha. 'Dina, did you feel drawn to making a purchase after your experience?'

Dina shook her head. 'No. I felt sad, but at peace.'

Ruth listened to them but continued to watch Martha with a slight frown on her face.

'Well, you know, it could have been a manifestation of Gaia,' Kira said, raising her voice to be heard above the mock groans from her friends. 'No, I'm serious. The natural planet needs our help, you can't deny that. We destroyed so much, it's only fair we help nature to rebuild as well. If we can't get more in tune with what's left of nature on the outside of City Forty-Two, soon there won't be anything left.'

'Kira, you don't seriously believe an ancient Greek deity is randomly stalking a handful of your friends.' Ruth sounded incredulous. 'What on earth would she want from us?'

Kira didn't know what to say.

MADSR: Cosmology Expert delivers final lecture before returning to City Fifteen. Dr Marshall Reynolds talks about the slowing of the universe oscillation and what will happen when the reverberations end. Register interest, VR plug-in available.

'Ruth - am I correct in thinking Marshall is the Professor delivering the Cosmology lecture tonight?' Martha said, changing the subject, wanting to know more about Ruth's mystery man. 'Are you two serious?'

'He is, and I don't think so,' Ruth replied. The others all looked at her, waiting for more details. 'There's honestly nothing to tell. He's a visiting lecturer. Goes back next week - bit obsessed with looking up at the stars and asking the big question.' She put on a silly voice and waggled her fingers upwards, 'Are we alone in the verse?'

'You sound smitten to me,' Kira teased, gently lifting Grace to burp her.

'Yes, well, smitten or not, he's gone next week so I'm free and clear of all that.'

Martha leaned over to give Ruth a brief hug.

'We all go through bad and come out good the other side. I have to believe that.' She stood up to get more wine.

'What was all that about?' Ruth asked Kira.

Kira shook her head, standing up.

'Not mine to tell, Ruthie.'

Kira called for everyone's attention.

'Hi, everyone – I'd like to thank you all for coming.' She pointed at the sleeping baby on her shoulder. 'Grace is going to sleep now but she's pleased you all came and she thanks you for the lovely gifts. We will come visit you all soon.'

The guests murmured good night Grace wishes as Kira took the baby into the bedroom.

ANTIC: More secret meetings at Corp HQ. Join the online discussion in social hub beta – share what you know, don't let Corporation keep you in the dark.

Sipping her wine, Martha noticed Jed was alone in the kitchen and went to stand with him.

'Anything?'

Without turning to face her, Jed spoke in a low voice. 'We got him Ma. You don't have to worry.'

She nodded slowly.

'What will happen to him?'

Jed felt uncomfortable talking about it but felt that he owed his friend the truth.

'Your father sent the order down. He's to be terminated.' He looked down at his wristplant. 'About now.'

Before he could say anymore there was a huge flash of light from outside the apartment window and a massive peal of thunder. Kira came hurrying out of the bedroom. Another series of flashes illuminated the windows from the outside. 'Lightening storm!' A couple of the younger guests cried.

Ingrid frowned looking down at her expanded wrist monitor. 'We're not scheduled a static storm tonight.'

'I guess tech isn't always a hundred percent,' Pete commented, taking Ingrid's hand.

She smiled, mellowed by the evening's wine. Everyone else continued to watch through the window as the lightening flashed, gradually slowing down in its intensity, the thunder growling above. When the storm stopped rumbling and the sky fell dark, heavy rain could be heard against the pane.

'What a night!' Kira's mother commented. 'I hope the skyway is still clear so we can get home.'

Kira reassured her. The party guests began talking about the weather and how they were planning to travel home. Martha touched Jed's arm tentatively, her face pale.

'Do you think that was caused by..' She trailed off.

'By termination? I don't think so Ma. Just a fluke.'

'That was no fluke,' Kira said joining the conversation. 'That was Gaia crying out in pain.'

Jed looked at his wife and shook his head ruefully while Martha stared out of the window.

An hour after the storm had passed, people started to leave the apartment. The soundproofing had kept Grace oblivious to the storm raging outside. Martha had gone to lie down in the bedroom and keep an eye on the sleeping baby. Family, friends and parents all left in small groups, many leaving with food parcels and unopened bottles of wine. By the time Kira managed to get her parents out of the door, she felt exhausted.

'Is that it?'

'Yep. Pete left with Ingrid, they were giggling.'

Jed raised his eyebrows at Kira in mock disbelief.

'I expect we'll hear all about that tomorrow,' Kira said.

She looked round the apartment in dismay. There were glasses, cups, bits of food and cake littered all over the place.

'Come on,' she said to Jed. 'Let's make a start on this lot. I decided not to use the clean up service thinking it wouldn't be that bad. We can at least get the washer on tonight.'

'I guess,' he said, less than enthusiastic. His wristplant beeped as a message from Pete came through

'Thank you beta test!'

Jed chuckled.

'Well, I think Pete's having a good evening.'

Kira's eyes widened.

'Apparently volunteering for tech trials at HQ is the way to my sisters heart. Who knew?'

'Is that Pete finally making some headway with Ingrid?' Martha asked, coming through from the bedroom as Jed nodded in response. 'I am sorry for missing the end of the party. I came over so tired I needed to lie down. I checked on Grace before I left the room, she's fine.'

Kira smiled gratefully as Martha looked at the mess in the apartment.

'Do you want some help?'

Jed replied by tossing Martha a recycling sack.
While they got to work Jed told the two women the news about the apartment next door. Kira squealed and jumped up and down like a little girl. She gave Martha a huge hug.

'This is brilliant Ma! You can move in, right next door - and be our free babysitter.'

Kira trailed off when she realised Martha wasn't matching her enthusiasm.

'Are you sure you don't need the space?' Martha asked.

Jed shook his head.

'Not right now and after everything you've been through, we'd be more than happy if you wanted to stay with us.' He wanted to hug Martha but he knew it might be too much too soon. Instead he changed the subject. 'Dina seemed nice.'

Both women nodded and Kira gushed, sounding a little like her mother.

'Oh, she is such a lovely young girl. She's just graduated but now she's on Ruth's PhD trail. I mean, poor thing. But you know, she's here all alone. Her parents died and she doesn't have anyone else except for Academy mates, and you know how they usually drift off. I told her she was welcome to come over anytime. In fact, we're actually going to do lunch next week.'

'It will be nice to have a new member in our little group, especially after Ingrid,' Martha added. They all remembered how awkward lunch had been the one and only time Jed's sister had deigned to come outside without her technology.

'She's a complicated person,' Jed said.

CORPCHAT: Share your best lightening shot for a chance to win extra water rations.

ANTIC: Terminators arrive at Force. What crime deserves such punishment?

ANON6: Corp just terminated a rapist!

CORP: Use of termination is strictly monitored and was sanctioned unanimously by the Board after reviewing a heinous crime. No further action is necessary.

ADDITIONAL MEETING OF CORPORATION
BOARD FOR CITY FORTY-TWO
DATE: 17th April 2215
VIRTUAL PRESENCE: R HAMBLE, J NICKS, Y
ASWAD and P BASJERE

AGENDA

1. UNSANCTIONED USE OF TERMINATORS
2. REDUCTION IN NAN-NAN SALES
3. INCREASE OF NATURALS

MINUTES

1. WHEN QUESTIONED HAMBLE DEFENDED
   UNSANCTIONED USE OF TERMINATORS IN
   PROTECTION OF DAUGHTER. IT WAS
   AGREED NO FURTHER ACTION TO BE
   TAKEN. HAMBLE WILL SUBMIT FULL
   REPORT.
2. IT WAS AGREED TO PUSH THE NEW NAN-NAN
   THROUGH THE SWEEPS AND OFFER
   REDUCED PRICES FOR THOSE UPGRADING
   FROM OLDER MODELS. ALL PARTS FOR
   EARLY MODELS TO BE WITHDRAWN FROM
   SALE. WATER CREDITS TO BE AWARDED TO
   THOSE WHO SUCCESSFULLY REFER.
3. ALL NATURALS TO BE LISTED AND ACTIVITY
   TAGGED FOR POTENTIAL UNREST. NOTHING
   TO REPORT SO FAR. BOARD TO CONSIDER
   REDUCING WATER CREDITS AS LAST
   RESORT.

ANY OTHER BUSINESS – NONE.

Chapter Six

Someone was crying.

Kira checked on Grace, who was sleeping peacefully. She could hear sobbing coming from the lounge. Creeping out of the bedroom so as not to wake Jed and the baby, Kira went to investigate.

'Ma, what's the matter?'

Martha lifted her tear-stained face and pointed at the news sweeps projected on the wall. Kira read them in silence. The rape case had finally been swept.

'It doesn't mention your name does it?'

'No,' Martha replied in a small voice.

'No-one will find out Ma.' Kira went over to where her friend was sitting on the couch and put an arm round her. 'It's going to be okay.'

Martha blew her nose.

'I took the wipe but I still know that it happened.' Martha gestured back to the wall. 'It was me. I was the victim everyone is talking about.'

'You know what the sweeps are like though, Ma.' Kira tried to comfort her. 'They would have found out about the Terminators eventually. Now it's been reported, it'll soon die down when Corporation floods the sweeps about something else. No-one will find out.'

Martha looked at Kira and squeezed her hand.

'Thank you.'

'You'll see,' said Kira. 'They'll be talking about the

latest tech in no time.'

Jed hurried into the lounge fully dressed.

'Morning love, Martha. I've got to go into work early,' Jed said, grabbing an auto-brew from the kitchen. 'There's been something on the sweeps about...'

'Yes,' Kira interrupted. 'We know.'

'Martha, I'm so sorry.' Jed kissed his wife on the top of her head. 'I'll let you know what happens Kira, love you.'

'Love you.' She watched him leave the apartment. 'I hope he doesn't get into trouble.'

'I had better speak to my father,' Martha said.

'Why?'

'If this is on the sweeps he will assume it originated from Pete or Jed.'

Kira bit her lip.

'Don't worry Kira,' Martha continued. 'I will vouch for them both.'

And she hugged her friend before getting up and returning to her new apartment. Kira didn't have time to dwell on anything as Grace began crying for attention and food.

Pete greeted Jed outside Force HQ.

'How's Martha?'

'Upset, but Kira's with her,' Jed replied. 'How did the sweeps get hold of the case details?'

Pete shrugged and followed his partner into the office. There was an instant summons from the Chief on both desks. The two detectives went straight to the Chief's door. Pete knocked.

'Yes?' the Chief barked.

Opening the door, Pete stuck his head into the room and the Chief beckoned them both in.

'Good, you're here. What the frag happened?' The Chief jabbed his finger in Jed's direction. 'I've got Hamble breathing down my neck and the fragging sweeps are full of a case no-one is supposed to know anything about.'

'It didn't come from us,' Jed said.

'Of course it didn't fragging come from you. You're not complete idiots.' Breathing hard the Chief motioned for the two detectives to sit down. 'Who else was involved?'

'No-one Sir,' Pete replied. 'We picked up Greenwood ourselves and carried out the questioning in meeting room one.'

'There was just the night guard,' Jed said. 'We didn't see anyone else.'

'Night guard, eh?' The Chief flicked through the screen in front of him then barked through the com to his secretary. 'Get Pearce in my office ASAP.'

The Chief lifted his gaze back to the two detectives. 'Can you think of anyone else?'

'Just the Terminators Sir,' Jed said.

'And Mr Hamble,' Pete added. 'And his man.'

The Chief rubbed his temples.

'Right,' he said. 'Hamble's on his way in, he wants to speak to both of you...' but before the Chief could continue, his office door banged open and Mr Hamble strode in.

'Hmmph.' Hamble surveyed the room. 'Which one of you broke protocol?'

The Chief stood up when Hamble entered and his face reddened in anger.

'You have no jurisdiction to barge in here and accuse my detectives.'

'They had no right to speak to the sweeps,' Mr Hamble retorted.

'My detectives don't speak to the sweeps. We have other lines of enquiry to investigate and a full report will be made.'

The two men glared at each other for a few moments.

'I expect instant updates,' Mr Hamble conceded. He turned and left the room without giving either detective a single glance.

Pete exhaled loudly but said nothing as the Chief shot him a sharp look.

'That'll be all. For now.' The Chief dismissed the two men from his office.

Jed's wristplant pinged, a message from Kira. *Martha is speaking to her Dad. Hope everything is alright? K x* Jed told Pete as they returned to their desks.

'I hope she tells him we had nothing to do with it,' Pete grumbled.

'I think he knows we didn't. He's just looking for someone to blame.'

Several hours later the night guard Pearce was escorted to holding in magno-binders, watched by a grim faced Chief.

There was no formal apology from Mr Hamble to Pete or Jed, but Martha assured them both that he had apologised to her for jumping to conclusions and that their jobs at Force HQ were safe.

CORP: *Our latest candidates for Corporation's Rising Star are:*
Miss Ingrid Jenkins, Corp Tech
Junior Dr Lewis Barnstable, Med Centre
Mr Vladimir Draganov, Science Division

INJEN: *Ecstatic to be nominated for Rising Star.*
I pledge to work even harder for Corporation.

Three weeks had passed since the leak at Force had been dealt with and an excited Ingrid was telling Jed, Kira and Pete over dinner about her nomination for Corporation Rising Star.

'It means I am a top pick for promotion.' Ingrid beamed at the others sat around the table. 'Isn't that exciting?'

Pete matched her smile, while Kira murmured her congratulations.

'Proud of you sis,' Jed said, as he leant over the

table and clinked glasses with her.

'I just never thought it would be me,' Ingrid gushed. 'The department has been so busy and everyone has been working hard, but it just goes to show – Corporation rewards loyalty and dedication.'

'Speaking of Corporation,' Kira said. 'Did you ever find out about the blue lady campaign Ingrid?'

'I told you before Kira, there was no such campaign.'

'Are you sure it's not top secret and you'd have to kill us if you told us?' Jed teased his sister, his voice full of amusement.

'It's not anything to do with Corporation at all.'

'So you admit there was a blue lady then?' Kira said.

'That's not what I mean.' Ingrid started to get red in the face.

'We've all seen her love, it's okay to admit you have too.' Pete was grinning with Kira and Jed and failed to realise how upset Ingrid was. She pushed her chair away from the table and stood up.

'I've just remembered, I've paperwork to finish at the office. Thank you for dinner Kira.'

Before anyone could stop her, Ingrid gathered up her coat and left the apartment. The others stared at each other for a moment.

'I'd better go and see if she's alright.' Pete said his goodbyes and followed his girlfriend out of the apartment.

'I'm sorry Jed,' said Kira. 'I didn't mean to upset her.'

Jed began to clear the dishes from the table.

'Don't worry about it hon, she's a corper. I'm sure we'll have them both over for dinner again soon.'

A month later and Ingrid was still giving Pete the cold shoulder, despite how well their relationship had been going. Ingrid claimed it was a busy time at work but Kira knew she'd caused an issue by raising the topic of the blue lady at dinner.

Kira spoke about the Gaia sightings with her other friends as they tried to figure out whether it was an advertising campaign, a nonsensical prank, or whether it could be the manifestation of an ancient goddess.

She was sure Ingrid had seen the blue lady and was desperate to apologise but all her efforts had met with a busy tone and Ingrid's sweep feed was full of work related posts.

INJEN: Latest development update – neural nets designed for colleagues to interface seamlessly in the workplace and increase efficiency.

'Are you still pinging Ingrid?' Ruth asked.

'Yes.'

'Don't bother K. She's so wrapped up in Corp these days, she probably thinks the blue lady is some kind of rival advertising.'

'A rival? To Corporation?' Dina was intrigued.

'I wish,' Ruth said.

Ruth, Dina, Martha and Kira had been meeting up regularly since Grace's homecoming party. The four women found they had a lot in common and enjoyed each other's company. Initially Dina had been Ruth's shadow, but gradually she had begun to express her own personality and individuality.

'Do you know why Martha wanted to see us all Kira?' Dina asked as she shook an old fashioned rattle at Grace.

'I do.'

'Well?'

'I'm not telling,' Kira grinned at Dina. 'Ma will be here soon, you'll just have to wait.'

'I hate waiting,' Dina grumbled.

Martha came through the door five minutes later, a huge box in her hands.

'Oh good, you are all here.'

The others called out hello and Dina pointed at the box.

'Is that for me?'

'Yes Dina,' Martha said. 'Let me show you what I have brought you.'

She took off her shoes, coat and bag and brought the box over to where the others were sat in the lounge.

'It's awesome you're part of the gang D,' Ruth playfully punched Dina in the arm.

'And it has been wonderful to talk to you about what I do at the Hydroponics Lab,' Martha said.

'I find it fascinating though Ma.' Dina was beginning to wonder where the conversation was going.

'You and Ben make such a cute couple,' Kira said. 'You're like the little sister I never had.'

'Okay, now you're going to make me cry,' Dina said as she tucked her blonde hair behind her ear.

Ruth and Kira watched as Martha opened the box she had put on the floor beside her. She gently lifted something up and held it out to Dina.

'Is that...' Dina spoke in hushed tones. 'Is that.. an actual tree?'

'It is a fern,' Martha said.

Kira got up and went over to the small altar in the corner of the room. She bent down and retrieved a small pot with a slightly bigger fern growing within it.

'This is George.' Kira looked fondly at her small plant.

'Mine lives in the bathroom,' Ruth said. 'It gets nice and steamy in there.'

The others laughed as Dina took the tiny fern from Martha and stroked the delicate fronds.

'This is amazing,' Dina said. 'It is real – isn't it?'

'Yes,' Martha replied. 'It is my personal project at SCID – I will have several to give away soon, but I wanted you to have one first.'

'Welcome to our family Dina.' Kira beamed down at the young girl who was still in awe of the small plant in her hands. 'I have something for you as well. Something for all of you.'

Kira put her fern back and picked up a small blue bag. She settled herself back down on the floor. Grace had rolled over to her tummy and was kicking her legs frantically.

'I've got her.' Martha picked the baby up and started bouncing Grace on her knee.

'Okay,' Kira said. 'I know you tease me about her, but with everything that we've seen and now that Dina is part of our extended family, I wanted you all to have one.'

She fished into the bag and pulled out three miniature female figurines, all painted blue – a match for the one on her altar.

'Oh Kira, thank you.' Dina peered at the statuette. 'She's beautiful.'

Martha and Ruth also looked curiously at the small yet exquisitely painted lady.

'I guess we can't blame the sightings on Corp anymore,' Ruth said.

'It's Gaia,' Kira said.

'How can you be so sure?' Martha asked.

'The blue lady experiences are too personal for them to be Corporation.' Kira reached over to take Grace from Martha. She was trying to eat the blue lady figurine. 'I don't believe they are adverts. And adverts for what exactly?'

As each of the women put away her tiny goddess, the conversation moved on to where they were headed for lunch that day.

DING: Nature is beautiful.

SCID – Scientific success in the hydroponics lab. Real ferns will be available to collect soon. Limited availability so register your interest with MAHA.

Chapter Seven

DING: So excited - touring Archive today!

MAHA: Thank you for the overwhelming response to the ferns. A new batch will be available soon, please register your interest with SCID.

Kira hummed as she made the morning synth-caf. The past three months had flown by, Grace was growing so fast. Now she was smiling and grabbing fingers, wide-eyed and interested in everything around her. Life as a family had certainly taken some adjusting to, and the sleepless nights had been so difficult they had come close to turning on the Nan-Nan, but Kira was glad they had stuck to their ideals.

But today - today was going to be a good day. Kira was going to meet Dina at Archive for their first official interview, although they'd spent lots of time together since meeting at the party. She would be introducing Grace to her colleagues for the first time and then give Dina the grand tour. Kira enjoyed taking people round Archive. Not only was it a grand building, it housed carefully preserved film, books, scrolls - even Egyptian papyri spanning thousands of years of history. It was awe inspiring to walk through the hallowed corridors of Archive, pointing out items of special interest to visitors and generally breathing in that delicious book smell. Jed used to laugh at Kira when she tried to explain the smell to him. He claimed she was imagining the whole thing, but everyone else who worked in Archive knew exactly what she meant. It was a truly special place.

Glancing at the wall, Kira realised she was going to be late. She hurried to get Grace dressed and assemble all the baby paraphernalia she would need to travel the few blocks down the road. That was the one thing she missed about being a non-parent - the ability to walk out the door on time.

Martha poked her head round the inner door at the end of the apartment.

'Is it safe?'

Kira laughed.

'Of course it is, Ma.'

Since Mr Hamble had organised the addition of the next door apartment to Kira and Jed's it had made sense for Martha to move in straight away. Especially as she had no inclination to go back to her parents. Being around her friends and baby Grace had helped her forget some of the awfulness that had happened to her.

'Are you seeing Dina today?'

'Yeah. We're meeting at Archive, I'm taking Grace with me too. Should be good. What about you?'

Martha grimaced.

'I have got a med check. I would rather not attend but if I do not go..'

'I know sweetie.'

That was the problem when your father was on the Corporation Board. There were good points like being able to live next door to your best friend, but it seemed your life was forever being scrutinised.

'May I cook for you both tonight?' Martha asked. 'I want to thank you again for letting me stay here.'

'Of course you can – especially if you can work your magic with what's in the cupboard.' Kira gave her friend a big hug. 'And we love having you next door.'

Grace began to babble over the wireless baby monitor.

'Time to get going.'

Martha gave Kira a little wave as the two women separated, each one intent on the day ahead.

Dina winced at the pain in her lower back. It had been eight weeks since her last period. She had eventually agreed to make an appointment at Corp Medical in case it was the result of something sinister. She would be able to have the treatment straight away and not risk any complications. Usually she made every attempt to avoid Corporation officials but Martha had been insistent that she have a check up, the appointment was booked for tomorrow. Dina looked in the mirror at how pale and tired she looked.

'Nothing a bit of make-up can't improve on,' she thought. She activated the '*truly natural*' option on her mirror and closed her eyes whilst the make up was applied.

Dina was looking forward to today. Not only would she get to spend some time with Kira and Grace, but she was going to be able to record the first part of her interview with Kira and, best of all, she was getting an insiders tour of Archive. She was sure not even Ruth had been in there. At least not officially, she thought, recalling Ruth's tales about adventures beyond the city walls. Now that she had left the comforting embrace of the Academy, Dina felt lucky to have found such a welcoming group of women who didn't treat her like a small child. It was so interesting to be able to have conversations about how life used to be, even if Kira's devotions to Gaia were a bit on the unusual side.

Dina checked herself in the mirror, turning her face from side to side. Much better. She applied a med-patch to her back, double checked her notes were in her bag and left the apartment.

The skimmer to Archive moved quickly through the airway. Dina struggled to find a comfortable position. She began to feel pain low down, deep inside her, like a hand was squeezing and tightening her womb rhythmically. She bit her lip at an intense cramp and started to worry. It had been a long time since she'd experienced severe period pain like this. She tried in vain to make herself think of something else and was so relieved when she arrived at Archive.

Dina saw Kira standing outside with Grace and hobbled over, hunched up to ease the pain in her abdomen.

'Dina! Are you okay?'

Dina gave a small nod.

'Bathroom?' she asked.

Kira led her through the doors and to the right.

'I'll be outside,' said Kira. 'Call me if you need me.'

As Dina went through to a cubicle, she gasped in pain and bent doubled. Half collapsing on the toilet she felt fluid leaving her body, and with some trepidation she wiped herself and looked to see what had happened. There was lots of blood. It wasn't the usual dark period colour, this was brighter, as if something had cut her inside. Dina searched frantically in her purse for her period pen hoping that it would be sufficient to stem the flow. After inserting the pen and finishing up, she stood and turned to see into the bowl. There were lots of clots and more blood. No wonder she had felt it leaving her body. She felt sick as she opened the cubicle door, then crunched her body up as the cramps returned.

'Kira,' she called weakly, then managed to repeat it louder.

The door to the bathroom opened, and Kira's face peered in.

'Yes sweetie?'

Dina couldn't speak, she pointed behind her. As Kira wheeled Grace's pram cube into the bathroom she wondered what on earth she was going to see. Looking into the cubicle Kira gasped when she saw the blood, and looked at Dina.

'This is your period? Tell me that isn't normal?'

Dina shook her head and said 'no' in a small voice before more cramps made her cry out. Kira touched her ear comm.

'I need medic transport for a young female from Archive.'

She continued speaking to the operator, calmly answering questions as she put her arm around Dina. When Kira finished the call she pulled the young girl in for a hug.

'They'll be here in five minutes Dina. Do you want me to call anyone?'

'No. There's no-one. Just you and Ruth and Ma. Will you come with me?'

'Of course I will. Can you make it outside to wait for the Med Van?'

Dina shook her head in misery.

'Okay, sweetie, it's okay. We'll just wait here, it's fine.' Kira tried to soothe her friend while they waited anxiously for the medics to arrive.

Martha frowned at the two medical staff having a heated discussion behind the glass, something must have gone wrong with the body scan but so far they weren't talking to her. At last they seemed to come to an agreement and a voice told her she could gather her things and go through to the waiting area.

'What about my results?'

The two medical agents looked at each other before one replied.

'If you could just wait next door we will ask the Senior Consultant to speak with you shortly.'

And they dimmed the partition preventing any further conversation.

Martha huffed, it was probably nothing but because her father was who he was, they had to make a fuss. If they made her wait around much longer she wouldn't have time to go and gather supplies to cook for Kira and Jed. She walked through to the outer office as the other door opened and an older man walked into the room.

'Miss Hamble?'

'Yes.'

'It appears we have a rather unusual set of circumstances. Your medical scan revealed an anomaly, of sorts.'

The consultant cleared his throat and rubbed his forehead as he struggled to find the right words.

'Am I sick?' Martha asked, suddenly worried.

'That remains to be seen,' the Consultant muttered, then realising he spoke aloud he coughed again and continued. 'To be blunt, you're pregnant.' He raised his hands and shoulders in a slight shrug. 'It's unclear as to how this has happened. Some genetic mutation perhaps. We'll have to run tests and keep you here, private rooms of course.'

'No. I will not be examined.'

The Consultant made sympathetic noises.

'It's quite a lot to take in my dear. Once your father arrives, I'm sure you'll begin to understand that staying here is the best course of action.'

Martha stood and stared at him in growing horror.

'You called my father? You had no right...' She broke off as the door banged open and they both turned to look at Mr Hamble entering.

'Good you're still here. What's going on? What's the emergency? Why couldn't I be informed over the phone?'

'I want to know why you were called at all.' Martha berated the Consultant. 'Don't you have any concept of patient confidentiality?'

'Martha, what confidentiality? What are you talking about?'

She held her hands to her stomach protectively.

'Apparently, you are going to be a grandfather.'

The consultant rushed to fill in the details in the surprised silence that followed, but trailed off when Mr Hamble held his hand up and looked directly at him.

'Who knows about this?'

'Myself and the two medical staff who carried out the scan.'

'I want them memory wiped, now. And you, you will sign a confidentiality disclosure and have all medical files relating to my daughter redacted immediately.'

'But the medical implications!' The Consultant pleaded.

'I don't care for implications!' Mr Hamble roared

making Martha and the Consultant jump. 'Do it. Now!'

The Consultant fled the room stammering affirmatives.

Martha sat down, knees drawn up, hugging herself, looking up at her father.

'I suppose you think I am abnormal too.'

'Martha. We need to keep this quiet while we decide what to do.' Mr Hamble began pacing the floor. 'I think you should move back home so I can have our personal medical staff see to you.'

'No Father. I need to process this in my own space, in my own time. I am not your little girl anymore – you do not control me.'

She stood up, moved past him and left the room.

'Martha!' Mr Hamble took a step after her but stopped when she allowed the door to bang shut behind her.

She walked numbly through the medical centre corridor and became aware of a voice calling her name. She looked around and saw Kira sat outside Emergencies.

'What are you doing here? Is Grace okay?' Martha asked looking around. Spotting the baby she put her hand to her chest in relief then frowned as she saw how worried Kira looked.

'It's Dina. She didn't feel well, and then there was an awful lot of blood and I didn't know what to do so I brought her here, and now they won't let me see her because I'm not family! I tried to explain to them that her family has passed and I'm listed as her emergency contact, but they wouldn't listen.'

Kira looked at the closed door and bit her lip, then looking back at Martha realised her friend looked ill as well.

'Are you alright Ma? You look pale - sit down, sit down.'

Kira helped Martha to a seat. Martha began to cry

as the realisation that her rape three months ago had left such a permanent mark. She felt incredibly vulnerable and lost as to what to do next.

'Kira,' she half whispered. 'I'm pregnant.'

Kira stared at her friend but before she had time to respond, Pete and Jed walked into the lobby.

'Are they here for me?'

Kira put a protective arm around her friend.

'What's going on?' Kira asked her husband.

'Why are you always in the thick of things my love?' Jed said, running his hand over his head. 'We got a call from Medical, we came. I don't know anymore, but I'm guessing it has something to do with us?'

Martha clutched Kira's arm tightly while Kira tried to explained.

'They won't let me in to see Dina. Something bad has happened, I told them she didn't have any family. We are her family for gods sake.'

Glancing back at Martha, Kira shook her head slightly as if to say it wasn't about her. Martha felt confused and then stiffened when she saw her father and the consultant coming down the corridor towards them.

'Do not let them take me Kira,' she whispered.

Mr Hamble eyed his daughter then spoke to Jed.

'Why are you here Jenkins?'

Jed was about to speak, but before he could say anything the Consultant cut in.

'I called him. We have.. another situation. It's nothing Corp Medical can't handle but I thought it would be prudent to involve the Force in case of any difficulties. The young woman in question has no family..'

'We *are* her family,' Kira said in a loud voice. 'I've been trying to tell you people that for the past half an hour!'

The Consultant looked startled at her outburst, but before he could continue Mr Hamble barked at him.

'What do you mean another incident?'

The Consultant stared at the angry, confused faces

around him.

'Perhaps we should move into one of the relative rooms? We can discuss everything in private there.'

'Very well,' Mr Hamble said. 'But we keep confidentialities already discussed. This has gone far enough as it is.'

They all walked into the side room indicated by the Consultant. Grace began to cry. Kira could feel her face getting redder and redder as, all fingers and thumbs, she struggled to get the baby out of the stroller and find her milk. Jed tried to help but she batted his hands away.

'I got this,' she said.

After a few uncomfortable moments, Kira sat down, settled Grace with her milk and motioned for the Consultant to begin.

'Well, about half an hour ago a young woman..'

'Dina Grey.' Kira interrupted again.

The Consultant scowled at her.

'Yes. Miss Grey came in to Medical experiencing severe stomach cramps and blood loss,' he paused, looking around the room. 'It appears she had a miscarriage. Whilst these are not unknown to Corp Medical, it has been almost fifty years since our last incident and there are certain protocols we must follow. One of which includes extensive medical testing and isolation of the patient. In order to begin this process we need family permission. It transpires that Miss Grey has no family,' he raised his voice in order to finish his sentence sensing Kira about to interrupt again. 'So we called Force for legal witnesses to the process.'

'You can't be serious,' Martha said, pale faced. 'You can't expect a young woman to surrender her freedom so you can prod her and poke her whilst she tries to come to terms with losing a baby she never knew she could have. It is inhuman!' She turned to stare at her father, imploring him. 'Father, you can't let them do this.'

'Yes, well. It's somewhat out of my hands Martha, without legal guardianship, I don't see what I can do.'

Martha rounded on him furiously.

'You sweep legislation to one side for me and then expect me to accept my friends being persecuted. I can't believe you will stand idly by and let the Corporation ruin Dina's life!' She leaned forward. 'She is nineteen Father, nineteen! I won't let her go through this alone. Let her come home with Kira and I. We will make sure sweeps do not get hold of this and we will allow Medical to treat her at home, non invasively.' She looked up at him with unshed tears in her eyes. 'Father please?'

Mr Hamble stared at his daughter for a moment.

'I'll have to pull some strings. Let me speak to my man.' Turning to the Consultant, he fixed him with a glare. 'I want this whole incident redacted. No evidence. Turn all files over to these two.' He pointed at Jed and Pete. 'I'll have my man come in and get you to sign a binding confidentiality. I'm sure I don't need to warn you of the consequences should a word of this be breathed to anyone.' He looked around the room glaring. 'Let's get this girl discharged, I want everyone out of here pronto.'

Pete stood.

'I'll get Dina discharged.'

'I'll come with you,' said Martha. She paused as she passed her father, touching his arm. 'Thank you, Daddy.'

Mr Hamble cleared his throat and spoke to Jed.

'I'll send my man over for agreements. I know you are all friends now but things change and I don't want to leave anything to chance. You will agree to never discuss this with anyone else, especially anyone with Anti-Corp ties.'

Scowling, he included Kira in his statement.

She flushed, knowing he was talking about Ruth. Although none of them knew the extent of her involvement with Anti-Corp, it was obvious she had some kind of tie.

The consultant coughed letting them know he was still in the room.

'Yes?' Mr Hamble asked.

'If the detective will follow me, I'll see about getting the memory wipes we discussed organised. I'd prefer to include myself with that course of action otherwise the temptation - you understand this is a double medical anomaly. I don't know that I could trust myself..' he trailed off under the stern gaze of Mr Hamble.

'Very well,' he nodded. 'Good man for volunteering, know your own weaknesses and act. Admirable, admirable.'

Jed gave his wife and daughter a kiss and whispered, 'see you later hon,' as he escorted the Consultant out of the room.

'Right then. I'll have some things sent over and get my man to organise the medical checks. Kira,' Mr Hamble paused as he tried to find the right words. 'My daughter.. ahem..it's important...' He trailed off as Kira came up to him and put her hand on his arm.

'It's okay, Mr Hamble. We love Martha very much and we won't let anything bad happen to her. I promise.'

He reddened and nodded, then patted her hand before leaving the room. Kira exhaled loudly and looked down at the little girl happily babbling away in her arms.

MED4C: *Hamble seen at Med Centre again. No Comment status released - again.*

ANTIC: *The number of authorised memory wipes has risen.*
What are Corporation trying to hide?

MAHA: *Healthy and happy – nothing to worry about. More ferns soon.*

Notes from Anti-Corp Meeting at Academy Student Bar,
June 30th 2215

- *Next beach trip planned for mid July to celebrate end
  of finals.*

- *September's drive for new recruits to be headed up by
  Bobby as usual. We've lost 17 members so it's
  important to replace and increase.*

- *Successful bugging of Corp Tech achieved – we should
  be able to find out what new tech is on its way.
  Corporation can't hide anything from us.*

- *Next on the bugging list is to get into Science Division
  so bring some ideas to our next meeting. We need to
  know what new genetics are being planned.*

- *Concerns raised again about the militant splinter group
  42nd **Army** who are now holding their own meetings
  and talking about extreme violent action against
  Corporation. Our leader Victor Bianchi will speak to
  their leader Zane and report back.*

*Meet again in a month's time. Bring all your ideas for new
rallies – let's keep fighting Corporation! Think free – be
free.*

Chapter Eight

CORP: Report suspicious behaviour for the good of your community. Illegal goods hurt Corporation, we care about you so look after us.

Ruth stubbed out her cigarette into an already overflowing ashtray. She didn't have many packets left and it would be several months before the next shipment arrived, but the nicotine kept her feeling calm and in control. The black market thrived with low tech solutions to everyday life, and there was nothing Corporation could do about it.

They had used 'The Event' to consolidate their power, and now a hundred years later most people could never imagine life without the omnipresent Corporation telling them what to do. When a younger, more idealistic Ruth had joined Anti-Corp she'd have done anything to effect change but both her and the movement had changed. These days she only passed on details of students who might be interested in joining Anti-Corp - being a lecturer of advanced studies had few perks, and certainly no high credit rewards, but what it did have was access to a steady stream of young, impressionable minds.

Ruth coughed as her lungs rebelled against the effects of the cigarettes, and looked down at the short list on the tablet in front of her. At the top of the list was Dina's name. Ruth picked up her stylus and carefully drew a thick line right through it.

Dina has been bought up in City Fifteen, the closest geographic city to Forty-Two. Fifteen was smaller with a lower gross profit margin, meaning Corporation had had no qualms in downgrading the city after the uprising. After they had relocated the orphans. Dina's parents had been extremely vocal against Corporation. Others had listened to them, and it was the Grey's suspicious deaths that had sparked the Fifteen riots. Dina had been too young to understand what had happened at the time, and when Ruth first heard about her background she thought Dina would've been desperate to join Anti-Corp. So far, she had shown no interest and Ruth didn't want to push the issue.

If she hadn't taken her to Kira's party, Dina would have never met Ben and never been distracted by that handsome face, and she would never have been invited to join the circle. Not that Ruth minded her inclusion. Being friends with Kira and Martha had originally been part of an Anti-Corp objective but after spending so much time with them Ruth had come to care for them both. It was one of the reasons why she was still on the fringe of Anti-Corp, involved with casual recruitment, rather than heading up new protests.

You can't be an activist and be best friends with the daughter of the Marketing Director of the Corporation Board. Victor had encouraged her to use Martha to discover Corporation weaknesses and opportunities for Anti-Corp to cast doubt over Corporation rule, but she had refused. Ruth shifted in her seat as she thought about the latest scheme she'd been involved with - using Pete's infatuation with Ingrid, Jed's sister, to plant a bug in her office at Corp Tech. Ruth hadn't been keen but felt sure Corporation security sweeps would catch the bug and remove it. Pete thought he'd been delivering a cute teddy to his lady. Ruth had no idea what Pete saw in Ingrid. He was a good looking guy, but Ingrid, she was tall and blonde, with the personality of a stick. The scheme had worked though. Detailed scans of the Corp Tech building had been downloaded by Victor and his team.

It would be the first time Anti-Corp had access to a high security Corporation facility, provided of course they could get past the security measures. Ruth shook her head, not her problem she tried to tell herself. Her ear comm pinged and Kira, sounding stressed, was on the line.

'Ruth? Can you do me a huge favour? Can you swing by Dina's place and pick up some overnight stuff for her? She's going to be staying with us for a little while. I can't talk now but I'll fill you in when you get here. Dina said you still have an access key?'

Ruth nodded, then realising Kira wouldn't be able to see her spoke aloud. 'Yeah, yeah I have. I'll go now. Is she alright? What's happened?'

'Just get over here Ruthie, it's too much to even try and put into words.' Kira clicked off.

Ruth gathered her things together. Whatever was going on sounded serious, trying to find new recruits could wait.

ANTIC: Calling all Academy Freshers – free drink and VR experience in the Quad today.

Martha held Dina's hand as they sat in the back of the private air car, courtesy of her father. Both women were preoccupied with their own thoughts, and said nothing to each other but each felt reassured at the close contact.

Kira and Jed sat in the seats in front of the two women, behind the driver. Kira looked back at her friends, then leaned over to Jed. In a low tone she spoke Jed's name to get his attention.

'Jed. What are we going to do now?'

Jed glanced up at the driver and whispered.

'There's barely any evidence left at the Medical Centre. Pete's on clean up and he won't leave anything behind. I suggest we get home and call a family meeting.'

He smiled at his wife, confident that Dina could be cared for and helped if she stayed with them. In a louder voice he added,

'It'll mean we'll have an extra guest, but luckily we have all the spare space. So I say, the more, the merrier.'

Kira leaned even closer towards him.

'Don't you think it's a bit odd, though?'

'How do you mean?'

'Well, first Martha's attack and all the sightings and now … this. A miscarriage for frag sake. They don't just happen Jed. It's clinically improbable. Since The Event I

84

mean. We physically can't have children – any of us. So how did Dina get pregnant?'

Jed hushed his wife.

'I don't know love. I'm sure this is an isolated incident. Just like Martha's attack – which is unrelated I might add.' He glanced at the driver who seemed oblivious to their topic of conversation. 'I don't think we need to worry about a sudden population explosion. Anyway, Corporation will investigate and let us know if we need to be concerned.'

'You are joking?'

'As for the 'sightings'. Kira, they were random projections for some product that never made it past initial tests. Ingrid says it happens all the time. It's just a coincidence that so many people we know were test subjects.'

Kira refused to give in.

'What about Mr Hamble then? Don't you think his behaviour is a little strange? I mean I know he loves his daughter but what's with all the secrecy. You have to agree that isn't *normal procedure* is it?'

As the aircar swung into parking for their apartment, Jed replied,

'You'd be surprised at what the Board gets brushed under the mat love.'

CORP: *Collect your updated water ration allocation and discover more ways to conserve with Corporation – we care about every drop.*

Ruth arrived at the apartment within half an hour of Kira calling her, laden with two large bags of Dina's clothes and other essentials. As Kira settled Grace on her play mat, Jed offered to make the drinks. Ruth took one look at Martha and Dina's pale faces, eyes red from crying and quietly asked what was going on. Neither answered, so she sat down with them and waited. Kira plonked herself on the floor, within arms reach of the baby.

'You want to start Ma?' she asked.

'Firstly I don't want to hear any wild fantasies about Anti Corp or resistance or any of that nonsense.' She glared at Ruth who held her hands up in mock submission. 'I mean it. We know you have ties with AC but this time you have to be on our side, otherwise you leave now.'

Ruth looked at the three women and saw how serious they all were.

'I'm in,' she said.

Martha looked over at Dina who gave her a slight nod. She continued.

'Dina had a miscarriage this morning, a medical anomaly. And I, well, I'm pregnant.'

Jed chose that particular moment to bring hot drinks over to the women and stopped in amazement at what Martha had said. The sudden scalding pain on his hand alerted him that he was spilling synth-caf everywhere.

'Ah! Frag, that's hot,' he cried, and danced around Grace trying not to lose any more burning liquid, rushing to get rid of the mugs. 'Pregnant? Pregnant! No wonder Mr Hamble is desperate for everyone to sign a disclosure. Oh, my fragging hand.'

Ruth's mouth hung open, her eyes wide - this was huge. This could be the sweep of the century.

'This could ruin Corporation.' Ruth spoke out loud and glanced quickly at Kira to see if she had heard her.

'But you won't say anything, will you Ruth,' Kira said.

'I won't tell anyone. I swear.' Ruth began fiddling with her thick hair hanging over her left shoulder. 'But have you thought about the implications? Corporation...'

'We have to decide what to do next,' Kira said, interrupting Ruth and trying to sound far more confident than she felt. 'Dina honey, you can stay here as long as you want. Do you want to call Ben and let him know what's happened?'

Dina shook her head while Ruth glowered at Kira.

'Not yet,' Dina said in a small voice. 'I'd like to go lie down to be honest.'

'Of course.'

Martha realised her presence was probably acting as a vicious reminder of what Dina had recently lost.

'I am so sorry Dina,' she said.

'I know.' Dina's voice trembled and her lower lip wobbled. 'I just can't talk about it right now.'

Tears began to roll down her cheeks. She put a hand out to stop the others from hugging her.

'Please, don't.'

Getting up from the floor, Kira gestured to Dina to follow her and took her through the adjoining door into the second apartment and found the spare room. She returned a few moments later and scooped baby Grace up for a cuddle, then turned to the others.

'What the frag is going on?'

Ruth tried to speak but Jed cleared his throat loudly.

'Before anyone says anything else, I have to remind you all this is still a Force investigation. I have to interview Dina and Martha officially because even though Mr Hamble has asked Corp Medical to purge their records, the information on their pregnancies has to go somewhere.'

He looked nervously at Martha as she realised what he was saying,

'You mean my case still exists?'

Jed nodded.

'Case, what case?' Ruth asked, frustrated at not being able to speak. 'Is this about what happened three months ago?'

Kira looked at Martha who was staring into space.

'Yes,' Kira explained. 'Martha was assaulted and Mr Hamble wanted it off permanent record.'

Jed chimed in.

'Only Force doesn't work for Corporation. We uphold the law and part of that law means keeping a record of crimes committed. It has the highest possible clearance attached to it. Only myself, Pete and the Chief have access.'

He turned to face Martha.

'No-one will ever see the details Ma but you can't let your father know that we kept the case file open. Pete and I nearly lost our jobs over the news sweep leak and if he knew the file still existed, well I don't think we would come out the other side this time.'

Martha shook her head. 'I won't say anything, Jed.'

'Wait a parse,' exclaimed Ruth. 'You mean Martha was the ra..I mean sexual assault that was swept? Does that mean you did or didn't catch him? Was the termination a cover too?'

Kira poked Ruth in the arm for being so thoughtless.

'Ow,' she muttered. 'Sorry Ma.' Ruth continued rubbing her arm. 'This is all news to me. Maybe if you'd kept me in the loop a bit more....'

Ruth hadn't known for sure that Martha had been the rape victim. She'd wondered at all the strange behaviour at the time, but feeling protective of her friend, Ruth had never reported those suspicions to Victor.

'Sorry, what?' She realised everyone was looking at her.

Jed repeated himself.

'I said, you can't breathe a word of this to anyone. You might think we are being ridiculous but I'm serious about this. We all know you have links to Anti-Corp but we choose to believe that you wouldn't put your friends in danger.'

Ruth shifted uncomfortably.

'It wasn't me who told the news sweeps about the rape – I only just found out about it!'

Grace started to fuss, reacting to the raised voices and Kira began to hush her, rocking her from side to side.

'I need to see to Grace,' she said taking the baby into the bedroom.

Neither Martha or Jed spoke. They watched Ruth

until she bowed her head and conceded.

'I'll sign whatever I need to sign.'

Satisfied, Jed stood up.

'I have to go back to the office – see you later ladies.'

'I have to go too,' said Ruth. 'Give D a hug from me Ma, I'll check in later. Bye Kira honey.'

If she hurried, Ruth would have time to delay the feed from her internal recorder and Victor would never learn about the real rape victim or the pregnancy or the miscarriage.

If she hurried.

Kira came out of the bedroom and saw Martha looking rather forlorn on the couch.

'Would you like to hold Grace?'

Martha smiled and nodded.

'I'll get some milk sorted,' Kira said. 'She's ready for a feed. Shall we order in tonight? I don't feel much like cooking, so I'm pretty sure you won't feel much like it either.'

'Sounds like an excellent idea to me. Should we check on Dina? She might want something.'

'No, let's leave her be. She needs to rest. I don't think any of us can do much for her right now. If she wants us, I'm sure she'll come through.'

Dina heard the murmur of voices through the apartment wall. It had sounded heated out there but now it seemed most people had left. She was curled up in a ball on the bed, feeling wrung out. She couldn't stop the tears from rolling down her face. She thought she had wanted to be on her own, but now that she was alone, her thoughts were all over the place.

How had this happened?

Why had it happened?

What did she do so wrong?

Dina tried to think back over the past three months. As

far as she could remember, she hadn't been involved in anything detrimental to her health. The aftermath effects of excessive alcohol and drug abuse could be eradicated through regular Corp Medical check-ups, so nearly everyone had tried one substance or other to excess. But since she'd graduated, Dina hadn't seen much of her old friends and had split her time between Ben and Kira's group.

The only odd thing that had happened to her in the last three months had been that weird encounter with the blue lady, if she had even seen her at all. She hadn't seen the bee like the others. But there had been dreams. Dreams of Dina floating in the warm embrace of her mother, watching tears roll down her beautiful face and hearing her whisper 'I'm so sorry, so very sorry.' Dina had few memories of her parents and although the image capture she had of her mother didn't match the beautiful face in her dreams - who else could it be?

Her chest constricted and she thought she might not be able to breath with the weight of the grief pressing down upon her. It wasn't in her plan to apply for Collection anytime soon, so why did it hurt so much? Why did the thought of her body rejecting the tiny fetus fill her with such misery? It should never have been possible in the first place.

Dina thought about Kira's belief in Gaia and the concept that the Earth had it's own spirit. She wondered at how such a peaceful idea could be responsible for the intense pain and loss she felt. I need to know more, she thought, and as soon as the idea began to grow, Dina felt a little bit stronger, filled with a purpose. This would make her feel better. She would get to the bottom of the blue lady, and she would find out why she and Martha had been made to suffer so much. But right now she needed someone to hold her, breathe with her, stroke her hair and tell her everything was going to be alright.

She touched her ear comm and called for Ben. There was no answer.

*ANTIC: Splash out and join Anti-Corp in today's protest –
free water for all.*

Ruth hurried round the corner to her apartment, and apologised as she ran into someone.

'Oh, it's you.'

'Ruthie baby!' Bobby Travelli, a skinny man with greasy hair blocked the entrance to her apartment. He gestured for her to open the door.

'Frag it,' thought Ruth.

She only had a small window of opportunity to stop the auto-download of the days conversations, and she wasn't sure yet whether she wanted Anti-Corp to learn about Dina's miscarriage, or that Martha Hamble was the rape case victim.

'What do you want Bobby?' she snapped.

'Inside,' he replied, and followed her through the doorway.

Bobby sat himself on the only chair in the compact front room, leaving Ruth standing. She glared at him and stood over by the small window, leaning against the wall.

'Well?'

'Victor is very disappointed, Ruthie. You haven't sent any newbies our way for a couple of weeks. We haven't heard anymore about the martyr's daughter. Some of us think you've gone soft.'

Bobby smiled and began to clean his fingernails with an old fashioned pocket knife. He looked more ridiculous than intimidating.

'Get to the point, Bobby.'

'We need someone in at Science Division. Victor has heard interesting things through the wire and he needs a body. He told me to let you know that your debt would be repaid in full, *if* you can put the right person in place.'

Ruth snorted.

'As if I'd believe that coming from you.'

'Believe or don't believe darling, I speak the truth. Victor said and I quote, *Quentin will finally be laid to eternal rest*.'

Bobby watched closely as a flash of pain crossed Ruth's face.

'You've given me your message, now get out!'

Bobby frowned at the viciousness of her tone.

'We need them in place as soon as Ruthie.'

'Out! Now!'

He put an info jack on the table as he stood up.

'All the details are on here. I'm going, I'm going,' he said quickly as she took a step towards him.

After Bobby had left, Ruth sat down heavily. This was it. This was the last job, the job she never thought would come. After this, Anti Corp would finally return Quentin's remains to her and she could lay him to rest, and it would all be over. She smiled, eyes brimming, at the small image capture on the table. Her laughing in the sunshine with a tall, dark haired man with beard and glasses. On their wedding day.

Shortly after that photo, Quentin had disappeared - a bad deal gone worse with Anti Corp. She had never found out what it was. She had been so desperate to lay him to rest she'd stayed with Anti-Corp, working for them in the hope that one day she'd have his remains returned to her. Victor had promised her he would find them. No-one understood why she had to have him back, but she wanted to say goodbye.

Feeling sickened by the whole situation, Ruth went into the bathroom, wiped her auto-record chip, and threw up.

Chapter Nine

Ingrid should have been concentrating on the figures in front of her. There was an important presentation coming up and if she wanted to be considered for promotion she needed to shine in front of the attending Board members. Glancing at the cute teddy sitting on the corner of her desk she smiled despite herself, and thought of Pete. Her Pete. Pete, Pete, Pete.

He was a pleasant distraction, and if Ingrid could relax enough to go with the moment she was certain she would enjoy herself. But she had worked so hard to get to where she was, and she didn't have time for a boyfriend – especially if it meant blowing her chances of promotion. Ingrid tried to push her focus back onto the technical specifications she should have memorised, but Pete's saucy grin kept invading her thoughts. In the end, she decided to call him.

'Hello - Pete?'

'Ingrid! Hi, how are you? Is everything alright?'

'I'm fine Pete. I was wondering, are you available at all this weekend?' Ingrid could feel her face getting hotter and hotter. 'I thought maybe we could do something together. If you want? If you're free?'

'This weekend, huh? I'm free, we can go out or stay in, whatever you like.'

'Let's stay in. I'll cook.' Ingrid felt happier than she had expected. 'See you Friday, at eight.'

Pete confirmed the details and clicked off.

'Right woman, time to focus,' she told herself, and bent over the data again.

The following day, the day of the presentation, Ingrid woke up feeling miserable. It felt like she'd spent the night downing shots and forgotten to take the hangover remover - yet she hadn't touched alcohol in months. She barely had enough energy to get out of bed, let alone complete her usual morning workout, and the thought of food had her running to the bathroom. Inviting Pete over now seemed a terrible mistake. Ingrid requested a mini health scan from her apartment, which had the complete health and well being programming installed.

'Anomaly detected. Referral to nearest medical centre advised.'

'Negative.' Ingrid paced her bedroom floor. 'Expand please.'

'Anomaly detected. Unable to determine exact specifics. Referral to nearest medical centre advised.'

It seemed this wasn't a random bug she could shake off with a health tonic. Ingrid felt a twinge of worry.

'Negative,' she replied looking at her diary for the day. If she hurried she could pop in to the on-site medical office at Corp Tech where she worked and still make it for her early morning presentation. Making sure she was impeccably groomed, Ingrid left her apartment mulling over in her mind whether or not to cancel Pete's visit.

Half an hour later she sat on a chair in the medical office while a fresh faced technician stammered apologies for inadequate equipment and alternated with excitement for her unique condition and assurances that a top level Consultant was on his way, and would be here soon. Ingrid wasn't listening. She was stunned. This was simply not possible. Not for *her*. Not for *anyone*. Not now, not today, not ever. A green shimmer waved its way across the room. Ingrid watched entranced as she picked out motes of gold and red. Then something warm embraced her deep inside and stretched to the ends of her being.

Before she had a chance to enjoy the feeling, her bosses neural network invaded her head shattering the colours into a myriad of rainbows.

Ingrid, where are you? We are ready to start and I need that presentation now!

A jolt went through her body. This is why you didn't call in sick she thought.

'I have to go. Tell the Consultant to make an appointment with me through my diary and,' she paused and looked directly at the Technician who appeared more shaken than she was. 'I assume this does come under medical discretion?'

'I'm not sure,' the technician replied. 'I have to tell my superior and then I expect they will tell yours – procedure, you understand.'

Ingrid nodded, gathering her things, and left the office. She wasn't sure whether it was a good idea for her bosses to be informed about her medical anomaly yet, but she also knew there was nothing she could do to prevent it.

Right now she had the presentation of her career to sail through, provided she was able to avoid vomiting everywhere.

ANTIC: Communication blackout at Force HQ – upload your feed and spread the sweep.

There was a lull in paperwork at Force, and Pete was whistling.

'You're in a good mood, Pete,' remarked Jed, leaning back in his chair and watching his friend in amusement.

'That I am, Jenks, that I am.'

'Care to elaborate?'

Pete grinned and sat on the corner of his partners desk.

'Ingrid called me,' he said. 'She wants to get together this weekend, just hang out, me and her.'

Jed was surprised, Ingrid never called anyone. Before he could say anything else, the Chief stuck his head round his door.

'Barnes, Jenkins, my office!'

Jed and Pete let out a collective sigh, and walked over.

'Sit down,' the Chief barked as they entered the doorway. They sat, exchanging glances.

'Now, you would tell me if this was some kind of joke wouldn't you? I mean one is unusual – two is unheard of but three! Three! And it's your fragging sister this time.'

'Ingrid? What's she supposed to have done?' Jed asked, a little startled whilst Pete half stood.

The Chief shot him a fierce look and Pete sat back down.

'She's only gone and got herself a fragging medical anomaly. The next thing you'll be telling me is that it's something in the water and everybody is going to have one.'

'Have one what, Sir?' Jed asked, frowning in confusion.

'A baby! A fragging naturally conceived bundle of fragging joy. The Board is going to have a fragging field day, and Hamble is breathing down my neck at the two revelations we've got already down at Corp Medical.'

Pete had grabbed Jed's arm whilst the Chief was speaking and appeared to be in some sort of shock.

'Pull yourself together Barnes, it's not the fragging apocalypse. At least not on my watch. Jenkins, you kept the file open on the rape case didn't you?'

'Yes, Chief.'

'And you added the rape baby and the miscarriage?'

'Those too, Chief.'

'Right, get the fragging paperwork completed for this other one and get to the bottom of this whole fragging debacle. I can't have babies springing out everywhere, there'll be uproar.' The Chief stopped, breathing hard and red in the face. He glared at both men. 'And if Anti-Corp gets hold of any of this, you two can kiss your shields goodbye. You find out what's going on and you put an end to it. I don't want out of control riots like those last century – too many people died. I won't have it. This ends now.'

Jed responded with a smart 'Yes Chief,' and dragged Pete out the office, through the department, and into the locker rooms. He chose an empty pod, and shoved Pete inside.

'Pete! Pete – buddy! Snap out of it.'

Jed clicked his fingers in front of his friends face and was about to resort to slapping his face when Pete spoke in a low voice.

'I'm going to be a Dad.'

He raised his eyes to look at Jed, and began to laugh.

'I'm going to be a Dad.'

Ingrid trembled as she made her way to the Managing Director's office. It was the first time she'd been officially summoned and she was desperately thinking back to the presentation to see if she could figure out what mistake she made. That could be the only reason for being summoned – a colossal mistake that would cost her her entire career. But she could not think of anything she had said or done out of place. As far as she was concerned everything had gone smoothly and management had listened to her projections with interest.

The light on the outer door glowed, confirming her identity. She tried to remain calm as she pushed the door open. A tall, thin man stood by the window, hands clasped behind him, looking at the city laid out below.

'Do you know why Corporation is so successful Miss Jenkins?' The Managing Director spoke without turning.

Before Ingrid could think of a response he continued.

'Because we *create* the demand, and we *supply* the demand.'

He turned to face her and pursed his lips.

'What you appear to have done, Miss Jenkins, is

find a niche market. I am not sure whether we can allow that niche to survive.'

Instinctively Ingrid's hand flew to her still flat stomach. She took an involuntary step backwards. The Managing Director walked back to his desk, sat down and gestured for Ingrid to do the same. She did so, wondering what he would say next. The Managing Director stared across the desk at Ingrid for a few moments.

'It appears you have powerful friends in high places, Miss Jenkins. You can thank them for your continued employment here at Corp Tech. You will remain in your current position until it becomes impossible for you to continue. You will submit to any and all medical investigations deemed necessary. You will not speak to the news sweeps. And when it becomes clear that you have a condition your only response will be 'No Comment'. Any questions?'

Ingrid shook her head, then remembering where she was, replied, 'No Sir.'

'Good. Dismissed.'

Once Ingrid had reached the outer door, she let out a huge breath and sagged against the wall as the door closed behind her. Clearly, she had Mr Hamble to thank for the intervention, but it looked like her dream of promotion was well and truly over.

'Thanks for nothing,' she spoke to her midriff, wishing the whole thing would go away. Unwilling to linger outside the Managing Director's office, Ingrid hurried down to her floor, and the relative sanctuary of her office. As she sat down, she wondered whether it would be possible to terminate the child. Having a baby now would be so ...... inconvenient. She hadn't planned for Collection anytime soon. Looking up at the Employee of the Month awards that lined her office wall, she felt swamped by a surge of helplessness. Pete would never forgive her. Ingrid picked up the teddy on her desk and fiddled with the old fashioned button on it's nose. She didn't think she'd be able to forgive herself either. This way at least she could test all the latest baby products first hand and drive that product area forward – promotion could always come from a different corner.

Dina held Martha's hair away from her face as she knelt in front of the toilet. Martha groaned and dry heaved again.

'Are you okay Ma?'

'I think so.'

Martha put a hand up to pat Dina's, and moved away from the toilet bowl. The two women sat on the bathroom floor and looked at each other.

'I am so sorry you have to deal with this,' Martha said, with one hand on her chest. 'It is probably the last thing you want.'

'Don't be silly. I'm happy to help you.' Dina tucked her hair behind her ear. 'Besides, if it happened once – who knows, maybe it will happen again and then I'll need your help.'

'Believe me Dina, I feel like I am dying. I would not wish this on anyone.'

Dina stood up and offered Martha a hand, helping her to her feet.

'Don't you have a Med Check today?'

'Yes,' Martha said, grimacing. 'I would rather not be poked and prodded by Corporation but if they can remove this morning sickness, then I will live with it.'

'I wish I could do more for you.'

'Oh Dina – you are already being the best friend I could ask for.'

And Martha leaned over to hug her before the two women went through the adjoining door to Kira and Jed's apartment.

Kira was sat on the floor deep in thought while Grace

entertained herself with various rattles and soft toys. Martha and Dina joined her.

'Anything wrong K?' Dina asked.

'That was Jed,' Kira said, pointing at the vid comm. 'He said Pete had huge news and they are all coming round here for dinner. Ingrid included. He's just getting in touch with Ben now.'

Dina gasped and Kira looked at her in concern.

'He said the whole gang needed to be here. I thought you two...'

'It doesn't matter. He can come. I don't mind.'

'You do not suppose Pete is going to...perhaps... propose?' Martha asked.

Kira burst out laughing, then stopped as she realised there was no other reason for them to all get together.

'He can't be, can he? Not after the run around Ingrid gave him.'

Yet the more she thought about it, it seemed the only explanation there could be.

'What about Ruth?' Martha said.

'Jed wants Ruth here too, but he couldn't get through to her. I tried her ear comm just now - it's nothing but static.'

Dina nodded.

'Sounds about right. She's probably off grid.' She stood up. 'I'll go round if you like, I need to speak to her about my placement, anyway.'

'You sure?' Kira asked.

'I've got to keep busy, Kira, otherwise,' and she trailed off, her eyes filling.

Martha reached up and squeezed her hand.

'It is okay, we understand, Dina. Whatever you need.'

Dina took a deep breath, and pushed her grief back down.

'I'll be back in time for the big announcement,' she said, blowing kisses at a gurgly Grace as she left.

'Do you think she is alright?' Kira asked.

Martha fiddled with a cushion.

'I think she is finding her own way of coping with the unbelievable. As we all are.'

Kira nodded.

'But she has been spending a lot of time with Ruth talking about the latest approved Anti Corp campaigns.'

'I know. She feels let down, and despite everything we've been doing, I think she feels abandoned. It can't be easy going through what's she going through without her parents.' Then realising what she said, Kira stammered. 'I... I... I... mean - you've got the same, I mean, it's tough and there's a lot going on and,' Kira trailed off as she realised Martha was laughing, then joined in.

'Oh, you know what I mean.'

'Yes, I know what you mean Kira.' Martha looked down at the happy baby. 'I still can't quite grasp the fact that I am growing one of these all by myself, without a lab.' Martha held her stomach and continued in a softer voice. 'Even if it was not my choice.'

Kira was teasing Grace with one of her soft toys, making her grab for the bunny ears.

'Have you thought any more about your father's offer of medical intervention?'

'Remove the baby? Do you believe that is the course of action I should take?'

'No!' Kira looked up at Martha in shock. 'I'd never suggest that Ma.'

'It is something I have considered. Taking the memory pain wipe helped but I still know I was raped, I just do not have any emotional feelings attached to what happened. Not knowing who the father of my child is – and the fact that I never asked for it – it makes me feel unclean on the inside. As if this baby is unclean.'

'Oh Ma,' Kira's eyes filled with tears. 'It's just an innocent baby, it never did anything wrong.' She looked at Grace playing happily. 'You're not ... I mean you wouldn't...' Kira choked off, unable to keep talking.

'No Kira, I am not going to remove it,' Martha said with a distant look on her face.

'That's good Ma, I know it's the right thing to do,' Kira said, wiping her face dry.

'I do have a Med Check appointment today though,' Martha continued in a faraway voice. 'I have told them to come to the apartment. I do not want to be poked and prodded at Med Centre.'

'Seems fair enough.'

'Yes,' Martha said, refocusing on Kira and Grace in front of her. 'I refuse to be a Corporation pin cushion. Do not misunderstand me, I want to get through this as safely as possible but women coped with pregnancy for centuries without being hooked up 24/7 to machines. Speaking of which, did you manage to get the materials I asked for at Archive?'

Kira shook her head.

'No, not yet but the request has gone through, so it shouldn't be a problem. We just need to wait for the repro and then you'll have all the texts you could possibly want. It is kinda exciting isn't it?'

Martha nodded, smiling back at her friend whilst at the same time panic butterflies fluttered madly around her chest.

Dina banged on the door again, she could hear movement inside. Ruth opened the door a crack.

'It's me. Ruth? What are you doing? Let me in.'

Dina tried to push the door wider.

'Dina, please, this isn't a great time.'

But Dina ignored her and pushed harder on the door. Ruth gave in and let her through.

'What do you want?' Ruth asked, not looking at Dina.

Dina looked around, expecting Ruth to have a visitor but realised no-one was there.

'Why wouldn't you let me in? What's going on?'

'Stuff,' Ruth said.

Dina coloured but carried on talking.

'Jed and Pete have called a family meeting. And they want you there too.'

Ruth looked up and raised her eyebrows.

'Me?'

'Yep. The whole gang. We tried to reach you, but no-one could get through.'

They both looked at the black screen of Ruth's vidcom. It was turned off.

'Why would you disconnect? Are you okay?' Dina asked, concern in her voice.

Ruth's bottom lip began to tremble.

'Hey, it's okay. I'm here Ruthie.'

Dina gave her friend a hug. Ruth clung to her and began to speak.

'It's all my fault - the news sweep leaks - everything. And I can't tell anyone because then you won't want anything to do with me anymore, and you guys are my only family. I just want him back, I just want him back.'

She choked off, incoherent with sobs.

'Want who back sweetie?' Dina asked.

They separated, and Ruth gestured for Dina to join her on the rug.

After a few moments to calm down, Ruth explained about her late husband's dealings with Anti-Corp, and how she had been putting candidates forward to join Anti-Corp and spy for them.

'Candidates?' Dina asked. 'Like me? You wanted me to spy for Anti-Corp? When were you going to ask me about that?'

Ruth wiped her nose on her sleeve.

'They backed me into a corner Dina, I had to do it. It was the only way to pay Quentin's debt, and get him back.'

Dina said nothing. The two women stared at each other in silence before Dina puffed out her cheeks.

'Frag's sake Ruth. Why didn't you tell anyone? Jed could've, I don't know, done something.'

Ruth looked back at Dina, her nose running, eyes red and puffy. She sniffed.

'I couldn't at first, I didn't know anyone well enough, and then when I did I'd already been helping Anti-Corp for a few years.'

'So you kept quiet, hoping it would go away?'

Ruth bristled, then gave in.

'More or less,' she agreed, her voice small.

'Well.' Dina stood. 'We have to get over to Kira's, so go sort yourself out.' She held out her hand to help Ruth up. 'We can hear what Pete and Jed have to say and then we can tell everyone together.'

Ruth's eyes widened.

'I don't think that's a great idea.'

'We're family, Ruth. And family helps each other, even when they make mistakes.'

Ruth still looked unsure, but Dina refused to hear another word. Now that Dina had people she cared for and who cared for her, she wasn't going to let anything bad happen.

To any of them.

By the time Ruth and Dina got back to Kira's, everyone else had arrived.

'Where's Grace?' Dina asked.

'Asleep in the bedroom. No distractions that way,' Kira explained.

Dina went and sat by Ben. Their relationship had cooled, both trying to come to terms with the miscarriage. But they were still friends. Ruth lingered near the front door, unsure where to sit, and not wanting to be there at all. Kira grabbed Ruth by the arm and pulled her into the loose circle that had formed in the centre of the lounge.

'You have the floor boys,' Kira said, smiling up at her husband.

Jed turned to look at Pete who stood up and took a

104

handheld scanner from his pocket.

'Before we begin, this is a bug catcher. I'm not saying anyone here can't be trusted.'

Pete paused and looked at Ruth. Ruth looked down at her hands, avoiding looking at anyone. Kira, Martha and Dina all looked at each other in confusion. This didn't sound like a proposal.

Pete continued.

'But something bigger than us is happening, and I for one want to get to the bottom of it without Corporation breathing down my neck.'

Ingrid frowned, but said nothing. Pete began the scanning with Jed. Kira leant over to Dina.

'What took you so long?'

Before Dina had a chance to reply the scanner beeped at Ingrid who reddened, flustered.

'It's my clearance chip. I forgot,' she said. 'Let me deactivate – sorry.'

She flicked her wrist, opening her internal screen. Despite many of them not wanting the invasiveness of top line Corp technology, they watched with interest. It was fascinating to see it in action.

'All done,' Ingrid said.

Pete smiled down at her, then realised the others were watching and quickly moved on through the group. Ruth was the last to be scanned. Another beep. They all looked at her in surprise.

'I didn't expect you to have tech,' Ingrid commented.

'It's not mine. It's Anti-Corps.'

Pete's face hardened as he put away the scanner

'So, we've found our mole.'

Dina jumped up. 'It's not like that Pete. Listen to what Ruth has to say.'

'Not until that bug has been removed.'

'Easy partner,' Jed intervened. 'Kira love, can you get the med kit please?'

Kira scrambled off the floor and went to the

105

kitchen, her head buzzing with a hundred questions, but she kept quiet, got the med kit and passed it to her husband. Jed knelt down beside Ruth, and took her left hand.

'Ruthie, this is going to hurt.'

Tears rolled down her face.

'Do it,' Pete said fiercely.

Everyone watched as Jed applied a numbing spray to Ruth's wrist and used the medical kit laser to slice open her arm. He deftly plucked the bug out and before her arm had chance to bleed, he had applied a coagulation foam and used invisible stitching to pull the flesh back together. Jed worked quickly, he was used to removing bugs from Anti-Corp activists. As he finished the group let out a collective breath, and Ruth cradled her arm.

'Talk,' Pete demanded.

FORMAL MEETING OF CORPORATION BOARD
FOR CITY FORTY-TWO
DATE: 2nd JULY 2215
VIRTUAL PRESENCE: R HAMBLE, J NICKS, Y
ASWAD and P BASJERE

AGENDA

1. UNPLANNED PREGNANCIES
2. CONTAINMENT
3. CONTROL
4. FILE 0

MINUTES

1. TWO PREGNANCIES AND ONE MISCARRIAGE
   HAVE BEEN REPORTED. MEDICAL HAVE NO
   EXPLANATIONS. SCIENCE DIVISION TO
   BEGIN INVESTIGATIONS ASAP.
2. SWEEPS WILL BE MONITORED. NON
   DISCLOSURES WILL BE SENT TO THE
   FAMILIES INVOLVED. MEMORY WIPES AT
   MED CENTRE HAVE BEEN ACTIONED.
3. R HAMBLE CONFIRMS PREGNANCY A AND
   MISCARRIAGE ARE CONTAINED. THEY WILL
   SUBMIT TO MED CHECKS AT HOME AND
   SAMPLES WILL BE SENT TO SCIENCE
   DIVISION. MD OF CORP TECH CONFIRMS
   PREGNANCY B IS CONTAINED AND WILL
   SUBMIT TO ALL CORP MED REQUIREMENTS.
4. IT WAS DECIDED NOT TO DISCUSS FILE 0 AT
   THIS TIME.

ANY OTHER BUSINESS – NONE

Chapter Ten

No-one spoke. Dina was holding Ruth's hand and the others were shaken by what Ruth had told them.

'Ruth.' Jed broke the silence. 'Now that your recorder has been removed – can we trust you?'

Ingrid's mouth twisted, but she held her tongue.

'I won't say anything to anyone,' Ruth said. 'But..'

'But what?' Pete demanded.

'But they'll know sooner or later the chip has been removed. So what do I tell them?'

'We could always arrest you.' Pete smiled grimly.

'Pete!' Kira wasn't impressed.

'No he's right, love.' Jed pointed at the deactivated bug on the floor. 'That way we'd have a legitimate reason for removing it. We're always doing Anti-Corp sweeps. Ruth can just say she got caught up in one.'

Kira still didn't look too pleased about the idea, but Ruth was nodding. Ben cleared his throat.

'If this wasn't the big reveal, why exactly were we all gathered here?' he said.

Pete and Ingrid looked at each other.

'We're having a baby,' Ingrid said.

Martha gasped, Dina looked shocked, and Kira's mouth simply hung open.

'I'm going to be a Dad!' Pete was grinning from ear to ear.

Ingrid looked less happy about their news and shook off the various attempts at congratulations.

'There are issues,' she said. 'My employer has been quite firm about my compliance with Corp Medical and my silence about the whole affair. But Pete...'

'Pete wanted his friends to know,' Pete said, still beaming.

'There is a more serious side to this as well,' Jed said. 'The Force is unofficially investigating why these pregnancies are happening. Only Pete and I are working the case - we are, after all, uniquely motivated to get answers.'

'That makes perfect sense to me,' Martha said, nodding.

Dina looked pensive. 'So, what's the plan?'

'I think Ruth's confession has actually helped us fill in some of the gaps,' Jed replied looking at Pete for confirmation. Pete reluctantly nodded.

'Ruth,' Jed continued. 'You told us that Anti-Corp wants to place someone in Science Division.' He looked at Dina. 'Do you think you would be up for that?'

'Now wait a minute,' Kira broke in, but Dina hushed her.

'Yes, I mean, I've got the right qualifications,' she said. 'If Ruth can help me get through selection.'

Ruth's face fell.

'Are you sure D?' she said. 'I mean, you'd be answering directly to Anti-Corp and they are definitely getting more and more aggressive.'

Dina lifted her chin slightly. 'I can do this. I want to know why my baby ... why I lost ... why this thing happened to me. And Martha and Ingrid. We all deserve an answer.'

'Okay Dina,' Jed said. 'Ruth, you organise getting Dina in at Science.' He paused, realising both women looked worried. 'Don't worry - I'll be your handler at this end. I'll get you set up with some top of the range surveillance gear and we'll plan all possible exit strategies.'

'What's a handler?' Dina asked.

'Exit strategies?' Ben said. 'What kind of danger do you think Dina is going to be in?'

'A handler is just a name for the person on the outside who looks after the people on the inside,' Jed explained. 'It's old world spy slang, but we still use it in field work. As for danger.' Jed glanced at Pete. 'It's hard to say.'

'Hard to say?' Ben exploded. 'What the frag does that mean? Just because Dina lost our baby doesn't make her expendable, you know.'

'Ben! Calm down.' Dina blushed. 'Not here.'

Jed went over to his cousin and put both hands on his shoulders.

'Ben - we're family. I would never willingly put you, or Dina, in a position of danger. That's why we are going to cover every angle. So nothing surprises us. Okay?'

Ben stared at Jed for a few moments, before reluctantly nodding.

'Anyone else got any objections?' When no-one replied Jed moved on. 'Based on Ruth's revelation that Anti-Corp wanted schematics of Corp Tech, Pete and I will put extra surveillance on Ingrid's building in case of terrorist attack. I doubt they'll be able to get through the security on that place, but again, we leave nothing to chance.'

'They know me there,' Pete added. 'So it won't look unusual if I drop by more regularly.'

Jed looked at his wristplant.

'We'd better get you processed Ruth, if you want to be out by the morning.'

'Is it really necessary to arrest her?' Kira spoke up again but Ruth put out an arm, forestalling any more discussion.

'Let's get it done,' she said. 'We don't have long before the recorder will attempt an auto info dump. It'll be okay K.'

Kira muttered under her breath and helped her friend get her things together. Before they were all about to leave, Kira hugged her husband and whispered, 'Look after her please.'

'I will,' Jed promised. 'We'll come straight back once it's all over.'

FORCE: Another successful bug sweep removed illegal software from Anti-Corp sympathisers. We remind citizens that bugs will not be tolerated.

Ingrid was looking for her coat when Martha decided to try and talk to her.

'Would you like to stay for a while? We could talk.'

'About what?' replied Ingrid, her expression blank.

Martha coloured, a little embarrassed.

'About the babies, our babies.'

'Oh, I haven't had time to think about it, to be honest. I ought to tell my mother first,' said Ingrid.

'Yes of course, I quite understand. If you ever do want to talk about them, I'm more than happy to,' Martha offered. 'Kira is getting some materials from Archives - you could look through them with me if you want to.'

'Perhaps,' Ingrid said. 'But Corp Medical are going to be keeping a close eye on me, so I'm sure there will be nothing to concern myself about. Are you going for your regular check ups?'

'I do not want to be constantly poked, prodded and monitored.'

Ingrid shrugged.

'I'm sure it's no different to normal medicals. Corporation will look after us you know.'

Martha smiled faintly, trying to ignore the look of incredulity she could see out of the corner of her eye on Kira's face.

Dina watched the exchange in silence. She would have avoided Corp Medical like Martha only now it didn't matter. Her tiny miracle no longer existed. She didn't blame Ben for getting upset - they hadn't talked about the loss in any detail. She didn't know what to say. He didn't know what to say either so they reverted to that safe place in dying relationships where you said nothing.

Ben coughed to get Dina's attention.

'I'm heading out,' he said. 'You want anything?'

Dina shook her head, but smiled in thanks.

'Are you leaving too, Ben?' Kira sounded disappointed. 'Are you sure you don't want to stay for dinner? There's plenty.'

'No thank you.'

'You won't say anything about what went on tonight will you, Ben?' Kira said.

Ben had his hand on the door. 'No, I won't,' he assured Kira without turning round.

ANTIC: Bug lovers rise up and join our ant farm, share and sweep the city.
'Divided we fall – together we are mighty!'

Kira watched him leave and chewed on her bottom lip.

'It'll be alright, Kira. Ben won't say anything.' Dina stood beside her.

'Huh?'

'Ben. He won't say anything. He doesn't want anyone to know about .... well you know.... about..... the failure.'

Dina tried not to cry. Kira turned and hugged her tight.

'You are not a failure love. You're a fighter.'

Martha murmured her agreement and even Ingrid patted Dina on the shoulder.

'Corporation will sort it out,' Ingrid said confidently. 'Things will go back to normal - Collection and control. The way it should be.'

The others stared at her, but Ingrid wasn't watching their faces. Instead she was accessing her mother's social calendar on her wristplant to see if she would be at home.

'I'll come round soon,' she said. 'I promise.' Then she air kissed them all, and left.

'What a Corper!' Dina exclaimed. 'I know she's your sister-in-law Kira, but she is such a tech-head.'

Kira nodded her agreement. A faint ding from the

kitchen reminded them of dinner.

'Let's eat,' Kira said, leading the others over to the counter as Grace began to cry. 'You serve, Ma. I'll go get the little one.'

CORP: NEW!! VR Extreme release their latest must-have experiences – drive a car (includes traffic jam simulator) – fly a plane across the desert – ski down a mountain – swim in the ocean. All these action packed ventures are waiting for you.
Order now through your local Corporation Rep.

The next morning saw a tired yet determined group of friends gather for their first planning meeting. Kira was bleary-eyed after getting up four times in the night with an extremely unhappy baby, and feeling resentful at how well-rested Jed looked. Martha and Dina had waited up for Ruth to get back from processing, and spent most of the night talking about how to get to the bottom of whatever it was that was happening to them.

'I had a strange dream last night,' Kira said, joining the others in the lounge with a cup of synth-caf in her hands. 'When I finally got to sleep that is.' She looked pointedly at her husband.

Jed, engrossed in the morning's sweeps, carried on eating breakfast unaware the remark was aimed at him.

'What?' he said, finally noticing the silence and speaking through a mouthful of food.

Kira ignored him, addressing Ruth, Martha and Dina.

'Anyway,' she said. 'I saw Gaia.'

'You saw Gaia,' Ruth repeated in disbelief.

'Yes, I did,' Kira replied, feeling defensive. 'She was walking towards me as the entire city around us exploded into a million pieces. As the pieces rained down they became trees and a lake and beautiful countryside. I couldn't hear her but I knew she was talking. It was odd because I was trying so hard to catch what she said, but I couldn't hear anything.'

'What did she look like?' Dina asked.

'Oh, she was beautiful. Blue skin and hair that moved around her on its own with flowers and creatures peeking out. Her eyes were like - '

'Eyes that sparkled like a thousand stars?' Jed asked, sitting up in the chair and paying attention.

'Well, yes,' Kira said, a little confused as to how Jed might know such a thing.

'That's who I saw. On Collection Day. In the street. When I saw the bee. You remember?' he said in excitement.

'A bee?' Martha said. 'I saw a bee.'

'Aren't they supposed to be extinct?' Ruth asked, but when no-one answered her, she shrugged. 'I thought they were extinct.'

Dina came to her rescue. 'Ruth's right, they are extinct. They're also familiars of Gaia.'

'What's a familiar?' Jed asked.

'Familiars are animal shaped spirits and bees are associated with Gaia.'

'How do you know that?' Ruth queried.

Dina flushed. 'I've been doing some research, reading ancient texts. I think I've dreamt of Gaia before too. At first I thought it was my mother, but the woman was more beautiful than I remembered.'

'What happened?' Kira asked, interested to know if Dina's dream could in anyway be connected to her own.

'I could hear her,' Dina said. 'She just kept on apologising. It was around the time I .... when I .... well, you know …..'

The group quietened, sensing Dina's reluctance to talk about her miscarriage.

Jed offered to refresh everyone's drinks, and walked away to the drinks machine with a handful of mugs.

'I did not know Jed believed,' Martha said to Kira in his

114

absence.

'I don't think he does Ma, not really. But even he has to admit strange things have happened to us. And the news sweeps aren't reporting any other pregnancies out there.'

'If it was widespread,' Ruth said. 'We'd definitely be hearing it on the sweeps.'

'Why?' Dina asked.

'Because Corporation wouldn't be able to stop every single person from uploading,' Ruth replied, then hesitated. 'Would they?'

'Who knows?' Dina shrugged.

'Speaking of Anti-Corp.' Kira changed the subject. 'Did they accept your arrest Ruth?'

'Yep. I've gotta report in later. I'm planing to get D up to speed by then, so I can give them their new mole and not get fitted with a new recorder. That's the last thing we need.'

'What's the last thing we need?' Jed asked, returning with fresh synth-caf.

'Ruth to be reactivated,' Kira said.

'Oh right, yeah. Well, it's not actually the *worst* thing that could happen. We've got some new tech that could hijack whatever Ruth transmits, and process it through our server first.' Jed paused, seeing puzzled faces in front of him. 'It means we can remove anything we don't want Anti-Corp hearing.'

'What about me?' Dina asked. 'What will I have?'

Jed fished around in the bag under his stool, and brought out a thin hollowed disc.

'This is what we call a jack-catcher. It'll fit around your neural jack and capture audio and data information.'

'So you can even read encrypted info dumps?' Ruth was fascinated.

'That's right,' Jed said. 'Anti-Corp might think they've got the upper hand over us at Force, but we are constantly evolving new ways to monitor and counter their actions. We don't want a repeat of the mob action we had after The Event.'

Even though no-one there had been alive then, regularly streamed audio and visual recordings of The Event and its aftermath kept the details fresh in people's minds. The recordings were played to provide a reminder of what had been lost, and what had been gained.

'We'd better get on with this then,' Ruth said. 'This is what I'm thinking...'

She outlined her plan to introduce Dina to her contact at Anti-Corp as a recent graduate, with all the right qualifications to be their Science Division insider. The others listened, each hoping that Dina would find out the answers to all their questions.

Later that afternoon Dina sat in Ruth's flat fiddling with her hair, trying to calm her nerves.

'You ready?' Ruth asked, looking at her wristplant to check the time.

'I guess so.'

Both women jumped when the door chimed, and Ruth went to open the door. The meet with Anti-Corp usually happened at the students own accommodation, but seeing as Dina was staying with Kira and company everyone felt meeting at Ruth's would be less suspicious. Bobby filled the doorway. He greeted Ruth then pushed by her, excited to meet his latest recruit.

'Well aren't you a sweet little chip,' Bobby said looking Dina up and down.

The group had decided to try and make Dina look as innocent as possible by dressing her in her University tunic and keeping hair and make-up simple and natural. So far it was working. Bobby ran through a few general queries about Dina's education and her areas of expertise, then sat back with a self-satisfied smile.

'Your credentials check out. You're exactly what we're looking for. I'm sure Ruthie has told you Dina, we have an interest in Science Division.'

'And what is it you want me to do?' Dina asked,

eyes wide.

'We want to know what it is they're cooking up in their placenta bars,' Bobby said, his grin fading as neither women reacted to his joke. He carried on. 'We want to know which genes are being spliced, what experiments they're working on - how exactly they plan to continue their vice-like hold over the masses. Everything really. That's where you come in.'

Bobby stopped speaking, waiting for Dina to guess.

'You want me to plant bugs?'

'Something like that. We'll start you off small with a couple of re-cons, see how you do. If they go well....'

Bobby noticed Ruth frowning hard at him.

'Now don't worry yourself Ruthie, we aren't going to get this little chip in any kind of trouble.'

Bobby cleared his throat and stood up, Dina mirrored his movement. He leant over and swiped his wristplant over Dina's.

'I've got your number, we'll send you your first job in a few days. Let's just leave it at that shall we. Ladies.' Grinning to himself he made his own way out of the apartment.

'Ugh,' Ruth shivered. 'That man is slime personified.'

'I think it went well though,' Dina said.

'He was a little bit vague for my liking,' Ruth replied. 'I'd like to know more but if Anti-Corp are planning something big I guess we'll find out eventually.'

A week after meeting Bobby, Dina stood in the foyer of Science Division gripping her access card, waiting to pass through security. She was wearing the bugged ear comm from Jed as well as carrying several listening devices scattered about her person. Both Jed and Ruth had assured Dina she would pass through security without a hitch, but standing in line waiting to be swept, Dina could feel sweat trickling down the back of her neck.

Thirty seconds later, and it was all over. She wished she didn't feel so clammy but at least the first hurdle had been negotiated. Now all she had to do was memorise the floor plan, find the places Anti-Corp wanted her to plant bugs in, and be the most unmemorable intern - all without getting caught.

An officious looking man came over to where Dina was standing by a moving staircase.

'You the new intern?'

'Yes, I'm Dina Grey,' she said, holding out her hand in greeting.

The man ignored her hand completely, turned and began walking away from her. He called 'Follow me' over his shoulder without even looking to see if she was and proceeded to ascend the moving staircase.

Dina decided against making small talk as she tried to keep up with him. He swept down an ordinary looking corridor with doors marked numerically, until they reached an empty lab. He retrieved a couple of passes from his pocket and passed them to Dina.

'We need you to clean up,' he said. 'The last intern fried the mechanism of our equipment-washer. While we wait for the parts we've got a bit of a backlog.'

He swung the door open to reveal tray upon tray upon tray of test-tubes and beakers, petri dishes and syringes.

'I thought it was all automated these days,' Dina said, somewhat surprised.

'Head of SD is a dinosaur,' the man said. 'He likes to keep some of the old traditions alive. When you're done, swipe this card and I'll come get you. Have fun.'

Dina surveyed the room in dismay. Was this some sort of initiation test? At least she was unsupervised, and as an added bonus there happened to be a map of the facility on the wall over the sink. It was looking less and less like a waste of time after all.

ANTIC: Outdated methods at Science Division – should we trust them with our futures? Upload your links and spread the sweep.

DING: Newest intern @ SCID – exciting times ahead!

Notes from Anti-Corp Meeting at Academy Student Bar, July 31ˢᵗ 2215

- *Well done to everyone who joined us for the beach party attempt. Even though our wall breech was unsuccessful at least it was well swept – the people deserve to know that outside is safe!*

- *We are in favourable talks with Professor Kamir to ensure any students who took part in the wall breech are given additional duties on campus rather than expulsion.*

- *Successful bugging of Science Division achieved – we are monitoring all feeds to find out what new experiments are being worked out and hope to have a full report by the next meeting.*

- *We'd like to remind members that anyone who decides to follow the 42ⁿᵈ Army should leave Anti-Corp – we do not share the same mission statement and cannot condone the use of excessive violence.*

- *Monitoring headquarters were broken into last week. Nothing was taken so we believe it may have been a student prank but if anyone has any information please come forward.*

- *We have located some nearby woodland outside the wall so submit your ideas for the theme of this year's fall ball.*

Meet again in a month's time. Bring all your ideas for new rallies – let's keep fighting Corporation! Think free – be free.

Chapter Eleven

*MADSR: Failed wall breach by Academy students –
Corpers calling for immediate expulsion. What do you
think? Voice your opinion in social hub beta and be heard.*

*CORP: City Forty-Two increases security measures on
perimeter wall.
Corporation keeps you safe from highly toxic HER levels.
We care.*

*ANTIC: HER levels are an urban myth.
Post your images from beyond the wall and fight
oppression.*

After a month into her assignment at Science Division,
Dina thought her brain might atrophy from boredom. Her
days were spent cleaning all the antiquated, yet still in use,
equipment and performing whatever menial task her
mentor didn't feel like doing. Some of these little jobs had
been quite interesting, taking her to different parts of the
building - useful for her double agent status - but mostly
she was reduced to filing of one kind or another.

Today was different. Today the head of Science
Division had specifically requested all interns to present
themselves outside the entrance to Banner Corridor, the
highest security clearance corridor in the complex, at 9am
sharp. Dina stood with the four other interns wondering
what was going to happen. There had been rumours about
an intern who mysteriously went missing when working
late on this particular floor. But Dina had done a bit of
digging and found out that the young man had been caught
in a comprising position with a senior lab technician. They
had both been quietly, but firmly, asked to leave.
Workplace gossip was useful and had helped Dina plant all
her bugs, but she hoped this gathering was not cause for
another sudden disappearance.

At 9am the automatic doors to Banner opened, and the five interns crossed the threshold. As the doors swung shut, Dr Basjere, Head of Science Division, exited a side room and joined the nervous group.

'Welcome,' he said, smiling at them all.

There were a few nervous thank-yous and foot shuffles.

'If you would all follow me please.' Dr Basjere set off down the corridor. 'Loyalty is a highly coveted trait. One that we look for in our staff. Here at Science Division we need you to be 100% committed to everything we do.'

Dr Basjere glanced over his shoulder to make sure everyone was still with him. He needn't have worried. The interns were hanging off his every word. Dina brought up the rear, wondering what Basjere was going to say next.

'We have decided that one of you will be our new full time scientist working on special projects. But before we make our final selection we have a tricky problem we would like you to take a look at. We welcome any thoughts and suggestions you might have.'

Dr Basjere stopped outside a pair of double doors.

'Please.' He gestured the interns inside. 'Enjoy this chance to look at the future.'

Dina and the other interns entered the room, and came to a standstill. They had entered the nerve hub of the entire division - the Idea Generation Room - a nirvana for anyone who wanted to work in Science Division. The place where the magic happened. Even Dina felt a tingle of excitement as she looked at the idea boards, floating mind maps, probability machines and, most wonderfully of all, the computer hive mind that ran everything.

The hive mind sat behind several layers of plexiglass, protected by intricate security levels, but the interns could still look at it through the window. And it was beautiful.

Dr Basjere had been talking to Dina, but she hadn't heard a word.

'Miss Grey, if you could?' he repeated.

122

Dina heard this time, and hurried to follow the other interns into one of the affectionately named 'fish bowls' - a workspace that cut you off from all outside interference and modulated it's background to whatever most inspired and motivated the individual. It was achieved through state of the art brain scans, and some dizzying computer programming that Science Division hoped to be able to begin beta testing in people's homes in the near future. That much Dina had been able to glean from one of her break-time gossips.

As the fish bowl closed around her, Dina caught a glimpse of a high-energy radiation warning sign from behind the hive computer. That was unexpected. HER weapons had been behind the devastating effects of The Event, and she had been taught the technology – and the means to recreate it - had been destroyed forever. The testing data popped up on the transparency in front of her. The fish bowl tuned into her own personal wavelength creating her optimal work environment, and she no longer had time to think about anything else.

Later that evening, Dina relayed her days' activities to Kira and the others over dinner. The glimpse of the high-energy radiation sign had everyone worried.

'I reckon that's what Anti-Corp is looking for,' said Ruth. 'If they had that kind of fire power, they could destroy Corporation.'

'And the rest of us,' Pete said.

'But why would anyone want to get rid of Corporation?' Ingrid asked, bemused.

Ingrid didn't come to all of the group meetings, but Pete had refused to exclude her from the essence of what they were trying to achieve. For her part, Ingrid had agreed not to divulge anything as long as it wasn't detrimental to Corporation.

'I didn't get a chance to investigate,' Dina said. 'But I think I did well with the testing so there is a possibility I'll get some additional access to Banner Corridor.'

'And what exactly is it that you think you'll be able to do?' Kira asked.

Dina shrugged, and round a mouthful of food she said thickly, 'I don't know. Snoop, improvise, you know, stuff.'

Jed cleared his throat.

'You don't need to do anything dangerous, Dina. We've got enough evidence to keep Anti-Corp tied up in Legal for a few years - thanks to your double-bugging.'

'Just try and get us a visual on the radiation sign,' Pete said. 'Then we can alert Science Division to the potential of an Anti-Corp attack.'

'Don't worry guys,' Dina said. 'I won't do anything stupid.'

Martha had been quiet throughout the exchange. She had been suffering with terrible morning sickness. Ingrid, however, seemed to be sailing through, looking more and more radiant as the days and weeks went by.

'You okay Ma?' Kira said gently.

'High-energy radiation,' Martha replied. 'It was a specialised HER weapon that caused our forebears sterility.'

The room fell still as everyone stopped talking and looked at her.

'As you may know, grow-your-own was extremely popular before The Event. People donated sperm and eggs for specific genetic modification. I believe during the bio-warfare they managed to modulate a HER to the right frequency to affect the DNA of reproductive gametes.'

'Only the power of the remodulated beams was underestimated,' Kira joined in. 'So before they realised the irreversible damage they'd caused, everyone left had already been affected.'

'Correct. With no viable human gametes available, Corporation began creating their own, hence establishing their strong power base. Of course, that is the short version, it took place over several decades.'

124

No-one spoke.

'You don't think Corporation are still dosing us do you?' Dina said finally. 'And somehow us three got immune, or missed a dose, or something?'

The others looked at her, then back at Martha.

'I can't say for certain. My area of expertise is plants, not people.'

'It's not possible,' Ingrid said. 'I know you want to find a bad guy to blame in all this but I refuse to believe that Corporation, who look after us from cradle to grave, would have anything to do with deliberately enforcing sterility. I mean what do they stand to gain?'

'Are you for real?' Ruth spluttered.

Ingrid sat up straighter, becoming red in the face at being directly challenged. Before she could reply, Ruth continued.

'Corporation have everything to gain. We are tame sheep herded from one technological marvel to another, never knowing the wonder of self miracles.'

Ruth was beginning to get angry, and Ingrid shrunk away from her tirade.

'Don't you think that Kira would love to be Grace's biological mother? Don't you think you should be able to decide whether you can grow life within your own body, and not some faceless suit in an office?'

Ruth took a breath to continue, but Kira put her hand on her arm and shook her head.

'Not now Ruthie.'

Ingrid blinked back tears, unused to being the focus of such anger.

'I think I'd like to go now, Pete. I'm feeling tired.'

She rose gracefully, air kissing her brother goodbye and waving slightly at the others. Pete clasped arms with Jed and tipped his hand to the rest as he walked out with Ingrid.

'Sorry Jed,' Ruth said. 'I know she's your sister but...'

'Don't worry about it, Ruth,' he replied. 'My sister

125

is a Corper through and through. If it's any consolation, I agree with you.'

'It's unlike you to be so aggressive though, Ruth,' said Martha.

'Sorry. I dunno know what came over me – I just felt so angry. I had to say something. It's this whole thing, it's got me on edge.'

'I'm glad I've got you in my corner, Ruthie,' said Kira, giving her friend a quick hug.

'Yeah, me too,' said Dina. 'I'd hate to be on the opposite side.'

Ruth nudged her in the ribs, and Dina laughed. Kira checked her wristplant.

'Look at the time – it's getting late. We'd better clear up,' she said, getting to her feet and collecting dishes. The others groaned as they reluctantly got up to help.

CORP: Visit your nearest Auto-Doc and get your latest health check. Corporation cares.

ANON88: Privileged few get lucky again – what about those who've waited years?

MADSR: No comment.

The following morning, Kira woke to a rapidly flashing handheld. She had over forty messages. Glancing across the bed, she saw Jed had even more. Grace was still sleeping, so Kira picked her handheld up, crept out of the bedroom, and went over to check the apartment vidcom and sync up. Fifteen more vid messages were waiting to be viewed. Something huge had happened last night. That, or something awful had happened to one of their parents. Kira quickly scrolled down the com in her hands, and with relief saw a message from her mother. And Jed's. And Martha's. And Martha's father - marked highly urgent - which remained at the top of the list as she continued to scroll. A scream from Martha's apartment startled Kira so

126

much she nearly dropped her handheld. Jed came running out the bedroom, looking around wildly as the connecting door to Martha's apartment banged open and a furious Martha burst through, trailed by a rather ashen faced Dina.

'She has betrayed all of us,' Martha fumed at Kira. 'She is a selfish, self-centred, miserable old hag and I am glad her husband is dead so he does not have to put up with her anymore.'

'What are you talking about Ma?' Jed asked.

'Have you not seen it? Do you not know what she has done to us? I will fragging kill her!'

Kira's eyes widened as Dina turned the expanded news feed on and let the sweeps fill the holo-projector on the wall of the lounge.

Another Corporation Cover Up but this time it's more than shady water deals. This time it affects every single one of us. The great and powerful Corporation have been trying to hide the facts but Anti-Corp, as always, has fought hard for the truth and we bring you the truth - the most incredible news since The Event.

NATURAL PREGNANCIES

That's right. You heard it here first. Anti-Corp has learnt that four women in our city have become naturally pregnant.

Martha Hamble (Corporation Marketing Director's daughter)
Ingrid Jenson (high flying exec at Corp Tech)
Ruth Maddocks (Corporation Educator)
Dina Grey (Student)

If you know any of these women we demand that you upload, share and spread the sweep. Urge them to tell their story about how they broke away from the oppression of Corporation. Let them tell you how you too can start building a new life. A free life. A life without Corporation.

There was more but Kira stopped reading.

'Wait. Ruth's pregnant? When did that happen?'

'Never mind that Kira, look at what she has done. She has betrayed us.' Martha was beginning to sound hysterical, but she carried on. 'I had one hundred and twenty four messages on my handheld this morning, and my ear comm will not stop ringing. I have barely had time to adjust to this myself, let alone feel ready to explain it to the entire city.'

There was a knock at the apartment door. Jed opened it. Ruth came in.

'You have got a fragging nerve,' Martha shouted at her as she flew towards the door. Kira managed to catch Martha's arm and slow her down, and Jed blocked her path to Ruth.

'It wasn't me,' Ruth implored, desperation in her voice.

Kira looked at Ruth more closely, she could see her eyes were red and puffy with dark shadows, and she was wearing the same clothes as yesterday.

'You didn't know did you?'

Ruth shook her head slowly. Jed guided Ruth over to the couch, and sat her down next to Dina. Martha, calming a little, allowed Kira to do the same with her. Jed's ear comm pinged.

'It's work. I have to go in.'

They all looked at him coolly.

'I think you should all just stay here for now,' he said. 'Let me see what I can find out.'

And he disappeared into the bedroom to get ready for work.

'Don't we have to attend the protest today?' Dina asked. No-one was listening.

'What the frag Ruth? What did you do?' Martha asked, her fingers curled into talons, as if she wanted to rake Ruth's eyes out.

Kira made shushing noises and gestures, trying to calm Martha down.

'I didn't *do* anything,' Ruth replied. 'I've not been feeling well so I went for a check up last night. It was just an auto-doc. I never spoke to an actual person. It found an anomaly.'

'An anomaly?' Martha said.

'Yeah. I got a tip to toe check. I did the scan and I saw … ' Ruth faltered looking at Dina. 'I saw the baby. I am so sorry Dina. It should've been you, not me. I don't understand.'

Jed reappeared from the bedroom with a wide-awake Grace. He passed the baby to Kira and said his quick goodbyes. As the front door closed behind him Martha sniffed loudly.

'Are we supposed to believe you got yourself pregnant and did not know anything about it until last night?' she said, acid dripping from every word.

'Look, I've not felt well,' Ruth said. 'But I thought it was just stress with getting Quentin back, and trying to find out what Anti-Corp are up to.'

Martha gestured to the sweeps still projecting on the wall.

'And all *this* just happens to be a coincidence?'

'Yeah. I don't have my mic chip Ma, and I'm not reporting back to Anti-Corp anymore. We've gotta find out where the info *did* leak from before it gets any worse.'

'How can it possibly get any worse?'

But before Ruth could respond, Grace began to cry, not used to the loud, aggressive voices. Kira scowled at them.

'You've made Gracie cry. Calm down the both of you. Dina, can you help me in the kitchen please sweetie.'

Ruth and Martha settled back into chairs on opposite sides of the lounge, glaring at one another, as Kira, Grace and Dina went into the kitchen to make baby milk and synth-caf.

CORP: We urge citizens to remain calm. No-one is at risk. Anomalies happen. For more information please visit your nearest Auto-Doc and get your free med check.

INJEN: NO COMMENT.

The apartment door banged open and Ingrid stood in the doorway quivering with rage.

'What have you done?' Ingrid shrieked at Ruth, who leapt up to defend herself.

Kira strode from the kitchen area into the lounge.

'That is enough. I have never, NEVER, seen such displays of rudeness and aggression in my home, and I will not have it. My home is a place of welcome and love, and I will not have you coming in here treating it like garbage. Do you understand?' Her gaze swept over all of them.

Ingrid, Martha and Ruth all remained silent as Kira continued.

'I am making synth-caf. We will sit down and discuss calmly how the sweeps got hold of this information. Mr Hamble has sent me an important message, and Jed has gone to work to find out what he can about the situation. Can you three control yourselves?'

Kira looked in disapproval at the three women, as Dina began to bring cups over to the lounge area. They all nodded mutely.

ANON88: How much did they pay Corporation? Why weren't we given a chance?
Protest against privileged pregnancies, sweep it out and join us.

Mr Hamble's message was brief and to the point. Kira settled herself with Grace on the couch, and read it aloud.

'Kira. Tell your friends the leak came from Force. It has been locked down. Inform the others that any contact with the sweeps goes against a legal directive from Corporation. I'll send my man over with the details. Yours

R. Hamble.'

By the time Kira had finished reading the message, Martha had calmed down enough to check her handheld. She confirmed that she had a near identical message.

'I suppose he knew we would come together over this,' Martha said, clearing her throat, and shifting in her seat. 'Ruth, I am so sorry I lost my temper. It was incredibly wrong of me to jump to conclusions. I know it is no excuse but I am feeling rather overwhelmed at the moment...'

She couldn't continue and the tears spilled down her face. Ruth was crying too, trying to tell Martha it was okay but not doing a very good job. Ingrid watched the two women curiously, feeling no desire to cry whatsoever.

'I hope Jed isn't going to get into trouble,' Dina said, once tears were dried and hugs exchanged. The others looked at her in alarm.

'What do you mean, Dina?' Kira asked.

'Well, if the leak came from Force, it must have come from the case files Jed has been keeping on all of us. I know he said his boss ordered him to do it, but it went against everything Mr Hamble told him to do. And if he finds out....do you remember how mad Mr Hamble was when the details of the attack got leaked?'

'I do,' Ingrid said. 'Pete nearly lost his job. So did Jed.'

'I guess we just have to wait for Jed to come back,' Kira said. 'And then we'll know more.'

A bleak silence settled on the women, each absorbed in their own thoughts. Ingrid stood.

'I'm going to be late for work,' she announced. 'I only came over here to find out what was going on. I have to go.'

'Are you sure it's safe?' Martha asked.

'It's fine. I have a driver. Management requirements now that....'

She pointed towards her stomach. The others said

their distracted goodbyes as she left.

'Sometimes I wish it were me and not Ingrid,' Kira spoke wistfully.

Ruth leant over and put her arm round Kira, hugging her gently.

'I hope Jed won't be too cross with us.' Dina broke the silence.

'Why would he be cross with you?' Kira asked.

'We have to go to the water protest today, remember? As part of my cover?'

'Oh – I'd forgotten all about that,' Kira said. 'I don't want to bring Grace to the protest.'

'Neither do I,' Dina said. 'It's okay – Ruth is coming with me.'

Martha was fiddling with her sleeve, listening to the others. 'I will come too.'

'Are you sure Ma?' Dina asked.

'Yes, I can't stay indoors all day. Not today.'

'What if someone recognises you?'

Martha shrugged. 'We will all have to adjust to our lives changing from now on.'

'I suppose so,' Kira said. 'You don't mind if I don't come, do you?'

The others all reassured Kira that they didn't and began planning their route to the protest.

'Have you seen the sweeps?'

'Yes. Corporation must have let something slip to result in four pregnancies.'

'It's a bit odd that they all know each other isn't it?'

'We didn't come here to talk about them.'

'Right. The meeting has moved to Corp Tech.'

'Are you sure?'

'Yes. The new secretary is ours. She's been waiting six years for Collection and after this morning's sweeps, she is feeling motivated.'

'Did you get the schematics?'

'Yes.'

'Any problems?'

'No. Anti-Corp think it was a student prank.'

'And they won't find the tech?'

'It's hidden well. All their files were downloaded yesterday. We have everything they have.'

'What's the plan?'

'There's a weakness on the south side.'

'Weak enough?'

'Should be.'

'What do we have?'

'Remotely controlled skimmer full of Ammonia Nitrate and wired with a remote detonation.'

'And it won't be checked?'

'It's already in place.'

Chapter Twelve

ANTIC: Biggest Corporation cover-up to date
Martha Hamble – pregnant!
Ruth Maddocks – pregnant!
Ingrid Jenkins – pregnant!
Dina Gray – pregnant!
Who do you know? Upload your links and spread the
sweep.

MED4AC: We can neither confirm or deny any medical
abnormalities at this time.

MSCHILD: Four!! How did that happen? It's not fair.

Jed caught the news sweep on his way to work. He was concerned - how the frag did the sweeps have all the details? And why did the sweep report Dina as pregnant and not a miscarriage? Nothing was making sense and Jed felt uneasy as he walked through the Community Hub and round the side of Force HQ.

When he got into work there was an immediate summons on his desk to the Chief's office. Knocking, then entering, Jed was relieved to see his partner Pete already there. He didn't recognise the other man. He was short and squat, dressed in a non-regulation grey suit, with greasy looking hair and a faint sneer on his face.

'Jenkins, sit down. You too Barnes. This is Agent Deveraux from Special Investigations. He'd like to know how the frag the sweeps got hold of our classified files.'

The Chief folded his hands on the desk in front of him, and waited for a response. Pete and Jed made a point of not looking at each other. Jed felt confident - he knew that neither of them had leaked the information.

'Sir, I have no idea. We followed protocol to the letter.'

'Have you checked all the internal coding for non

Force elements?' Pete asked.

Jed raised his eyebrows in surprise at that. It was not like Pete to think of the techy solution. Ingrid must be rubbing off on him.

'It's alright detectives,' Agent Deveraux said, smiling with no real warmth behind it. 'We know you didn't leak the information. The both of you are so tightly entwined in this mess on a personal level I believe a leak of this nature would be the last course of action either of you would take.'

Agent Deveraux handed Pete and Jed an info jack each.

'This is everything we have on Anti-Corps movements in the past six months. I think you might be surprised at how widespread their little spies are.'

The agent paused as if deciding whether or not to reveal any more details. He thumbed his earlobe whilst moving back to stand at the side of the Chief's desk.

'In fact,' Deveraux said. 'We also know about your own personal infiltration.'

Pete and Jed tried to keep their face neutral.

'Anti-Corp are not the only ones who look to the student body for convenient bug placers gentlemen. Your apartment has been under surveillance for several months now. Audio only – of course.'

Jed's jaw tightened. The Chief interrupted, glaring at the Agent.

'What Deveraux is trying to say is that he wants you to continue in your infiltration of Anti-Corp. Find out everything you can because we will not be left on the sidelines holding our arses when this thing kicks off.' The Chief breathed heavily through his nose.

Jed addressed Deveraux.

'I assume you'll be removing that bug immediately. Now that we're on the same page.'

The Agent shrugged.

'Sure. Just make sure you use the info jacks I've given you to get up to speed and then continue to update us with your progress.'

Jed nodded, then looked at the Chief.

'Anything else, Sir?'

'I want you heading up a team for today's protest, Jenkins. I will not allow these fragging activists to get away with anything. If one of them so much as puts a toe out of line you arrest first, ask questions later. That'll be all.'

ANTIC: *No Comment says Corporation in the face of medical miracles – new experiment gone wrong sparks health scares – check your womb today!*

ANON6: *Martha Hamble was the rape victim!!!*

ANON88: *Serves her right – Corpers deserve it.*

JMBISH: *Have some respect you sweep vultures and leave the poor girl alone!*

MAHA: *Thank you for the supportive messages. I am keeping the baby.*

ANTIC: *We support MAHA.*

'What the frag are SI doing bugging your fragging apartment?' Pete asked when the two men were back at their desks, his face red, fists clenched. Jed ran a hand through his hair as he sat. His head felt like it was fizzing. Everything seemed to be running out of control. Four women falling pregnant. All of them he, and especially Kira, knew. One of them suffering a miscarriage. And now that their little spy stunt had stumbled on the HER source, things were getting more and more serious.

'I think we need to get ourselves up to spec.' Pete waved the info jack at his partner.

'I agree,' Jed said, 'I'll just send Kira a quick message.'

Hi love, it was an internal leak – we're on it. Tell everyone to stay in and stay safe. I'll fill you in when I get home. Love you xx J.

It took several hours to go through the data on the jacks. Jed was surprised, and a little impressed, at how far Anti-Corp had managed to infiltrate. They had people in every division of Corporation, with access to every level. It was clear to Jed they were planning to release the information about HER from Science Division, but there was no indication as to a time-frame.

The protest planned for this afternoon was about water restrictions. It was being held outside Corporation HQ, about as far from Science Division as you could get.

Anti-Corp were meant to be demonstrating *peacefully,* but the Chief didn't trust them - especially after the Special Investigation bombshell. He wanted as many Force operatives on site, and that meant riot gear, as per procedure. Since the pregnancies had been leaked over the news sweep that morning, people were becoming restless. Jed had felt it when he'd walked through the Community Hub on his way to work. There had been a lot of muttering and hostility, much of it broadcast through the news feed and aimed towards the pregnant women. Fortunately, Jed knew Martha and Ingrid had enough sense to keep away from the Hubs, but it didn't stop him worrying about them. Especially his sister, who still believed Corporation could do no wrong.

The Corporation kept a tight control over water allowance. It was the most precious resource there was – if the reports that no usable water existed outside the city were true, that is. Jed had always listened with interest to Ruth's descriptions of what she found beyond the city. Most young people made a foray, but Jed had never got round to it. Then he'd made Detective. And then he'd gotten Grace. It was too much to risk for the sake of idle curiosity. Besides, what possible reason could the

Corporation have to lie about water. It made no sense to Jed. Catching up with the others on his riot team, Jed exchanged greetings with them and then went through his own kit check. Just because they weren't expecting trouble didn't mean he shouldn't be prepared. After gearing up he went to find his partner.

ANTIC: Fight Corporation for water rights - today at noon.

Pete was whistling as he grabbed his stuff from his desk.

'Why do you sound so happy?' Jed asked.

'Half day. I'm off for the weekend, so no responsibilities. And best of all I'm spending it all with Ingrid and …'

Pete remembered where he was and stopped speaking, looking around to see if anyone was listening. Jed knew he meant Ingrid and the unborn baby. He was pleased for his friend, especially now Pete would become family, but he was still caught up in everything they'd learnt this morning.

'Don't you think you should stay here?' Jed said. 'Now that we know more about....well, everything.'

A ping came through Pete's wristplant. He glanced down and grunted.

'Guess whose working late. Again. That woman is a workaholic.'

'You could always stay for protest watch.'

'No thanks,' Pete paused. 'I've got...' He looked round again then continued in a quieter tone. 'Little person things to do. And as for the rest of it.' He waved his hand. 'There's nothing we can do right now. They've put extra security measures in place at Science Division and the other girls are all at home today right?'

Jed agreed with Pete, but he did not feel happy about it.

'Alright Pete. Take care out there, who knows what information they'll leak next. I've got to get my team ready.

Have a good one.'

Jed clapped his friend on the back before heading out.

Ingrid sat at her desk. A single droplet of sweat trickled down the side of her face.

'Air-con!'

A tinny voice replied. 'Air temperature is at an optimum nineteen degrees Celsius.'

It seemed natural pregnancy came with pitfall after pitfall, even with regular check ups. Even so, Ingrid didn't want to feel like she was being parboiled from the inside out if she could help it. Perhaps her electronics weren't functioning properly. The med-tech had told her that changes in her magnetic auras due to the pregnancy could affect her implants, and as some of the tech was in beta test, there were still kinks in the software. A cool breeze swept over her as the doors to her office opened. It was her boss.

Ingrid, you look cooked. He projected with his telepathic neural implants - the latest thing being developed. They were full of bugs and blinking out all the time – Ingrid's especially.

A green shimmer waved its way across the room. Ingrid watched, entranced, picking out motes of gold and red. She felt the fire within embrace her and stretch to the ends of her being. There was something. A noise. A noise that didn't belong. It shattered the colours into a myriad of rainbows as her bosses neural network invaded again.

I'm serious – I need those figures stat. Meeting in t-minus 10.

Her boss left the room and a jolt went through Ingrid's body as she remembered what she was supposed to have been working on. This is why you aren't finishing on time, she thought to herself.

Ingrid tapped her receiver and bought up the screen, amalgamating sales and losses. The figures looked good. Only a handful of off radars, and those would be picked up by Agency. A curl of steam wound its way out of her nostril. Butterflies fluttered in her womb as more sweat trickled down her back.

Dina pushed her way to the front of the crowd, looking for Ruth. Despite the morning's sweeps they'd decided it would be prudent if both of them were present at the peaceful protest but they'd travelled separately. Who knew how many Anti-Corp eyes were watching them, and being seen at a public event should help maintain their cover, bringing Ruth one step closer to her husbands body.

Dina wished Anti Corp would hurry up with whatever it was they wanted from Science Division. She was looking forward to her next session in the fish bowl, and it seemed she was a front runner for permanent selection.

Bobby appeared next to her.

'Hello my little pregnant chip.'

'I'm not pregnant,' Dina snapped.

'That's not what the sweeps say.'

'Yeah, well, sometimes the sweeps are wrong.'

There was a tense silence as Dina scanned the crowd looking for Ruth and Martha, wishing Bobby would go away. Finally he spoke.

'Great job on the planting. We've got everything we need.'

Dina turned to look at him.

'So I'm done?'

'For now,' Bobby confirmed. 'Although we can always use more soldiers. Especially as you are so uniquely qualified to fight against Corporation.' He took her wrist and pressed his own wristplant to her tech, transferring contact details. 'You can reach me anytime.' He smiled down at Dina, his eyes twinkling, full of mischief.

'Thanks,' Dina muttered, as he melted back into the crowd.

'Air-con,' Ingrid asked again, not bothering to hear the reply.

She messaged the office intern for ice, and when the cup appeared on her desk – the contents began to melt. The cold squares quickly ran into liquid as she picked up the cup. A ripple shuddered through the water as tiny bubbles started to form. She put the cup down, noting her melted fingerprints on the surface. It was stifling in her office, there was no air and the *heat*. She began to panic. I'm with child. I can't be sick. What is wrong? Ingrid dialled through to the Med Centre, and requested a check up. She sat half panting as they checked her vitals remotely.

'Infant is fine.'

'What about me?'

'Carrier is normal. Keep up the good work.'

She couldn't believe it. Her hair was stuck to her scalp, her tunic was moulded to her body, and steam was rising. From the back of her hands. She looked at her reflection in the window by the side of her desk and thought she saw flickers of flame in her eyes. What was happening?

'What was all that about?' asked Ruth breathlessly, as she and Martha pushed past protestors to stand next to Dina.

'Do you think we should all be here?' Dina asked. 'Aren't you worried at being recognised?'

'We can't stay locked away forever,' Martha said. 'Besides, isn't Jed working this protest? I'm sure we'll be safe.'

'Never mind us,' Ruth said, 'What did Bobby say?'

'Well, he congratulated me on my pregnancy,' Dina sniffed. 'And apparently I'm all done, for now. At Science Division. They've got what they wanted.'

'I hope you told him to frag off,' Ruth said sharply.

Dina looked down at her feet, hunching her shoulders.

'We should let Jed know,' Martha said, reaching for her ear comm.

Dina grabbed her hand.

'Not here. Later.' Dina gestured at the crowd. 'We just need to show our faces briefly and then we can get back to Kira's. We can fill everyone in then.'

Ruth linked one arm through Dina's and one through Martha's, and the three women began to meander through the protestors. As they passed by the Force defenders, Jed raised his eyebrows at them, but the women smiled serenely at him and continued on their slow circuit.

'Asking for trouble,' Jed muttered, scanning the crowd for troublemakers.

There was a commotion to the left. A man and a women, dressed in garish purple with identical cropped heads, were pushing through the throng roughly, trying to get to where Martha and the others were.

'I know who you are,' shouted the woman. 'You're Hamble's daughter – you're one of the affected.'

Jed discreetly called for back up, and began to make his way over to the women.

'Aren't you going to say anything?' The woman sounded slightly hysterical.

'Yes, I am Martha Hamble. My handle is MAHA, and I will post an update later.'

'I don't want some sweeping update. I want answers. Now!'

The woman pushed Martha hard. Martha wind-milled her arms but lost her balance and fell backwards with a jolt. Jed quickly grabbed the aggressive woman and magno-bound her arms behind her back.

'Get off me!' she screamed as she fought the restraints. 'You can't touch me. Filthy Force scum.'

'Martha – are you okay?' Jed called out.

Dina and Ruth were helping Martha back up. She looked pale and shaken.

'We'll take her home and do a Med check,' Ruth said, using her body to block access to Martha's as they forced their way out of the crowd.

Jed jabbed his finger at two nearby Force

142

Officials. 'You two. Go with them, see them safely home.'

The woman who had attacked Martha was still struggling. Jed touched his ear comm.

'I need an offender transport from Corp HQ protest, now.'

The butterflies rippled inside her. Ingrid got up, hot, exhausted, melting, and walked across the floor in a burning daze. The door was open. The corridor felt cooler and she knew that if she got out of the building she would feel so much better. She could feel heat absorb her, reflect out of her, resonate with her soul and the child within. Suddenly tendrils of flame were licking her skin in bursts of heat. Her electronics fell out, breaking as they hit the ground. It felt like the sun burnt twice as brightly as Ingrid exploded into flames, and woke up with a start. She looked around wildly, before realising she was still at her desk and despite feeling a little warm, she certainly wasn't on fire.

Since finding out she was pregnant this wasn't the first time Ingrid had had a dream about catching fire at work, although what it was supposed to mean was beyond her. She had put it down to an odd side effect from changes in her hormone levels, and her reluctance to go into work this morning after a distressing heat dream, was pure laziness. Just because she was growing a life inside her and not in a laboratory like it was supposed to be, didn't mean she had the luxury of lying around all day. Ingrid was under way too much scrutiny to show any sign of weakness, especially today with the information leak to the sweeps.

A ping on Ingrid's console refocused her attention to the figures in front of her. She had to get this done. She had plans. Suddenly her desk started to move as the floor fell away and a gaping chasm opened up beneath her. Ingrid held her stomach as she tumbled down, her last thoughts of Pete.

A boom rang through the air as the ground shook and a

plume of smoke appeared across the city. All around Jed urgent instructions could be heard from Force Control.

'Terrorist attack at Corp Tech. Calling all units for immediate scramble. Terrorist attack at Corp Tech. Calling all units for immediate scramble.'

'Frag!'

Jed looked at his wristplant. Ingrid was still at work. Releasing the aggressive protestor, Jed gathered his team. All the Force skimmers were parked nearby, Jed and his team were in the air and on their way within moments of receiving the call.

ANON76: Corp Tech explodes – live feed available.

When he arrived at the scene, Jed looked at the wreckage in dismay. There was nothing left of the building except a pile of smouldering rubble. Dust hung thick on the air. Force operatives donned their breathing gear and a Detective organised the safety barrier. Jed quickly found the first on scene operative.

'Was anyone inside?' Jed asked, his voice sounding thick in his ears.

'Most likely, Sir. Apparently there was a meeting on the upper floors but we haven't sent teams into the rubble yet.'

'The list? Do you have the list?'

The operative passed over his handheld. Jed frantically scanned the list, checking, checking.

There. Her name. Ingrid Jenkins. Present. She hadn't left yet.

'Frag it. She shouldn't even be there.'

'Sir?'

'I'll head a team up. Let's get moving.' Jed commandeered the handheld and yelled for his unit to fall in behind.

They headed over to the destruction. Drones hovered above making their own scans. Several had stopped above a patch of rubble, beeping, indicating life signs beneath. Quickly, Jed divided his unit into two teams. Heading up one of the teams, he began to shift the rubble aside using pressure blasts where needed.

The second team found a body first. Jed's heart pounded in his chest as he craned his neck to see. It was a brunette. Relief rushed through his body, he didn't even stop to feel guilty – he had to find his sister. One of his operatives uncovered a man's shoe and Jed wanted to scream in frustration but they had to help anyone they found. After shifting a pile of rubble the man's leg ended abruptly and one of the rescuers threw up behind a broken chair. This was taking too long. Jed blasted some ceiling wreckage into smaller pieces and a pale arm flopped out with the debris.

'Halt,' Jed yelled.

He knew that arm. He knew that hand. It couldn't be. He began to scrabble desperately with his hands at the debris, gradually clearing enough away for the team to help him pull the inert body out of the wreckage.

It was Ingrid.

And she was not breathing.

'Medic!' Jed screamed.

A medic rushed over. Jed cradled his sister's head on his lap, unaware of the tears streaming down his face. The medic ran his scanner over Ingrid's body, then jerked it back in surprise.

'This one's gone,' he said. 'But there's an anomaly.'

Before he could continue his report, Jed finished it for him.

'Her name is Ingrid. And she's pregnant.'

The medic yelled over to his colleagues. 'I need a gurney - stat.' He tried to move Ingrid from Jed's lap, but Jed shoved him away roughly. 'Sir. We may be able to save the baby.'

One of the Force operatives put a hand on the medic's shoulder, bent down and whispered in his ear. The medic looked up in dismay at Jed clinging on to his dead sister's body.

'I had no idea,' he said. 'I'm so sorry for your loss, but we have to act quickly if we hope to save the child.'

It took four of Jed's unit to pull him away from Ingrid's body. Two more medics ran over with a gurney. Jed was still fighting the men holding him as his sister was air lifted away.

'No! That's my sister. She's not... you can't....get off.'

As the med van disappeared, the fight dropped out of Jed. He sagged into the arms of his men. A skimmer flew into the crime scene, and somebody hurtled off at a run. A young operative tried in vain to stop Pete.

'Sir. You can't enter here. It's a cordon..'

Pete carried on. When he saw Jed, he stopped in his tracks. Jed lifted his tear stained face and shook his head as his friend fell to his knees and howled in pain. For a brief moment, everyone stopped to look.

Pete's howl reverberated around the wreckage, as he poured his grief into it. Without warning, he broke off, staggered to his feet and grabbed Jed by the arms.

'The baby? What about the baby? Not the baby?'

Jed couldn't answer. He didn't know. The medic who had organised Ingrid's gurney came cautiously over to the two men.

'We sent the body to Science Division. I'm sure they'll do everything they can to save the baby but,' he hesitated. 'It didn't look good.'

Not waiting to see whether the two men understood what he had told them, the medic hurried over to another body being pulled from the wreckage. Pete and Jed looked dimly at each other, neither one able to comprehend what had happened.

EMERGENCY MEETING OF CORPORATION
BOARD FOR CITY FORTY-TWO
DATE: 1ˢᵗ August 2215
VIRTUAL PRESENCE: J NICKS, Y ASWAD and P
BASJERE
R HAMBLE INJURED – MINUTES SENT
THROUGH

AGENDA

1. ATTACK ON CORP TECH
2. DECISION ON PREGNANCY B
3. PUBLIC UNREST
4. CONTINGENCY PLAN

MINUTES

1. UNWARRANTED ATTACK ON CORP TECH
   HAS REVEALED SERIOUS SECURITY BREACH
   – NEW MEASURES TO BE PUT IN PLACE. ALL
   EFFORTS MUST BE MADE TO RECOVER
   PROJECT WORK & RE-HOUSE IN SECURE
   LOCATION. FAMILIES TO BE SENT
   CONDOLENCES. ORDERS FOR TERMINATION
   APPROVED ON CULPRITS.
2. PREGNANCY B UPDATE – HOST DIED IN
   ATTACK. BABY WAS VIABLE BUT DECISION
   MADE TO TERMINATE FOR MEDICAL STUDY.
3. LEVEL OF PUBLIC UNREST NOT TO BE
   TOLERATED. FORCE MUST EXERCISE
   GREATER CONTROL. CORPORATION TO FILL
   THE SWEEPS WITH POSITIVE MESSAGES
   AND TURN FOCUS.
4. CONTINGENCY PLAN A READY FOR
   EXECUTION – BOARD MEMBERS WILL BE
   ABLE TO LEAVE THE CITY UNTIL SITUATION
   RECTIFIED.
ANY OTHER BUSINESS – NONE

147

Chapter Thirteen

*CORP: Use your locator tech to check on your loved ones.
Corporation looks after you.*

*ANTIC: Our leader, Victor Bianchi speaks out against
today's violent action.
"Radicals have used our peaceful movement as a terrorist
springboard."*

Twenty minutes after being air lifted to the Medical Centre, Ingrid's body lay within a suspension field in the operating theatre. Several medical staff and two senior consultants, one taller than the other, stood around her.

'And you're sure they don't want the fetus to survive?' The taller consultant asked, reluctant to act. 'If we continue to supply oxygen, there's a very good chance it can be saved.'

'The Board want us to carry out an investigation into how this happened. That means autopsy for both mother and child.' His older colleague replied.

'We can't just let the baby die. Surely emphasis should be on saving the child. I mean, it's a medical marvel, think of what might be possible.'

'This is why we have strict directives. Dead mother – dead child.'

Both consultants looked at Ingrid's lifeless body for a moment longer. The older consultant shook his head and gave the signal to turn off life support. If anyone in the room was shocked, they hid it well. The two consultants watched as the rapid heartbeat of the fetus began to slow and become erratic, before fading away altogether. Neither of them noticed the recorder nestled in the corner of the room, it's small red light flashing, capturing both image and sound.

MED4AC: Let's ignore the Hippocratic Oath shall we?

ANTIC: !!!INSTANT UPDATE!!!!
Ingrid Jenkins killed in building terror attack.
Corporation murders baby – watch the unbelievable
footage and spread the sweep.
Stand for the people – join Anti-Corp – justice for Baby J.

Kira stared in shock at the news sweep.

Anti-Corp, who had reported her sister-in-law's death, were blaming Corporation for her murder and using Ingrid and the baby as martyrs for their cause.

Kira threw the remote at the wall, cutting off the transmission. Collecting herself she went over to Grace's cube and stroked her baby's cheek gently as she slept.

Her sister in law was dead. And her unborn child. Dead. In a senseless attack by a radical arm of Anti-Corp. How could this have happened? How did they go from being a group of friends – each the inexplicable recipient of an amazing, beautiful gift - to a family ripped apart, shattered by grief?

MED4AC: Hamble, Marketing Director of Corporation,
rebuilding spine at Corp Medical.

The vid com chimed. Kira answered when she saw who it was.

'Kira? Are you okay? You're not hurt are you? Is my granddaughter alright?'

'Yes Mum. I'm okay.'

'I heard what happened, I can't believe it. Your father and I were still getting over the shock of finding out all your friends were pregnant and then, and then, oh Kira – it's just awful. That poor baby. And Ingrid. Oh my dear, is there anything we can do?'

For once Kira's mother fell silent. Kira looked at her mother's loving, concerned face, and her shoulders shook as the tears fell.

'Oh my poor sweet girl. We'll be right over.' Before Kira had chance to say otherwise, her mum signed off.

Martha came out of her side of the apartment, face ashen, her hair in disarray.

'Kira, my father... he was in the building when....when the attack happened.'

'Oh no – is he okay?'

'He is alive but he is in surgery. The med centre said something about a damaged spinal cord. I have to go and see him. Mother is too scared to leave the house. I can't leave him there all alone.'

'I understand sweetie, but do you think it's safe for you to leave the apartment? By yourself I mean.'

'I will not be by myself,' Martha said. 'Jed has assigned us all a Force shadow, did you not know?'

'No. I can't get through to him. I'm so worried, Ma. His sister just died and..'

'Ingrid is dead? What about the baby?'

'You didn't know?' Kira was confused. 'But how did you know about the attack on Corp Tech?'

'I turned the news sweep on and saw the coverage but before I could read anything I got the call about my father.' She shook her head in disbelief. 'Ingrid is dead? I can't believe it. Where is Pete?'

'I don't know. I can't get through to Jed. I don't know what's happening. I just know that Ingrid and the baby are.... Oh Ma....they're gone. They're just gone, Ma. And I don't understand why it happened. The baby... the baby... it never even started. Why? Why would they do this? I can't.....'

Kira stopped talking as the tears took over.

'Oh Kira.' Martha embraced her, stroking her hair as she cried. 'Poor, poor Ingrid,' she whispered. 'And the baby, that poor innocent baby. Oh Kira.'

After a few moments, Kira pushed Martha gently away, and both women dried their eyes. Martha held a protective hand over her stomach.

'I can't believe Anti-Corp wanted to kill them. It had to have been a mistake. Not a baby, Kira. What possible threat could it have been? Or Ingrid for that matter.'

Kira shrugged, her face a picture of misery. Grace woke up and began to cry.

Martha took the Force skimmer provided to the Med Centre. She had to make sure her father was alright. She didn't think she could cope with more bad news.

As Martha reached the side wing of the Medical Centre reserved for VIPs, she saw a red-faced medical officer scurrying away from a closed door. Without knocking, she entered the room and looked in dismay at the amount of electronics surrounding her father.

'Hmm. You came then.' Mr Hamble gestured at all the equipment around him. 'Don't worry about all this. I'm regrowing part of my spine - nothing to it. No need to fuss.'

Martha came over and kissed him gently on the head. 'Oh Daddy. What happened?'

'It was those idiotic anarchists. Blowing up a perfectly respectable building for no good reason. The meeting got moved. Shouldn't have fragging been there in the first place.'

'Did you hear about Ingrid? Jed's sister?' Martha asked.

Mr Hamble's bushy eyebrows drew into a frown. 'Bad business. Just terrible. And the loss of the child. Bad business.'

'How did you know about that? Do they project the sweeps in here?'

Mr Hamble looked uncomfortable. He tried to adjust his position on the hospital bed but gave up when he realised he had no control over his lower limbs yet.

'Father?' Martha demanded. 'What do you know?'

Mr Hamble breathed heavily out of his nose. 'It wasn't my call.' He looked uncomfortable. 'They decided not to save the fetus. It was a board decision. The bodies are to be investigated by Science Division to find out what is going wrong.'

'Going wrong,' Martha repeated, feeling nauseous as she considered her own condition and how the Board must be viewing her.

'Not that there's anything wrong with you,' Mr Hamble said hastily looking in concern at his pale faced daughter. 'It's just an anomaly. That's all.'

Martha took a seat on the chair beside the bed. Several uncomfortable minutes passed until Mr Hamble cleared his voice.

'It isn't safe for you to be here. You should be careful, now that everyone knows who you are and what's happened. In fact, I've been thinking.' He began fiddling with one of the wires sticking out of his arm. 'I want you to leave the city. There's a place, a wilderness camp. Away from the city. It's a test base, highly confidential, to see whether we can exist outside the walls, I want you to go there. You and the others.' He paused as if trying to find the right words. 'You are all in danger. We don't know how people are going to react. The attack today, those idiots blowing up that building. I can't risk you. Any of you. You must go.' He looked up at Martha, waiting for her reply.

'A wilderness camp? What about the radiation levels?' Martha asked.

Hamble tried to move again and gave up with a grunt. 'There's no radiation at Camp Eden. It's a safe place.'

Martha put her hand on his arm before replying. 'I will let the others know, but if they decide to stay, I am staying with them. This is happening to all of us, we need to stick together.'

'I suppose that's the best I'm going to get.'

Jed sat with Pete in the interview room, waiting for their debrief to begin. Pete hadn't said a word since breaking down at the scene of Ingrid's murder. The door opened and the Chief came in, followed by Agent Deveraux.

'Detectives,' the Chief said.

Agent Deveraux came over and put a hand on Jed's shoulder. 'I'm sorry for your loss,' he said, in a low voice.

Jed stiffened and turned his head to look up at Deveraux, but the Agent had already moved over to Pete and was repeating the gesture.

Pete said nothing.

The Chief settled himself behind his desk while Deveraux leant against the wall, off to one side. Jed looked warily from one to the other, bracing himself for the worst.

'I've read your statement Jenkins,' the Chief began. 'And Deveraux confirms that Special Investigations monitoring did not pick up any chatter from your Anti-Corp infiltration team relating to the attack.'

Jed cast an uneasy eye on Pete, expecting a reaction.

Nothing.

'We know you didn't know. Frag, none of us knew the target was Corp Tech - it was all pointing towards Science Division. I want you to pull your girl out of there and all association with Anti-Corp stops.'

The Chief glared at Jed, expecting him to protest, but Jed nodded.

'We'll provide some additional eyes on you all, keep you safe in the interim,' Deveraux said.

'Safe?'

The Agent looked at the Chief, who nodded. Deveraux walked closer to the desk. 'We moved on your information about finding high-energy radiation signs at Science Division. Miss Hamble's suggestion about its use was right.' Deveraux paused to make sure he had their complete attention. 'Corporation have been deliberately treating the water and forcing us to remain sterile.'

Pete finally reacted.

'Are you saying that my baby was some sort of secret science experiment?' he said, his voice hoarse and thick with emotion.

'No, Detective Barnes. I am saying that the entire population has been a fragging experiment,' Deveraux replied.

'We are the law,' the Chief said, interrupting him.

'We are not Corporation. We are not paid by Corporation and we are going to get to the fragging bottom of this. Barnes, Jenkins, I want you two to take the rest of the week. Grieve. Do what you need to do. This investigation will still be here when you get back.'

'So we're just supposed to carry on and pretend that we don't know that we've been kept in the dark our entire lives?' Jed shouted. 'What am I supposed to tell my wife? I won't lie to her, she deserves the truth and . . . '

Agent Deveraux held up a hand to stop Jed's tirade. 'We will be issuing a release – to inform everyone – but first we need all the facts. There is no need to create mass panic.'

'What about Anti-Corp and what happened today?' Jed asked.

'Those responsible will be brought to justice,' the Chief said.

Pete leapt up, his chair flying backwards. 'Not if I get there first,' he snarled, and left the room.

Jed made to go after him but the Chief stopped him.

'Make sure he doesn't do anything he'll regret, Jenkins.'

'I'll try, Sir.' He followed his friend out of the office.

The Chief turned in his chair to face Deveraux 'What do you think about Barnes?'

'I think he'll solve our problem,' Deveraux replied. 'Shame to lose a good man though.'

Pete was in the skimmer bay by the time Jed caught up with him.

'Where are you going?' Jed asked.

'I'm going to kill them,' Pete said. 'I'm going to kill them all.'

'I need you, Pete. We all need you. Here, now. Please.'

Jed stretched out a hand. Pete began pacing up and

down the corridor before spinning and punching the wall with a loud roar. Then he waited a moment, his fist in the wall, his head bowed before looking up at Jed, and giving a small nod.

'Alright,' he said grimly. 'But I will see this through, Jed.'

'I know.'

At the apartment, Jed's parents had arrived. They were sitting in the lounge, shell-shocked, while a puffy-eyed Kira tried and failed to make light conversation. When Jed and Pete entered the apartment, Gretchen - Jed's mother - seemed to grow paler.

'Jeddidiah, my boy. My sweet boy.'

Gretchen held her arms out to her son, and Jed crossed the floor to greet his mother, clasping hands with his father before kneeling on the floor besides them both.

Kira came over to Pete standing near the doorway, and burrowed herself into his chest. Pete stood a good foot taller than Kira, and could hardly make out what she was saying as she sobbed her sympathy and grief into his shirt. He gently hugged her back, fighting against the waves of pain that lashed through him. These five broken people clung to each other, drowning in their personal grief.

It wasn't until Grace began to cry that they moved. Jed's father came over to Pete and pulled him into a bear hug before going into the kitchen area, while Jed stood up and hugged his wife. They went through to the bedroom together to find out what Grace needed. Mrs Jenkins had been left alone so Pete approached her cautiously. They hadn't made much progress in getting to know each other, and he didn't want to upset her further.

Gretchen looked up at Pete and took one of his hands in hers.

'We lost our daughter, Peter. And you, you lost your love. No-one can ever, ever give her back to us.'

She dropped his hand and began crying again, loud racking sobs that shook her whole body. Mr Jenkins returned to the couch and gathered her into his arms. Pete stood awkwardly not knowing what to do. He jumped when Jed touched his shoulder.

'Help me make synth-caf?' Jed asked.

JENHUB: A private funeral for Ingrid Jenkins and child has been held at the request of the family. All messages of condolences to be sent to the link within.

It was the day after the funeral. Science Division had refused to release the body....bodies. Protestors had thronged outside the End of Days Chapel forcing the agents from Special Investigation to work hard to keep Jed's family and friends safe. Pete had remained impassive throughout. Not reacting to the service, the farewells, Jed's emotional eulogy – nothing. It was as if he simply wasn't there. The men assigned to protect him had reported no unusual behaviour, but Jed was still concerned. Pete's girlfriend had died in a terrorist attack and Corporation had let his baby die. For the good of science. Pete should've been raging.

MED4AC: Dina Grey miscarried. Now only two pregnancies left.

DING: Looking for BEJE – please get in touch.

The apartment was subdued. Even Grace was quiet.

'Can I get you anything hon?' Kira asked from the doorway as Jed lay in bed.

'No.'

He lay on his side, staring at the wall. Kira closed the door behind her, she didn't know what else to do.

'Anything?' asked Dina.

Kira shook her head.

'He just needs time,' Martha said.

'I know. I just feel so helpless. How are you doing D? Now that everyone knows about...' Kira trailed off.

'I'm okay. It had to come out sooner or later. I just wish I could get hold of Ben.'

'Still incommunicado, huh?'

'Yeah.' Dina tucked her hair behind her ear. 'He wasn't in Corp Tech, I know that much, but I can't find him.'

The mood of the apartment took over the three women, and they stopped talking. Martha fiddled with her Gaia statue while Kira looked off into space, and Dina played with the baby.

It had been three days since the attack.

MED4AC: Miscarriage Q&A session to be held later today in social hub beta.
Ask your question now, sweep your friends, join in the discussion.

'Are you speaking at the Q&A session, D?' Kira asked, casting about for something to talk about.

'No way. I don't want to rehash everything with a bunch of strangers.' Dina squished a soft ball in her hands. 'Women won't leave me alone as it is – asking questions about my private life. I wish it would all go away.'

'I am certain it will blow over eventually,' Martha said, leaning over to rescue the toy from Dina's hands.

'Blow over? Have they left you alone yet?'

Martha gave the ball back to Grace. She had received some nasty sweeps regarding the rape but on the whole people had been supportive, especially when they learned she had decided to keep the baby.

'People just want to identify with you,' Martha explained. 'They want to be able to say it could have been me.'

'I wish it *had* been someone else,' Dina said bitterly. 'I wish everything had happened to someone else.'

Kira regarded her young friend. 'Everything?'

Dina coloured, and tucked her hair behind her ear again. 'I just think that if I hadn't agreed to the whole stupid undercover thing, Ingrid would still be with us.' Dina's voice wobbled and she fought not to cry.

'It wasn't your fault sweetie,' Kira said. 'They would've found someone else.'

It didn't make Dina feel any better. She felt responsible for Ingrid's death no matter how many times Kira tried to convince her otherwise. If Force hadn't been focusing on Science Division, they might have found out about the terrorist attack on Corp Tech in time.

'It is lovely having you stay here with us Dina.' Martha tried to lighten the mood.

'Thanks. I know it's only temporary, but..'

'Temporary? Who said it was temporary?'

'Well, I didn't think you'd want me here when the baby comes.'

'Oh stop being so soft.' Martha threw a pillow at Dina. 'I would love you to be here – if you still want to.'

Dina hugged the pillow, hiding her face. When she looked up, she had tears in her eyes. 'Yes,' she said. 'Yes I do.'

The bedroom door opened and Jed came through. His eyes were bloodshot, and he hadn't shaved. Sitting down next to Kira, he put his head on her shoulder.

'Are you alright, love?'

'No,' Jed replied. 'But I will be.' There was a pause. 'Has anyone heard from Ruth?'

'I didn't see her at the funeral,' Dina said. 'Did she have the details K?'

'Yes, but I think maybe she felt she wouldn't be welcome.'

'Is Pete still angry at her?' Martha asked.

Jed ran a hand over his face, considering his words. 'He hasn't forgiven her for her part in staging the building attack.'

'Her part?' Martha said, frowning. 'She had nothing to do with the bombing.'

Jed looked uncomfortable. 'Ruth gave Pete a teddy bear to give to....Ingrid.' Jed swallowed the lump of emotion that threatened to overwhelm him. 'It was found in the wreckage. There was a scanner inside. Force techies think it was used to get schematics of the building.'

'But she didn't know what they were going to do with it – surely?' Dina looked appalled.

'No she didn't,' Jed admitted. 'Pete thinks she should've known what was going to happen, and that she should've come forward earlier.'

'No wonder she hasn't shown her face,' Kira said. 'I hope she's alright.'

'I'm sure Ruth will be in touch, K.' Dina looked down at her hand-held and sent Ruth another ping. 'When she's ready.'

ANON88: I hope it shatters you like my dreams have shattered.

In the end, it was a brick through the window that decided it for Ruth. Her apartment was in a low-tech high rise, and it didn't have automated security settings. Thanks to the sweeps reporting every last detail about the two remaining pregnant women, Ruth was easy to find, and therefore easy to attack. The people were angry and frightened and it didn't take much to stir them into action. Ruth finally replied to one of Dina's pings and told her what had been happening.

Ruthie! Are you okay? It's not safe for you to be there. Come to Kira's and be with the rest of us. There are Force Operatives on their way to get you. D x

'I didn't know if I should come,' Ruth said as she was deposited on the doorstep by two Force agents an hour later.

Jed had answered the door, and he pulled Ruth over the threshold. Once inside he hugged her and whispered, 'It wasn't your fault.'

Soon Ruth had been hugged and welcomed by everyone.

'Where have you been?' Dina asked.

159

'Anti-Corp released Quentin's remains. They'd already cremated him, so...' Ruth broke off, unable to speak.

'Hey, hey Ruthie.' Kira hugged her friend. 'It's alright. He's at peace now.'

'I'm okay. I'm okay. He bought the remains over himself.'

'He?' Martha asked.

'Victor – the head of Anti-Corp.'

'Oh wow,' Dina said. 'What did he say?'

Jed leaned forward, intent on Ruth's every word.

'He said they would never have kept him that long, if they'd known.' Ruth sniffed.

'Known what?' Jed asked.

Ruth's voice took on a harsher tone. 'That evil pig of a bastard Bobby never told Victor I was Quentin's wife. Bobby used it as his own personal leverage to keep me working for Anti-Corp.' Ruth looked at Jed red-eyed. 'I swear Jed, if you don't terminate that piece of crap – I will.'

'Ruth!' Kira exclaimed, shocked.

'I'm not sorry K,' Ruth said, tears running down her face. 'He kept my husband away from me all those years.'

Kira whispered to Jed to go make some more drinks while the others tried to comfort Ruth.

Martha and Ruth were comparing their bumps when the door pinged and Pete entered. His jaw tightened as he noticed Ruth sitting on the couch. He walked over to the kitchen where Jed and Kira were stood, and handed a bag of food to Kira.

'Pity meals,' Pete explained. 'I don't want them.'

'Thanks,' Kira said, touching Pete's hand before taking the bag and putting it on the counter.

'Do you want me to pick you up tomorrow?' Jed asked, clapping a hand on his partner's shoulder.

'No.'

'You sure?' Jed said. 'It's our first day back after....'

Pete shot another disapproving glance over towards the rest of the women in the lounge. 'I'm sure.' He turned to leave but Jed put a hand on his friend's arm to hold him back.

'I'm going to tell the others,' Jed said. 'About the water. Will you stay?'

Pete shook him off. 'You do it,' he said. 'I've got something else to do. I'll see you tomorrow.'

Jed watched his partner leave in concern. He felt anxious about telling his wife and friends what he had learnt and wished Pete had stayed. Walking over to the others, he clapped his hands together, getting their attention.

'I have some news. It's about what Dina discovered at Science Division. Corporation have been treating the water deliberately. Making us sterile. And they've been doing it for years.'

CORP: Safety is our number one priority – upgrade your security now.
Speak to your local Corporation Representative.

EMERGENCY MEETING OF CORPORATION
BOARD FOR CITY FORTY-TWO
DATE: 5th August 2215
VIRTUAL PRESENCE: J NICKS, Y ASWAD and P
BASJERE R HAMBLE INJURED – MINUTES SENT
THROUGH

AGENDA
1. ANTI-CORP INVOLVEMENT IN CORP TECH
   ATTACK
2. CONTROL OF REMAINING PREGNANCIES
   UPDATE
3. IMPROVING CORPORATION IMAGE
4. FILE 0

MINUTES
1. VICTOR BIANCHI, LEADER OF ANTI-CORP
   HAS SPOKEN TO THE BOARD AND DENIED
   INVOLVEMENT IN THE ATTACK ON CORP
   TECH. THE BOARD ACCEPTS HIS
   STATEMENT AND IS PUSHING FORWARD
   TERMINATION FOR ALL MEMBERS OF 42nd
   ARMY.
2. PREGNANCY A AND C ARE LIVING AT THE
   SAME ADDRESS. BOTH HAVE REFUSED
   MEDICAL AND ARE UNDER FORCE
   PROTECTION. ONCE PUBLIC UPSET CEASES,
   GREATER EFFORTS WILL BE MADE TO
   BRING THEM UNDER CONTROL.
3. PR WILL WORK ON A NEW CAMPAIGN TO
   IMPROVE CORPORATION IMAGE. SPIN IS
   NEEDED ON FETUS TERMINATION.
4. FILE 0 IS REDUNDANT. SPECIAL
   INVESTIGATIONS KNOWS ABOUT THE
   WATER TREATMENT. CONTINGENCY PLAN A
   IS STILL RELEVANT.

ANY OTHER BUSINESS – NONE

*Notes from Anti-Corp Meeting at Academy Student Bar,
August 5th 2215*

- *We are still reeling from the Corp Tech attack – Victor
  has urged everyone to publicly denounce the attack
  using their personal handles on the sweeps.*

- *Victor has spoken with the Board and they have
  accepted his statement that the attack was planned and
  executed by the 42nd Army who have nothing to do with
  Anti-Corp.*

- *Victor is arranging to speak to the leaders of 42nd Army
  and ask them to surrender themselves to the authorities.*

- *If anyone has any contact with members of the 42nd
  Army they must disconnect now or risk being added to
  the list for termination.*

- *All bugs are to be deactivated. All files and records kept
  on Corporation buildings and members are to be
  destroyed.*

- *At this time it is unclear whether Anti-Corp will
  continue to meet.*

Think free – be free.

Chapter Fourteen

CORP: *We remind citizens that individual safety is a priority.*
We put you first.

Everyone began talking at once.

'What do you mean treating the water?'

'Is it safe?'

'Will Grace be okay?'

Ruth and Martha looked at each other, concern mirrored in their faces.

'Will my baby be okay?' They spoke in unison.

'Why doesn't everyone know about it?' Dina asked.

'I don't have all the facts yet,' Jed said, moving to sit down next to Kira. 'Special Investigations are putting together a sweep release and the case is still open, but with the current mood in the city – well, they didn't want to risk any more panic.'

'The water, Jed, is it safe?' Kira asked, clutching at his arm.

'I think so. We are all still here aren't we?' Jed patted her hand, trying not to show his own concern.

'If Science Division have been using High Energy Radiation to treat our water, it must have been a continuous low dosage designed to attack reproductive cells only and prevent them from repairing themselves,' Martha said thoughtfully.

'So Corporation have lied to us and stopped us from having children.' Ruth glared at Jed. 'Why would they do that?'

'I'm sorry Ruth.' Jed ran a hand through his hair. 'I have no idea. I'm back in work tomorrow. As soon as I find out more you girls will be the first to know. I promise.'

'Can we sweep about it?' Dina asked.

Jed looked at her.

She coloured slightly, 'I guess not.'

The group lapsed into thoughtful silence as Grace burbled happily on her tummy, and began to crawl across the floor to where an interesting looking handbag was within easy reach.

'I have more news.' Martha spoke in a low tone.

'Oh no,' Kira said. 'It's your Dad isn't it – is he okay? Was he badly hurt?'

'He is having his spine regrown, but he will be fine. He has a rather odd request of everyone, he wants us to leave the city. He says there is a place we will be safe. Some kind of wilderness camp.'

'Camp Eden?' Ruth interrupted, sounding excited. 'I've heard all sorts of rumours about it - a hidden science base investigating how tech and nature can co-exist. It's a hang over though, right? From before The Event. It's not funded directly by Corp.'

'I don't know I'm afraid.'

Jed jumped in. 'Not funded by Corp? Like Force and Special Investigations? I thought they were the only ones.'

'No, no, no,' Ruth said. 'But they are probably all that's left now.'

'I never heard about this before.' Dina sounded sceptical.

'When Corporation first came into control there were still factions who disagreed with the way governance was heading,' Jed explained. 'They pooled their resources into setting up independent checks, to stop Corporation becoming a ruthless juggernaut.'

'They've done a fragging poor job,' Dina commented.

'Dina!' Kira exclaimed.

'Sorry K, but just look at where we are now, and what we've lost.'

Kira and Dina both looked a little embarrassed at their outbursts, but before they could say anything else Grace distracted everyone by pulling the abandoned NanNan box over onto the floor, narrowly missing herself.

Kira leapt up in dismay, the conversation forgotten.

ANON33: No charges brought against those responsible for building attack yet – who's guilty? Share your thoughts and spread the sweep.

Later that night, Kira and Jed lay in bed looking up at the ceiling, both wrapped up in their own thoughts.

'Jed? Do you think we should leave the city?'

'I don't want anything to happen to you hon. But I don't know if Camp Eden is the right answer,' Jed replied. 'I think we should wait.'

'Wait for what?' Her anger flared. 'Another building to blow up? Another loved one to die?'

She calmed down when her husband put his arm round her and pulled her close.

'We should wait to find out what Special Investigations have to say. Let me go in to work tomorrow and learn more.'

Kira snuggled into Jed's chest and spoke in a small voice. 'I don't think Anti-Corp will let this go quietly. Once they find out about the water treatment things are going to escalate quickly.'

Jed stroked his wife's head and made small shushing noises. 'Let's not start panicking yet. You've all got a security detail and the apartment is protected. I won't let anything happen to you or Grace, or anyone. I promise.'

Jed waited for her reply, but Kira's breathing had slowed and become deeper. Feeling safe in his arms she had finally relaxed and let the stress of the last few days leave her body, falling into a deep sleep. Jed continued to stroke her head and stare up at the ceiling.

Dina was checking her dailies. There were a lot of random approaches from people all over the city asking about her miscarriage – some apologetic and supportive, others downright nasty. Still nothing from Ben but she did notice one from Pete. He had never messaged her before and he'd only been over that afternoon. She clicked through.

Dina. Can you give me your Anti-Corp contact please? Force wants us to start investigating individuals involved with AC and 42nd Army and I think your guy would be a good place to start. Cheers, Pete.

Dina replied instantly, giving him Bobby's name and number, as well as a brief description. She would do anything to help apprehend those responsible for Ingrid's murder.

Jed was surprised to see an empty chair opposite his desk when he got to work. He double checked his messages, certain that Pete had told him to meet at the office.

Several hours later and Jed was starting to worry. Pete wasn't answering his ear comm, and hadn't sent any messages to say why he had been delayed. They were due to meet with the Chief in five. Jed knocked on the Chief's door.

'Come in!'

Jed poked his head into the Chief's office. 'Sir? Have you heard from Barnes?'

The Chief looked up at Jed from his desk monitor. 'Who am I? His mother?'

'No Sir.' Jed came fully into the room. 'He hasn't come in yet.'

The Chief was about to answer when Agent Deveraux entered, without knocking.

'Update Barnes later,' said the Chief as he glared at Deveraux. 'Take a seat Jenkins.'

Jed sat down in the only available chair, leaving Deveraux to stand. The agent gazed at the Chief for a moment before clearing his throat.

'We're here to discuss how we tell the city about the water treatment – or if indeed, we should.'

'Are you serious?' Jed said. 'You can't keep something like this a secret.'

'Corporation managed to do it for at least the past fifty years.'

'Corporation is why we are in this mess,' the Chief said. 'Get on it with Deveraux.'

Deveraux began pacing back and forth. '*If* we tell the public, I think we should release the information slowly.'

'Slowly – as in telling the privileged first you mean.' Jed snorted. 'Because they don't sweep. No, you can't contain this to one sector. It's all or nothing.'

'Jenkins is right,' the Chief said. 'We have to beat the rumour mongers on this. What are your recommendations Detective?'

'Well Sir, I think a simple sweep with links to more information should work. We put Force operatives out on the street as a precaution, and ride out the reaction.'

'Ride out the reaction – that sounds like a solid plan,' Deveraux said sarcastically.

Jed closed his eyes briefly and pinched the bridge of his nose.

'What's your contribution?' the Chief said, pointing at Deveraux.

'I still think the less said the better...'

'The less said the better?' Jed stood up in anger. 'My sister just died thanks to factions fighting with each other – I seriously doubt continuing to lie to my city is the way forward.' He breathed heavily through his nose.

'Detective,' the Chief barked. 'Sit down.'

Jed looked at his boss, and shook his head.

'With respect Sir, I'm going to find my partner.' Jed glared at Deveraux before leaving the room. The Agent raised an eyebrow at the Chief.

'And you're just going to let him go like that?'

'It's none of your fragging business how I run my department.' The Chief stood up and held the door open for the Agent. 'I'll get public relations to draw something up and send it over.'

Deveraux stared at the Chief in silence for a moment, then shrugged and left, the door banging shut behind him.

After walking out of the Chief's office, Jed had gone to find tech support and ask them to activate Pete's tracker. It had led him to the East Sector. There had been a series of unexplained deaths in this abandoned sector last year, and Corporation had initially declared it a hazardous, no-go area. Once the buildings had been cleared drifters had moved in, and then refused to move on. It was a low priority problem as far as Corporation were concerned, preferring to have all undesirables in one place.

Jed entered East sector cautiously. He'd not been here before. There was something odd about it. He realised there were patches of greenery amongst the buildings. Splashes of moss growing on walls, tendrils of ivy winding themselves round abandoned gates, and small clumps of grass and wild flowers dotting the walkways. He slowed the skimmer and brought out the tracker. Pete was two streets away to the left. Suddenly Jed heard shots fired and men yelling from that direction. He touched his ear comm and demanded back up before skimming over to investigate.

Pete rested, his back against the wall. Just a few moments. Just to catch his breath. He'd surprised everyone. They hadn't stood a chance. And now they were dead. All of them. Yet Pete felt no relief. Instead he felt cold, and alone. A trickle of blood ran over the hand Pete had pressed to his stomach, but he didn't notice. He was thinking about how he'd arrived at this moment. His beautiful Ingrid was dead - their unborn child murdered before it even had a chance. She would have been a wonderful mother.

Despite his best efforts he had not been able to get around Special Investigations' lock down at Science Division, so Pete didn't even know if it had been a boy or a girl. Better to think of his Ingrid as alive and smiling with her blonde hair hanging round her face and her blue eyes twinkling.

Tears ran unnoticed down Pete's face. He was losing the feeling in his legs. He felt so tired it made sense to stay here and rest. He'd get up in a minute. He ought to thank Dina. And speak to Jed. But his hand was wet and sticky. A small, alarmed part of his brain was telling him to keep pressure on the wound, so he left his hand there and thought about the morning's events.

It hadn't taken him long to find Bobby. He'd hacked into the Corporation mainframe using the next gen code Ingrid had shown him, and then he'd been able to pinpoint a five block radius via Bobby's ear comm digits. He'd had to skim the streets a few times, but finally Bobby had come round the corner, whistling to himself. It had been easy for him to stun Bobby and load him into the skimmer. Once Pete had tied Bobby up and applied a certain amount of persuasive pressure, he had been only too happy to talk.

'I'm a low level guy,' he'd protested. 'I just pass messages.'

Pete hadn't believed him. So he removed Bobby's left hand. After all why should he have both his hands, when Pete's Ingrid was gone. It had taken a while for the stump to stop bleeding and for Bobby to stop yelling, but once Pete had threatened to chop the other hand off, things had gone better.

'I wasn't at Corp Tech,' Bobby spluttered. 'I was with some of my girls at the protest.'   Pete knew he was lying. A scumbag scrabbling to say anything to save his worthless life. Once Pete had passed electricity through the raw, dripping stump to refocus his prisoner, he'd been forced to administer some revival drugs. All he wanted to know was where to find the ringleaders. Bobby had told him that Victor, leader of Anti-Corp, was meeting the leaders of the 42nd Army, here, in the abandoned Eastern sector of the city. Everyone responsible for Ingrid's death would be in the same place. Pete had made certain of that. One shot through Bobby's head and the smoking laser hole had sent the lowlife away permanently. It had been a kindness in the end and Pete had his information.

It seemed to be getting darker in the building. Pete blinked and tried to focus. There was a burnt out laser gun next to him, no shots left. He'd have to wait until he felt strong enough to get up. It didn't look like anyone else in the room would be getting up anytime soon. He started to laugh but the blood caught in his throat. He began coughing instead.

'Pete!'

Someone was coming, shouting his name. He tried to reply but couldn't stop coughing up blood.

Jed ran up the corridor, noting the bodies by the doorway at the end. They'd been shot through the head. Instant death. He paused to look at his scanner. Only one sign of life. Pete's tracker confirmed he was inside. Somewhere. Jed tried to open the door but something was blocking it, he pushed hard until it gave way. Behind the door - another dead body. And there were three more in the room. Pete was propped up against the left wall. He didn't look good. Jed rushed over.

'Pete – Pete! Can you hear me?'

Jed ran a quick diagnostic, taking note of the laser shot to the stomach. He applied a vacuum patch and administered pain relief to the side of Pete's neck.

'I got them,' Pete mumbled. 'Did you see? I got them.'

'Easy brother,' Jed whispered. 'Easy.'

Force sirens wailed through the air as back up arrived and a fully armed unit came dashing into the room, followed by a medic. The medic sent a drone to scan the room as he hurried over to Pete's slumped body.

'Anything administered?'

'Vacuum seal and pain relief,' Jed answered. 'I just got here.'

The drone beeped to confirm the rest of the bodies were dead, and the medic motioned Jed to help him get Pete onto the hover gurney. The team leader, from the Force unit that had entered with the medic, came over to

Jed.

'Detective? I'll get the scene bagged and tagged, but we'll need your statement.'

'I need to go with my partner,' Jed said.

'Of course. Back at HQ?' The team leader clapped a hand on Jed's shoulder before getting back to his unit.

The medic was steering the stretcher out the door as Jed hurried to catch up.

'I'll ride with you.'

ANON64: Shots fired in abandoned sector East. What happened? Sweep and share!!

Jed was pacing up and down in the waiting area as the Chief and Agent Deveraux came through.

'Anything?' the Chief asked.

'We've only just arrived, Sir.'

Before Jed could say anything else the door to the emergency examination room opened.

'The patient has refused treatment,' said the female medic standing in the doorway. 'There's nothing more we can do. If you want to say goodbye, now is the time.'

The medic gestured towards the open door. Jed looked at it, and did not move. Agent Deveraux made to walk towards the open emergency room, but the Chief held out an arm and stopped him.

'Chief, with respect, we need to speak to Detective Barnes.'

'I'll do it,' Jed said. 'He's my partner.'

Pete's eyes were shut when Jed walked in. The medical staff had cleaned him up, but his breathing was shallow and blood seeped out of the dressing on his torso. Pain flitted across his face, and his hand clutched the sheet beneath him.

'Pete?'

Pete opened his eyes and gradually focused.

Jed gazed at his dying partner. 'Why did you do it?'

'I had to,' Pete whispered. 'You understand?' He gripped onto Jed's arm. 'I had nothing left.' Pete let go of Jed's arm, and closed his eyes, his breath rasping in his chest.

'For Ingrid.'

Agent Deveraux collared Jed as he left the room.

'What did he say?'

'He admitted killing them, if that's what you mean.'

Deveraux glanced at the Chief, made his excuses and left. The Chief came over to stand by Jed.

'Did you know Barnes was going to do this?'

Jed stared at him for a moment before answering. 'No, but you did. You and Deveraux. You were hoping he'd solve your 42nd Army problem for you. Well, he has. And now he's going to die - and for what?'

'Jenkins, ...'

Jed turned and started to walk away. Before he'd gone far, he turned and shook his finger towards his boss. 'You shouldn't have let this happen,' he said, walking back and handing in his badge and laser gun.

The Chief watched Jed disappear round the corner before going to sit with his dying detective.

MED4AC: Force Detective injured in shoot-out.

Chapter Fifteen

FORCE: ****ALL SWEEPS**IMPORTANT ANNOUNCEMENT**ALL SWEEPS****
Citizen Update: Corporation have been artificially treating the water supply.
We urge citizens not to panic and to continue using water available while city governance formulate a replacement source.
This is a city-wide top priority.
Click through for more details and help desk access.

MSCHILD: *No children and now no water? Are Corporation trying to kill us?*

MADSR: *I have been drinking the water. I do not have a secret water supply!!!*

MED4AC: *We do not have a separate water supply. Please continue to use your water ration as normal. Click through for more information on signs of dehydration.*

ANON88: *This is all part of Corp's plan – we must fight back! Where are 42nd Army?*
Join me and fight back!

CORP: *Extra water rations are available. Your safety is our priority.*

ANON64: *Don't drink the water! There must be a secret supply!*
Raid your nearest Corporation outlet and share the sweep!

MED4AC: *Shoot out Detective dies.*

C42N: *Leaders of Anti-Corp and the 42nd Army have been killed.*

Force Detective responsible has died.

ANON27: Mob rules – mob rules – mob rules – mob rules!!

When Jed walked through the door to the apartment, Kira ran to him in tears, and hugged him tight.

'Jed,' she sobbed. 'Have you seen the sweeps? It looks like everyone has gone mad. And Pete – is Pete?'

Jed buried his head into his wife's shoulder, and tried hard not to cry. They stood, holding one another for several minutes before he was able to speak.

'Pete's gone.'

Kira's hand flew to her mouth and she stumbled backwards a little.

'No – oh no, not Pete.' Tears fell down her face. 'What happened?'

'He went after those responsible for …. for Ingrid.' Jed took a deep breath to steady his voice. 'He was... he was... I found him.'

'Oh honey.' Kira took her husband in her arms again. 'I am so sorry.'

Jed took a shower and changed while Kira saw to Grace. Neither spoke for a while as they tried to process what had happened. Eventually they found themselves sat on the couch together.

'Are you okay?' Kira asked, leaning forward to kiss her husband on the cheek.

'I honestly don't know.' Jed tried to smile. 'So much has happened in such a short time.' He ran a hand through his hair. 'I quit Force.'

'You quit!'

'I had no choice. They knew what Pete was going to do and they did nothing to stop him.'

Kira looked down at her hands. 'What will we do now?'

Jed shrugged. Seeing that his wife looked so upset,

Jed pulled her in for a hug and began to stroke her hair. 'Everything will be alright – you'll see.' He changed the subject. 'Where are the others?'

'Martha and Dina went to Science Division, and Ruth went to help out at Academy.'

'Do they still have their Force escorts?'

'I think so.'

'Good – they'll get back safely then.'

'Jed, I'm scared. Is it safe for them to be out there? The sweeps...'

'Never mind the sweeps,' Jed interrupted. 'I know who's on escort duty, so I'll call them and get them to bring the girls back, okay?'

Kira sniffed.

'It'll be alright sweetheart,' Jed said. 'I love you.'

'Love you too.'

MAHA: I am working with other scientists to find a cure for the water supply.

'Ma'am?'

Martha looked at the Force Operative who was trying to get her attention. 'Yes?'

'I have orders to bring you back home.'

'But we only just arrived,' Martha protested.

'Sorry Ma'am. Science Division is now under Force lock-down. It's not going anywhere.'

Grumbling to herself, Martha went to find Dina who was in one of the fishbowls.

'Dina,' Martha called. 'We have to go.'

'But we just got here!'

'I know, but our escort detail have orders and they are locking down the facility.'

Dina grimaced as she left the fishbowl. She hadn't even had time to begin calculations on how long it would take for the water to be clear of contaminants.

As the two women walked back down the corridor, the way was blocked by several people watching something. They drew closer and saw Dr Basjere, Head of Science Division and Corporation Board Member, being led away in magno-binders.

'I wouldn't like to be in his shoes right now,' Dina commented.

Martha watched, her face ashen then reached for her ear comm to call her father.

'Father?'

'Martha.'

'Are you okay?'

'Why – what's happened?' Mr Hamble answered her gruffly.

'I just saw Dr Basjere get arrested.....Are you?...Will you?...'

'Spit it out, girl.'

There was a pause as Martha worked up the courage to ask a question she already knew the answer to.

'Are you going to be arrested?'

Silence.

Mr Hamble cleared his throat. 'I have volunteered to come in for questioning once my spine has been regrown. The Chief and I have an understanding – of sorts.'

Martha felt light-headed and leant on the wall for support.

'Everything will be fine.' Mr Hamble reassured his daughter. 'I've got my man on the case. Are you at home?'

'I am at Science Division but...'

Before Martha could finish, her father bellowed down the connection.

'Get yourself home NOW – it's not safe. I'll talk to you later.' And he terminated the call.

'Ma'am?'

Martha looked up, still feeling a little dazed.

'This way Ma'am.'

Dina linked Martha's arm, and the two of them followed the operative out of Science Division and into a waiting skimmer.

'You want me to leave now?'

'Yes Ma'am. This way please, Ma'am.'

'Alright, alright – there's no need to Ma'am me to death.'

Ruth had only just arrived at Academy but the campus was largely deserted as students had gone to protest at Corp HQ about the water. There wasn't much she could do anyway so she meekly followed the operative back to the skimmer.

ANON88: They had to have known – what makes them special? They have to pay!

C42N: There have been city-wide attacks on Corporation buildings and one residential apartment block believed to be the home of R. Maddocks – the pregnant anomaly.

FORCE: All violent activity will be penalised harshly. Think for yourself and don't regret your actions.

'What about Archive?' Kira asked, pacing up and down the bedroom.

'Archive will be fine love,' Jed said. 'It's probably the most secure building in the entire city.'

Kira came to sit on the bed beside Jed. 'It's getting aggressive out there. What are we going to do?'

'I think you should go to Camp Eden.'

'Mr Hamble's suggestion?'

'Yes,' said Jed. 'You know Martha got shoved at the protest?' Kira nodded. 'People know who you are and they're angry. I don't want anything bad to happen to you. To any of you.' He gestured at the wall where the news feed display hung. 'You've seen the sweeps. They just looted Ruth's apartment, and she had that brick through the window.' Jed took Kira's hands in his own. 'It's not safe in the city for any of you. I can't protect you Kira, and I can't

178

lose anyone else.'

Jed's voice began to break as he fought to keep his emotions in check.

Kira turned and fished a packed bag out from under the bed, and looked a little shamefaced at her husband. He took her hand again, and gave it a squeeze. This was the right thing to do.

'Martha and Dina will be back soon,' Jed said. 'I've told Ruth's Force escort to bring her here as well. I made some calls when you were changing Grace. There's a private hover on its way over to take you to Camp Eden. You all need to be out of the city for a few days. I'll let you know when it's safe to come back.'

'What about my parents? Your parents? Our other friends? I feel like I'm running away. I should stay here and help, or something.'

'You are at a higher risk than anyone else, love. Thanks to the sweeps everyone knows you are friends with two of the mother-to-be anomalies. They know you lost another friend in the terrorist attack. And they know about Pete.'

Jed had to stop as the words stuck in his throat. Kira leaned in and hugged him.

'What about you? What are you going to do?'

'I'll look after what's left of our families.'

'Are you going to reply to your boss?'

Jed puffed out his cheeks and fiddled with his wristplant. The Chief had been calling him every hour on the hour. Each call had gone to message.

'I will, I promise.'

There was a happy gurgling sound as Grace crawled off the side of the bed, only to be caught by the surrounding hover field and gently lifted back up. Both parents turned to look.

'Ingrid sent it over,' Kira said. 'It was the last thing she did before...' Kira dashed tears away from her eyes, and leant over to scoop up Grace.

'We're going on a trip Gracie,' she said, and began

smooshing her face into Grace and kissing the delighted baby.

'Kira? Jed?' Martha called out sharply as she entered the apartment.

'In here,' Kira replied.

Martha came rushing through the doorway to the bedroom looking pale, her eyes red from crying. Dina trailed behind looking shocked.

'What happened?' Kira said as she thrust Grace into Jed's arms and came over to Martha. 'Are you okay?'

Martha clutched at Kira's arms and then, her legs sagging, she pulled them both to the floor and began crying.

'They found him. They just went in and....' Martha gulped for air. 'Oh Kira. They killed him. They killed my daddy.'

Martha collapsed into wails of anguish as Kira looked over her head in disbelief at Dina. Jed leaned over and grabbed his ear comm from the side of the bed. Reattaching himself, he dialled through to the Chief.

'Sir? Detective Jenkins - reporting for duty.'

There was a long silence.

'About fragging time Detective, get in here ASAP.'

Jed dithered about where to put Grace, who was trying to grab his ear comm, when Kira got his attention by waving her hands and pointing to the play cube. Kissing his wife's head and giving Dina a quick hug, Jed left them trying to comfort Martha on the bedroom floor.

Enough was enough. He was going to make sure there was a peaceful end to this uprising, and he was going to make fragging sure no-one else he loved died.

MED4AC: Roger Hamble, Marketing Director for Corporation dies from complications.

ANON88: One down, one arrested, two to go! Don't let them get away with poisoning us!!

The two remaining Corporation Board members met in secret, in an underground skimmer bay.

'We have to leave.'

'I agree.'

'Where shall we go?'

'It's too risky for us to travel together. Go South. I hear they're pro Corp down South.'

'What about you?'

'I'm going North. I have family North, they'll protect me.'

They parted with a formal handshake, each returning to their private, blacked out skimmers, confident that they could escape the city unscathed. Neither one had stopped to think about whether their drivers watched the sweeps. Neither one checked to see whether their skimmer was on auto pilot. Neither one saw the collision coming.

Neither one survived.

As Jed travelled into work, Ruth returned to the apartment. Martha had gone for a lie down so Kira explained what had happened to Mr Hamble.

'Frag! What the frag? Are we safe here? Did you see what the bastards did to my flat? What are we going to do?'

'We are going to Camp Eden,' Kira announced. 'Pack a bag you two, essentials only. We've got secure transport out there.'

'But what about everything that's happening?' Dina said. 'We can't just leave – can we?'

Ruth held one hand over her belly protectively. 'I actually agree with K. It's not safe for us here at the moment. Let's give Force time to calm everything down.' Ruth looked down at herself. 'Kira – have you got any clothes I can borrow?'

'I'm sure I'll have something, sweetie,' Kira said, and the two women headed off into Kira's bedroom.

Dina went reluctantly to her side of the expanded apartment, poked her head round the adjoining door and heard soft sobbing coming from the far bedroom. She hesitated, not wanting to intrude. She knocked on Martha's door and opened it.

'Martha? Are you okay?'

Dina winced, realising what she'd said. Of course Martha wasn't okay. Her father had been killed. The sobbing continued. Dina ventured into Martha's bedroom. She spotted Martha sat on the floor in the corner of the room, knees drawn up, head bent down on crossed arms, shoulders shaking as she cried.

'Martha?'

'Go away.'

'We have to pack. We're leaving for Camp Eden,' Dina paused. 'Shall I pack your stuff?'

No answer.

Dina found an empty bag and began gathering things she thought they might need. Not knowing where they were headed made it tricky, but she put together a few changes of clothes for each of them and various small pieces of tech that might come in useful out in the middle of nowhere.

Martha continued to sob.

Dina left her where she was and walked back through the adjoining door, putting her bags down with the others in a pile in Kira and Jed's lounge.

'Kira,' she called. 'I've got our stuff but Martha, she's just.... I don't know what to do.'

Before Kira could reply, the door chimed and two Force operatives entered.

'Ma'am,' one of the operatives greeted Kira. 'We're here to transport you to Camp Eden. It's getting ugly out there, we have to leave immediately.'

Kira smiled bravely, hoping her fear didn't show. 'I'll get Martha. You two take the bags. I'll meet you down there.'

With Grace snuggled close to her in her baby

wrap, Kira went through to Martha's room. 'Martha. Get up. It's time to go.'

Martha lifted her tear stained face and looked at Kira. 'To the middle of nowhere? How do you even know we will be safe there?'

Kira held out her hand. 'Because your father told us to go. He loved you, Martha, and he wanted to protect you and his grandchild. Come on Ma. Do it for your baby.'

Martha looked dully at the proffered hand for a moment, before finally grasping it and pulling herself up off the floor. 'I haven't packed.'

'Don't worry, Dina packed you some stuff. It's going to be okay.'

As the transporter travelled through the city, Kira was glad of the blacked out windows and additional security.

C42N: The number of people hurt in widespread riots has increased. Force are reminding citizens to stay at home and avoid areas of aggression.

ANON88: Who's in the secret skimmer? Who's getting preferential treatment?

MED4AC: We urge non-emergency cases to visit their nearest auto-doc.
We DO NOT have a separate water supply.
Please consider whether it is medically necessary for you to attend Med Centre.

C42N: Blacked out private skimmer seen travelling through City Forty-Two. Sweep if you know who's inside.

A brick hit the window, making the women jump.

'It's alright ladies,' one of the Operatives said through the intercom. 'This skimmer is equipped with unbreakable windows. You're quite safe.'

Despite the reassurance, a sense of unease lay over

all of them, as they continued to travel towards the city limits.

Ruth leant over and patted Kira's hand. 'I'm sure Jed will be fine.'

Kira smiled weakly, and looked back out the window. She didn't think anyone in authority would be safe right now. Hopefully, the people would realise they weren't achieving anything by their actions, and go home. Until they did, Kira hoped Jed stayed out of harms way.

The transporter left the rioters behind and the streets got emptier and emptier. The women began to calm down, each of them feeling mentally exhausted by what they'd been through the past few days. One by one, they drifted off to sleep, lulled by the hum of the transporter's engine and the mild sedative the Force operatives had released into the back of the vehicle.

'Feels wrong, drugging them like this,' commented the older of the two operatives.

'Orders are orders. Detective Jenkins didn't want them getting scared,' the other said. 'And we've still got to make it past city limits.'

City Forty-Two was contained within a forcefield, which apart from one or two weak spots, kept the citizens safe from the alleged toxicity of the ravaged world outside. The residual radiation from the HER wars was the reason the human race had been divided up into small cities dotted throughout the continents – in order to save what was left.

As the transporter approached the official city exit, the two Force operatives started scanning the surroundings for any violent activity. Jed had been worried that angry citizens might gather at the city gate demanding to be let out, but fear of what was outside had kept them away. The transporter stopped briefly, and one of the operatives punched in an access code. Gradually a hole in the shimmering forcefield grew large enough to allow the transporter through, then closed behind them as they left the city behind.

Kira leant her head against the now opaque window. She felt relaxed and at peace. The sedative was beginning to wear off, but she no longer felt as scared. The others still slept, and Grace was tucked within the baby wrap, nestled close.

Kira pressed the intercom to allow her to speak to the Force Operatives.

'Do you know how much further we have to travel?'

'No Ma'am – it's a preset course. The transporter is on auto cruise.'

'Oh. I see.'

'But I'm sure it won't be long,' reassured one of the operatives.

Kira went back to staring out of the window. Lulled by the hum of the transporter she closed her eyes again, and drifted. She was stood in a meadow - sweet smelling grass and wild flowers all around her. Bees hummed in the air, and Grace played by her feet.

'I'm so glad you came.' A melodious voice spoke to her.

Kira turned in slow motion and was unsurprised to see the beautiful blue lady stood next to her.

'Are you sure you want us here? It's so beautiful,' Kira asked.

'I am not complete without you. All things must balance. It is time. We are here.'

'We're here. Ma'am?' said one of the Force Operatives. 'We've arrived.'

Kira looked around blearily, realising that the transporter had stopped and one of the operatives was speaking to her. The others were waking up.

'We're here?'

'Where is everything?'

'Who's that?'

'We're just the travel detail, Ma'am,' said the Force Operative opening the transporter door and looking at

Kira. 'If you're ready?'

The operative gestured that they should exit the transport. Kira turned to look at the others.

'Are you ready?'

Dina and Ruth both gave small nods while Martha looked expressionless, eyes still red from crying. She gave a half shrug, and allowed herself to be led out the transporter with the others. After their bags had been deposited on the ground next to them, the transporter turned around and left.

There were two large marquees set up on either side of the camp clearing – one looked like it was used for cooking and eating, the other had its flaps down and nothing was visible. A communal area had been set up towards the rear of the clearing and there were several wooden huts down one side, half hidden by the encroaching forest.

A small Indian man waited patiently for them at the camp entrance, dressed in khaki trousers and tunic, his brown feet bare.

'Welcome to Camp Eden,' he said. 'I'm Moham, I'll be your guide – anything you need or want to know about, just ask.'

Dina grabbed her bag and began to walk forward while the others hung back. 'Where is everyone else?' she asked, looking around with interest.

'They will be back later,' Moham said. 'Can I offer you some refreshment?'

He gestured for the women to follow him further into the clearing. Dina fell in behind, while the others looked doubtfully at each other. After brief hesitation, they picked up their bags and slowly followed. Everything seemed to have been set up to blend in with the scenery as much as possible, making full use of the natural materials available.   Moham stopped beneath the canopy at the far end of the clearing. A number of cushions lay scattered around an empty fire pit.

'This is our communal area,' he gestured. 'Sit,

make yourselves comfortable, and I will get some tea brewing.'

Moham returned to the open sided marquee at the beginning of the camp, leaving the women alone. They stood motionless for a moment before Martha dropped her bag with a thump. No-one spoke as they sat down. They waited to see what would happen next.

'Hey, we get signal,' Dina said as she checked her handheld for updates.

The others followed her lead, even Martha, checking to see what they'd missed. There was a video message for Martha. From her father. Martha activated her ear comm to receive the audio file as well, and watched her father speak to her from his hospital bed, tears rolling down her face.

'Martha. I hope that you never get this message. But if you are watching this, then events have got out of hand. I want you to know that your mother and I love you very much. We always have. I am so proud of you. Throughout your life you have thought about what you wanted, and not let me, or Corporation, or anyone else get in your way. I admire that. I want you to do that now – be strong, be yourself. Be Martha Hamble.'

In the recording, Mr Hamble rubbed his eyes quickly and cleared his throat. There was a brief smile to camera, and the video message stopped.

Martha let out a huge breath. The others watched her in concern.

'Are you alright, Ma?' Kira asked.

'I will be. I will be.'

Chapter Sixteen

It had been one day since the girls had left the city limits. One day since Jed had returned to Force. One day of utter madness. Ordinarily peaceful citizens were trashing public buildings and spaces, whilst others looted service points for foodstuffs. No-one was going to work except for Medical and Force personnel. Force might not be under Corporation jurisdiction but they signified authority, and were therefore a target for the ire of the people.

Jed was exhausted. He'd been on call for twenty-four hours straight and needed a break. Uncontaminated water was the biggest issue. So far, scientists at Science Division had confirmed that now the HER treatment had stopped, the water would return to normal - in time. However, no-one knew how long that might take. Everyone needed water but no-one wanted to use it, and the medical centre emergency service was close to breaking point trying to keep up with the number of dehydration cases.

Jed self-administered a stimulant and waited for the adrenalin to kick in. It was all too easy to fake the body into feeling full of energy, but if he didn't eat something soon he might become the next emergency patient. The Chief poked his head out of his office door, and seeing Jed motioned him to come through.

'Sir,' Jed said, entering the Chief's office.

The Chief was slumped in his chair.

'Deveraux believes we might be ready to start opening talks between what's left of the city leadership. Get this whole thing under control.'

Suddenly the room pitched into darkness as the power cut out.

'Initiate the fragging emergency back up system,' the Chief barked at an internal comms panel. A dull glow emanated from the floor as safety lights came on throughout the building.

'Report!'

But the screens remained dark. The Force's interface had insufficient power to run it's diagnostic system. The Chief muttered under his breath before getting up. 'Get me a technician in here now!' he yelled, sticking his head out his door.

The Chief came back to his desk and jabbed a finger at the unresponsive screen before pushing it away. 'Jenkins, procedure states that we must facilitate negotiations between the highest city representatives. If I had my way I'd terminate the whole fragging lot of them. But you need to find them, bring them here, and set up a holding area.' The Chief rummaged through his desk. 'No-one leaves until we get this mess under control.' He found what he was looking for and handed an info jack to Jed. 'This tells you who to round up. With any luck, they'll be tucked up at home. Anyone located in a trouble zone is to be bound and held for punishment. I will not have them destroy my city.'

The Chief held Jed's eye for a moment, before waving him out of the room and stabbing thick fingers at the unresponsive screens in front of him again.

Jed headed for the skimmer bay – they were solar powered so at least they still worked. As he entered, a number of operatives looked up expectantly.

'I need two volunteers.'

'I'll go,' volunteered a freckly, fresh-faced young man, bouncing eagerly to his feet. 'Operative Griggs, Sir.'

He was followed with a sigh by a larger, heavy set, older man Jed recognised from the Corp Tech disaster site. 'Me too.'

'What's your name?' Jed asked as he handed them both riot gear to put on.

'Ash, Sir. Matthew Ash.'

'Okay men, this is us.' Jed pointed to the closest skimmer and the three of them got on board, Jed taking the front seat. 'Our job is to collect the most senior city representatives and bring them back to Force HQ.'

He whacked the jack into an info port. A list popped up on the display. The first name was Roger Hamble. Jed pinched the bridge of his nose.

Strike one.

An hour later Jed stood in an underground parking lot looking at the crashed skimmers and mangled remains of two more city leaders – who also happened to be Board Directors, and the next names on the list. Jed tried calling through to Med Centre for a deceased body pick-up, but his call wouldn't connect. The power was still out and the general comms grid looked like it was down too.

'Griggs,' Jed called out. 'I need you to go to Med Centre and get a body pick-up organised. We'll seal the scene and move on.'

'Yes, Detective.'

Griggs saluted, and headed out to the Med Centre on foot while Ash took out a black disc from the kit in the back of the skimmer. He placed the disc in front of the crash site and activated the forcefield. It shimmered as it spread up and over the crime scene, sealing in all the evidence and solidifying so that only a member of Force would be able to deactivate it. Jed nodded in approval then climbed back into the Force skimmer and checked the next name on his list. Professor Kamir, Head of Academy.

Hopefully, he was still alive.

Jed manoeuvred the skimmer across the city, dismayed at the level of vandalism and destruction. It seemed the power cut had calmed some people down, they'd returned to their homes and their emergency energy sources. Passing the charred remains of Corp Tech, Jed felt a stab of pain in his chest. But he didn't want to think about his sister and her fledgling family. Or the fact that his partner was gone. And with Kira and Grace out of the city, it felt like there was nothing left to fight for. The city's blackness matched his mood. They rounded the corner and Jed stared at the brilliance radiating out from Academy.

'Separate power grid obviously,' Jed muttered as they parked up.

Students milled around all over the grounds, but there was little sign of the violence that had ravaged the rest of the city. Jed checked his riot gear was firmly in place and armed his stunners. The Academy was the birth place of Anti-Corp. Members of Force might not be welcome.

They left the skimmer and assessed the area. Jed and Operative Ash breathed a sigh of relief. The students looked scared and lost, not angry or violent. No-one said a word or approached them as they walked through the quad into the main building.

'Where can we find Professor Kamir?' Operative Ash asked a frightened looking girl sitting behind the front desk. The girl stared back at him, wide-eyed.

'C'mon, it's this way,' Jed said, turning left, not waiting to see if Ash was following him.

Jed remembered the way from his wife's enthusiastic description of her tour of Academy. He roughly pushed away thoughts of Kira and Grace. Now was not the time to start worrying about his family. He had work to do. Focus. Jed stopped outside a blue door engraved with a huge, many branched, old tree – the crest of the Academy. He rapped twice, before entering the room.

'May I help you?'

An older man turned from a bookcase to look at them. He was tall with white hair sweeping across his brow and, despite his age, stood firm, radiating a quiet strength.

'Professor Kamir, I'm Detective Jenkins. This is Operative Ash. We've come to bring you to Force HQ as part of the city leaders protocol.'

'Ah.' The Professor placed a book back on the shelf. 'May I collect my coat?'

Jed nodded, and watched the elderly yet spry man stride over to retrieve his hat and coat.

'Lead on Detective.'

Jed touched his ear comm, intending to call through to the Chief, but remembered the defunct network.

'Do you have call access?' he asked the professor.

'Yes - we run on a separate grid. In case of student pranks. It seems to have worked rather in our favour today, eh.'

Jed went over to the touchscreen on the Professor's desk, and used his Force chip to log in and override the system. The connection was grainy with no picture.

'Ah,' said the Professor, peering over his shoulder. 'You'll probably only get sound working if it's down at that end. No power, see.'

Jed nodded. 'Chief? It's Jenkins.'

'Jenkins?' The Chief's voice sounded tinny and far away. 'Report.'

'We've got one so far, Sir. Fourth on the list.'

'Where the frag are the first three?'

'Dead, Sir.'

'Hmmph. Who's left?'

'Well, you Sir. And the Surgeon General from Med Centre. We're going there next.' Jed scratched the side of his head. 'Is there anyone else I should round up, Sir?'

'No. Get back here, ASAP.'

'Sir.' Jed clicked off and cleared the screen down. Operative Ash and Professor Kamir followed him out of the office, and back to the skimmer.

At Med Centre it looked like something out of an old disaster movie – harassed medical staff flitted from corridor to corridor, emergency lighting cast an eerie glow over everything with muffled shouts and various machines beeping erratically in the background. People milled about, some groaning, some holding their injuries close, whilst others looked vacant - in shock. They'd all come for answers.

The desk warden leapt to his feet as Jed approached. 'You've bought a squad for us then?'

'No. Sorry. I'm here for the Surgeon General. Do you know where he is?'

'But we need you here – we can't cope.' The desk warden spluttered. 'People just keep showing up.'

Jed gave a small shrug, then pointed at Operative Ash.

'You can have him. I'll let HQ know you need more bodies. The Surgeon General?'

The desk warden scowled at Jed and pointed to a corridor on the left. 'He's in surgery.'

Jed left Ash in the foyer and headed down to surgery. There were people everywhere. Jed had to fend off several persistent citizens begging him for answers. At this rate, it looked like Jed might have to fight his way out of Med Centre.

Reaching the surgical wards, Jed cast about for a med tech who might be able to point him in the right direction. The consultant he'd seen at Med Centre before came out of a side room, his sandy brown hair looking dishevelled and his medical tunic crumpled.

'Detective,' he said, greeting Jed in the corridor.

'I'm looking for the Surgeon General.'

'Well, you've found him. Your men will just have to wait like everyone else. We're doing this on a first come, first served basis – apart from emergencies of course.'

'You don't understand. You need to come with me to Force HQ. Now.'

'Well, I can't leave *now,*' the Surgeon General replied, and tried to walk past Jed. But Jed stood his ground. The Surgeon General was red in the face. 'Don't you people realise what's happening out there? It's mass panic. I have a duty of care to look after these idiots whether I like it or not. I don't have time for your emergency.'

The consultant attempted to brush past Jed again who continued to block his way and took out his magno-binders.

'I charge you as a city representative to take part in the protection of the city,' he said. 'I will take you to Force HQ where you will begin the protocols that will end this crisis. We can do it with magnos, or without – your choice.'

The Surgeon General glared at Jed. 'I want a Force unit in place to back up my people.'

Jed tucked the magnos back into their holder. 'I've left one operative in reception and requested back up,' he said. 'We're stretched thin ourselves. It's the best I can do.'

The Surgeon General's shoulders slumped in defeat. 'Can I at least get my jacket?'

Returning to Force HQ with two city representatives had Jed on edge, contemplating what the consequences would be if anything should happen to the skimmer. He scanned the streets ahead for any signs of a mob, but the skimmer made it to Force HQ with only one detour. Jed herded the two men into meeting room one. As he entered, Jed was reminded of the last interview he had conducted in this room. It felt like a hundred years ago.

'Make yourselves comfortable. I'll send in some refreshments.'

'You can't keep us here indefinitely,' the Surgeon General shouted, as Jed left the room to inform the Chief he had two city representatives.

'I think you'll find that until city protection protocol is completed – he can,' Professor Kamir said, smiling as he sat down in the most comfortable chair in the room.

Jed secured the door on his way out of the room. Walking over to the Chief's office, he snagged a junior recruit and put in a request for a team to go to Med Centre and help keep the peace.

Whatever that meant.

Jed entered the Chief's office without knocking. The Chief and Agent Deveraux were waiting for him.

'Any problems?' Deveraux asked.

'Nope.'

'Let's get this fragging thing over and done with then,' the Chief grumbled. 'Jenkins, I need you to bring in the Anti-Corp representative. He's in holding cell four.'

'Sir'

As Jed walked down to holding the power came back on and the corridor was suddenly bathed in light. Reaching the cells he wondered who was left from Anti-Corp. Pete had been thorough when he hunted down those responsible for Ingrid's death. Who else could there be?

Chapter Seventeen

ANON88: What gives Hamble the right to abandon the rest of us?
I hope she gets radiation sickness.

MAHA: Yes I left City Forty-Two but I will be back.

Kira couldn't see who was speaking. She knew she was asleep, her limbs felt heavy, and although she was seeing light around her, she couldn't see a person or place.

'I'm so glad you came.' The voice made Kira feel warm and safe, protected.

'I'm so glad we came here,' Dina said. 'Wake up Kira.' Dina poked Kira in the ribs, and once she was sure Kira was awake, she tossed something at her. It was green and round. 'It's an apple Kira – an actual apple. Grown in soil, taken from a tree. And it's all ready to eat. Try it, Kira – it tastes so much better than the synth ones.' Dina's eyes sparkled as she bounced from foot to foot with excitement.

'Where's Grace?'

'She's fine. Martha has her, they're exploring the orchards. That's where apples grow, you know. You can get red ones too. This place is just amazing.'

'Yeah,' Kira muttered, as she pulled on her trousers and went in search of her daughter.

Kira found Grace crawling through the grass, cooing and burbling, as she explored the undergrowth. Martha and Ruth sat nearby, drinking tea.

'Good morning,' Martha said. 'Did you manage to get any sleep?'

Kira bent down to check on Grace before plopping on the floor next to the others. She idly plucked a stem of grass and began turning it round in her hands.

'Eventually. Thanks for getting up with Grace, Ma.'

'My pleasure, after all I need the practice.'

Martha and Kira smiled at each other as Ruth stretched her feet out into the grass. 'Isn't Camp Eden great?' she said. 'So peaceful.'

Kira looked pensive. 'Aren't you worried about what's happening at home? Whether our friends and families are alright?'

'Of course K,' Ruth replied. 'But just being here makes me feel better – like everything is going to be alright.'

Kira looked down at Grace, playing happily.

'Everything is going to be alright, Kira.' Martha leaned over and put her hand on Kira's knee. 'Jed will be okay.'

Kira sniffed and nodded. 'The camp does seem lovely. But where exactly are we? What is this place?'

A man's voice came from behind them. 'Why, it's Eden, of course. Birthplace of man, but without the sin.'

Ruth snorted in response, then began coughing as her tea went down the wrong way. A tanned man in his thirties with a shock of dark hair came to sit on the grass with them, gently patting Ruth on the back until she waved away his assistance. Kira eyed him doubtfully.

'I'm Max, lead scientist at Eden,' he said, and he held out his hand for Kira to shake. She took it, then looked around.

'Where's the rest of your team?'

'Resting, I hope. We got back late last night. We heard all about your arrival from Moham. Have you got everything you need?'

Kira nodded, not knowing what to ask for, even if she did need something.

'Now that we're all here,' Dina asked. 'Can you tell us about Eden, Max?'

Max settled himself more comfortably on the ground. 'Okay,' he said. 'Where shall I start? After The Event, much of the Earth was uninhabitable because of the radiation levels. We had created a self-inflicted mass

197

extinction event.' Max paused to pour himself some tea, and looked around to make sure he had everyone's attention. 'You all know your history – our predecessors congregated inside specially built cities and barricaded themselves from the harmful effects. There was recycled water, synth food, and of course, the safe embrace of Corporation.'

The women all nodded. Grace tried some grass and decided it wasn't very tasty.

'About fifty years ago a high ranking official decided it was time to find out what was going on outside, so they sent a team of scientists to these coordinates with orders to report back.' Max shrugged. 'They never returned. The report was logged and archived, and that was that. I found out about it a year ago, and sent a petition in to the Board to try again.'

'And you were successful?' Ruth asked in surprise.

'No, not at first. It took a lot of lobbying and a lot of private funding but we made it. We've been here about six months now.'

'What have you been researching?' Martha said.

'The Gaia Effect, mostly – seeing whether the Earth has managed to adapt and heal itself.'

'The Gaia Effect?' Kira asked intrigued.

'Yes,' Max said, warming to the topic. 'Nature has eventually worked her magic - cleaning the soil, the air and the water. The Earth has tried to rebalance old ecosystems and develop new ones. Some species haven't survived of course, but others have triumphed.' Max swept an arm out across the camp excitedly. 'In some places luscious forests and swelling grasslands cover the ruins of past cities while animals, birds and insects roam free amongst the disappearing debris of man. Plants have recolonised and freshwater lakes and rivers are teeming with fish and other aquatic life.'

As he paused for breath, Dina leant forward to catch his attention.

'Then in a way, moving mankind into self

198

contained city modules did the Earth a favour,' she said. 'Forcing ourselves to figure out how to recycle our waste and water has given the Earth a chance to heal.'

'That's right,' Max said, taking a large swallow of tea.

'What about the other team – did you find anything?' Kira asked.

'No, just the remains of their camp and the results of the seeds they'd planted.'

'Which is why you have apples,' Dina exclaimed as Max grinned at her.

'The other team – what happened?' Martha looked around for some trace of them.

Max shifted, looking a little uncomfortable, and seemed to gather his thoughts before speaking again. 'Expeditions don't always go to plan,' he said. 'Sometimes there are causalities. Anything could've happened to them. The important thing is, we are here now.'

'Why have you survived when the other team didn't?' Kira asked.

'We have access to clean, fresh water - it may not have been available to them,' Max explained. 'There's no radiation here, which means....' He was interrupted by Dina.

'Which means you can grow and plant and eat and drink and live! Outside, Kira. No more cities. No more Corporation!'

'I think I would still like indoor plumbing,' Martha remarked. Dina shushed her.

'Why doesn't everyone know about this place, Ma?' Kira asked.

'It was classified, one of Father's secrets. I do not think he even told the rest of the Board. He was trying to do the right thing Kira. I know he was.'

Martha's eyes brimmed with tears as she fought to hold it together. Max cleared his throat. 'That's right. Mr Hamble was our benefactor and we reported directly to him.' He added then continued more softly. 'We are all terribly sorry for your loss Martha.'

Martha acknowledged him with a nod and wiped her eyes on the back of her hand.

'What happens now?' Kira turned back to Max.

Max puffed out his cheeks. 'I don't know. I'm a bit behind on the sweeps – we've been off campus for a while but we still get access here. I checked this morning and it looks like they're having a city reps meeting to try and diffuse the situation. I'm guessing Camp Eden is still a secret?'

'Yes, my husband – he's a Force Detective – he sent us here for safety, because of the children.'

'Children?' Max asked a little confused, pointing to Grace. 'Don't you mean child?'

Ruth and Martha shared a smile then pointed to their stomachs. Max stared at the women.

'You mean, you two are..'

'Yes, we are,' said Ruth with a smile.

'How? Did they finally come clean then?' Max looked at the two women and seeing them both look confused, he elaborated. 'About the treated water. Corporation I mean.'

'You knew?' Dina demanded.

'It was top level but Hamble briefed me fully. He said that our work was more important than we knew because of the mistakes Corporation had made. I didn't think they would just stop treating the water and tell everyone.'

'They didn't,' Kira said, amused at Max's confusion.

'So, how....how did you.. I mean, I know how, but why...'

Max was getting redder by the second. Kira took pity on him.

'We only just found out about the water supply, us and the rest of the city. That's why we are here. To keep safe. As for how Martha and Ruth got pregnant – I call it divine intervention.'

Max choked on his tea, and after receiving vigorous pats on the back from Dina, he was able to speak again.

'Divine intervention?' he croaked. 'Like God – you actually believe?'

'No, not God. I'm thinking even older,' Kira said, a faint smile on her face. 'It's not something many people remember but you might know about her given your work here – Gaia, the spirit of the Earth.'

Max interrupted excitedly. 'Oh we believe! She's real. We've all seen her.'

The women looked quickly at each other, then stared at Max in disbelief. Grace broke the silence by clambering up to Kira and demanding to be fed. Everyone started talking at once until Kira raised her voice over the top of them.

'Hey – can I please feed my daughter and then Max, you need to tell us more.'

The women gathered up their things and went back to the communal area where the rest of the science team were beginning to gather. Kira went through to the kitchen area, looking around for their supplies. After hunting for a few minutes, she found Grace's bottle and milk and came out of the tent to join the rest. Max made the introductions.

'This is my team – Dr Gina Ayres, flora and fauna and Dr Mitch Guardis, geology and radiation.' He pointed at two, virtually identical sun-kissed people, dressed in the same khaki shorts and top as the rest of the team. 'You've already met Moham, he looks after us.' He gestured to the group of women. 'Everyone, this is Kira Jenkins, Martha Hamble, Dina Grey and Ruth Maddocks. Oh, and not forgetting, little Gracie.'

The group chuckled as they settled themselves on the various cushions. Kira and her friends faced Max and his team.

'It will be easier to show you,' Max said as he turned on the camp's holo recorder.

The women all watched with interest as the video began to play, showing the science team members helping themselves to food. Suddenly Dr Ayres, who was facing outwards, dropped her cup, the others followed her gaze reacting in similar shock - but the holo recorder didn't show yet what they were looking at.

'Wait for it,' Max said, as the recorder panned slowly round. It seemed to take an age, but finally the women could see what the science team had seen. It was a big blue blur. Kira's heart sank in disappointment. A blue blur wasn't evidence. But as she continued to watch, the blur began to glow brighter and brighter until the image of a woman revealed itself. The light faded, and a beautiful blue woman stood before them. Her eyes sparkled like a thousand stars and flowers grew out of her hair which hung down her back, touching the floor. The blue woman was naked, yet covered in shapes which moved and danced across her skin. Kira realised they were animals, and watched delighted as a swarm of bees lifted out of her skin and flew lazily away. Kira glanced over at the others. Dina and Martha were smiling and crying, Ruth looked like she'd seen a ghost. The recording fizzed out.

'She's real,' breathed Kira.

'She came to me in my dreams and told me.... told me... she was sorry.' Dina was sobbing.

Martha could only nod, fighting the vague memories of her attack, memories which threatened to overwhelm her.

'I thought it was the drugs,' Ruth murmured, half to herself. 'I didn't know it was real.'

Max turned the feed off. 'It took a while to find the information in Archives but we ran a full search, and that's when we discovered her name. Like you said Kira - the spirit of the Earth, Gaia.'

'We think she's happy that we came,' broke in Dr Ayres, sounding breathless, as if she still didn't entirely believe it herself.

'We've only seen her the once but it was as if she was saying I know you're here, and it's okay,' Dr Guardis added.

'We have to tell the city,' Ruth declared.

'Are you mad?' Dina exclaimed loudly.

Grace began to cry, and Kira comforted her, while Dina apologised.

Ruth continued. 'I'm serious. So much has happened. The pregnancies, the Anti Corp attacks, Corp lying to everyone. Surely Gaia is a message of hope. Surely everyone deserves to hear that.'

'But how do we prove it?' Kira asked. 'One holo recording, which could have been doctored - no offence - and the dreams of a few random women. It's hardly rock solid evidence.'

'You of all people should know your religious history, Ruth,' Dina added. 'Every time believers of one deity try to sway believers of another, it ends in bloody wars. You can't force faith on people.'

'I'm not talking about forcing faith on people,' Ruth snapped back. 'She's real. We've seen her, the scientists here have seen her, and others deserve to know Gaia is real. They deserve to know that hope exists.'

'I understand what you are trying to say Ruth,' Martha reassured her. 'But the people are not ready. They are still reeling from the lies of Corporation. What they need is solid leadership and transparency. Belief in the spirit of the Earth may follow. But looking after our basic needs has to come first.'

Martha stopped talking, trying to gauge how the others felt.

'You sound like a politician,' Dina said.

'Well, I am a Hamble.'

Chapter Eighteen

C42N: Click through for the latest riot images and live feeds.

MAHA: Our city needs transparent leadership from those who care.

ANON88: What gives MAHA the right to stick her nose in?

ANON6: I agree with MAHA. New governance for the people, by the people.

ANON27: Everyone should be able to do what they want.

MADSR: Now is the time to elect fairly, no more Corp rule.

Jed walked Ben to the meeting room in silence. With so many questions swirling around in his head, Jed didn't know where to start. As they reached the meeting room door, Ben grabbed his cousin's arm and stopped him.

'It's not what you think,' Ben said. 'I'm the only one left. The only one they could find.'

Jed stared at him for a moment before shaking his arm free and opening the door. When the two men entered the room the others were already seated. The Chief gestured to the two empty chairs.

'Take a seat. Both of you.'

Jed sat slowly, unsure why he was being included in the meeting. His cousin looked at the remaining chair suspiciously before also sitting, with a glare for the rest of the room.

'Auto - capture on,' Agent Deveraux said, the holo humming as it began to record. '6th October 2215. This meeting calls forward the remaining high ranking officials in accordance with city breakdown procedure 3.0. In attendance are Chief Tony Minkov from Force. Professor Faisal Kamir , Head of Academy. Surgeon General William Lee from Med Centre. Agent Jack Deveraux, Special Investigations. Representing Anti-Corp is Ben Jenkins, and the public protector, Detective Jed Jenkins.'

Jed looked up in surprise but Deveraux avoided his gaze and licked his lips before continuing.

'Corporation Board Member, Roger Hamble – unable to attend, deceased. Corporation Board Member, Julia Nicks – unable to attend, deceased. Corporation Board Member, Yassin Aswad – unable to attend, deceased. Corporation Board Member, Patrick Basjere – unable to attend, bound by law.'

A glowing panel appeared on the table in front of each man. Silently, they all pressed their hands down upon the panel and a DNA sample was taken confirming their identity.

'Declaration of truth initiated. Please repeat after me.' And Deveraux led the men through the declaration.

'I understand that from this moment on I represent the best interests of City Forty-Two. When questioned I vow to share all information truthfully. As a city representative I will uphold the law in all decision making. I understand that failure to do so will result in the loss of my freedom and rights. I make this declaration of my own free will.'

Once the declaration had been completed, the illuminated panels faded, and Deveraux called up the procedural guidance for a city representative meeting on the large screen at the back of the room.

As per procedural guidance 3.0
All decisions must be made unanimously and in one session. The recording will then be sealed to prevent tampering and made available for public record.

Step One: Identify the threat to the City

Step Two: Facilitate solution
Step Three: Identify those responsible for threat
Step Four: Action containment
Step Five: Update leadership

Each man took his time reading through the expected steps.

'Seems pretty fragging obvious what the threat is.' The Chief was the first to speak.

'Corporation lies,' Ben said.

'Anti-Corp terrorism more like,' the Chief snarled.

'Arguing semantics won't get us anywhere,' Professor Kamir said. 'The threat is clearly the hysterical masses running amok outside. We need immediate crowd pacification with regular info jack updates on the water crisis. Rumour mongoring certainly isn't helping the situation.'

'And you think gassing the populace will?' the Surgeon General asked, incredulous.

'I never said gassing,' Professor Kamir replied. 'But that might be the only course of action available if we can't agree on how to calm the people down.'

'The issue is clean, fresh water, supplied freely without any Corporation involvement,' Jed said, trying to refocus the conversation.

The Chief jabbed his finger into the table. 'Yes - but where are we going to get a free uncontaminated water source from?'

'Aren't people working on the filtering system at Science Dept?' the Surgeon General asked, looking at Agent Deveraux.

'They are,' Deveraux conceded. 'But we have to wait for the levels of radiation to dissipate. Nothing we can do about that.'

'So we need a miracle.' The Surgeon General snorted.

'There's a place, outside the city limits,' Jed said. 'It's called Camp Eden.'

'Camp Eden?' the Professor scoffed. 'Fifty years ago there was an expedition outside, the whole crew died.'

'Another expedition went last year. They are all still alive and well.'

Jed tried to say more but Ben cut across him angrily.

'And how do *you* know that? Another Corporation cover up? Or is this perhaps a Special Investigations top secret hideaway? Replacing one oppressive regime with another.'

'I know because my wife is there,' Jed replied calmly.

'Special Investigations have no involvement with Camp... what do you call it?' Deveraux said, looking flustered as he tapped away furiously on his handheld.

'Camp Eden was financed by Mr Hamble...'

Ben leapt to his feet. 'So it IS a Corporation cover up,' he yelled.

'Will you *stop* interrupting me Ben? For frag sake man, sit down – I sent my wife and child out there.' Jed coloured a little when he realised everyone was staring at him. 'They have some tech there. We should be able to set up a live link, and you can talk to the people on the ground. I've told you everything I know.'

The Chief rubbed his jaw. 'I'll get a tech team in to set up the link. It might take a short while. Let's pause the holo and reconvene in an hour.'

Deveraux pressed some buttons on the holo, putting it on hold, and was the first to stand. 'I need a synth-caf,' he said to no-one in particular, and rushed out of the room.

The others followed at a slower pace, but the Chief gestured for Jed to hang back.

'What about him?' Jed pointed to Ben leaving the room.

'He has a detail, they won't let him go far.' The Chief huffed. 'This is a fragging mess we're in Jenkins. This Camp Whatsaface better not be some rich boy's playground.'

Jed swallowed. He hoped it wasn't as well.

*C42N: City Forty-Two Representatives meet to end crisis.
Sweep your view across.*

*ANON88: Who gave them the power to decide what we
want?*

Forty-five minutes later, a live feed was streaming between
Force and Camp Eden. An extremely brown, slightly
dishevelled, man stood in the main tent with Kira and
Martha off to one side.

'Hi hon. Are you okay? Where's Grace?' Jed spoke
to the screen, ignoring the man for the moment.

'Hi. We're fine, we're all fine. Grace is playing in
the orchard with Dina and Ruth. Jed – this is Dr Max
Carter, he's in charge here.'

The two men nodded at each other.

'Before we begin, Kira, there's something you
should know,' Jed said. He stopped talking as the door
opened to the meeting room and the city representatives
filed back in. Each resumed their seats around the table,
turning so they could all see the video link.

'What's Ben doing there?' Kira whispered to
Martha, who shrugged in response.

Jed stayed standing, and began the introductions.

'Gentlemen, may I introduce Dr Max Carter, head
of the Camp Eden project. Also present are my wife, Kira
Jenkins, and Martha Hamble, who some of you know I
believe.' There were murmured greetings. Jed carried on.
'Max, ladies – this is William Lee Surgeon General of Med
Centre, Head of Academy Professor Faisal Kamir, Agent
Jack Deveraux from Special Investigations, Force Chief
Tony Minkov and you already know Ben.' Jed paused,
shooting a glance at his cousin. 'He's the Anti-Corp
representative.'

Kira gasped while Martha merely looked on. Max

was a little bemused at their reaction but decided to wait and find out what was happening. Jed walked round the table to take his seat.

'How can I help gentlemen?' Max rubbed his hands together nervously.

'You can start by telling us exactly what you're doing out there,' the Professor said, sounding disgruntled. 'And why Academy has no knowledge of this *expedition*, if it can even be classed as such.'

Max grimaced, and ran a hand through his hair. 'Well, you heard of the failed attempt fifty years ago to set up Camp Eden?'

The Professor nodded and gestured for him to get on with it.

'I found out about it, and thought it was fascinating. I spent a year lobbying anyone I could to fund a new expedition. Mr Hamble was the only person of authority who would listen to my bid. Academy officials told me I was wasting my time, so I never got to pitch to you directly.'

'We get a lot of funding bids,' the Professor said. 'There is a process, you know.'

'So Hamble paid you to do what? Watch the grass grow?' the Chief said gruffly.

Max barked a laugh. 'We came to test the air, soil and water for contaminants. And to see if we could discover what had happened to the original expedition members.'

'And?' the Surgeon General leant forward.

'All our testing came back negative.'

There was a collective sigh of disappointment in the room.

'No, no – negative for contaminants. The radiation levels have gone, we have a fresh water supply here. Mother Nature has begun to heal herself.'

'Begun?' asked Ben, frowning.

'We've been scouting further afield and the bombing sites are still arid. A nearby lake is devoid of life

209

but with a little human engineering we could help things along. We've been working on a new way of..'

'Yes, yes. All very interesting I'm sure,' the Professor interrupted. 'The real question is how do we get your fresh water to the city? If indeed it is clear of contaminants.'

'We'd need to corroborate your findings,' the Surgeon General agreed. 'Can you send some samples to us for verification?'

'We can bring them,' Kira said. 'That is, if it's safe for us to come home?'

Jed tried to sound more confident then he felt. 'I'm working on it.'

Kira looked upset. There was a pause in the discussion as everyone in the meeting room tried to think of a suitable solution for transporting the water into the city. Ben cleared his throat. 'I might have a way we can get the water to the city.'

The others looked at him in surprise.

'Anti-Corp uses the ancient sewer system sometimes - to get in and out of the city undetected. With a little hi-tech investment, the tunnel walls could be resealed and water flow guided to the abandoned water works. Which would also need servicing but they should still work.'

'We'd need some serious man power,' Jed said, looking at his boss. 'And I think I know where we can get that from.'

The Chief rubbed his hands together. 'I like your thinking Jenkins.'

'Care to explain?' Deveraux asked.

'We round up everyone involved in the rioting, and split them into work teams,' Jed said. 'Force operatives can oversee.'

Ben slapped his hands on the table. 'You want to make the people pay for Corporation's cock up? It should be corpers who fix this, not the man on the street.'

'We all need to work together to fix this, Ben.

Water shortage is a serious problem – take your head out of your ass and grow up. It's about time the people of City Forty-Two did something for themselves.'

Jed was breathing hard. He glanced at his wife on the video screen and she gave him a discrete thumbs up. His face twitched as he tried not to grin, and muttered his apology to the Chief.

'I agree,' the Surgeon General said, surprising himself for speaking up. He carried on quickly. 'We face a hole in governance. Rather than allowing miscreants to ruin our city further, we must all come together.'

The Professor was nodding. 'A new, shared governance. Focused on the problems at hand. It is the only way.'

Martha had been listening to the discussion with interest. She waved her hand to get the room's attention. 'Are we going to open the city walls then?'

'I don't see how else we can solve the water issue, unless you have another idea?' Jed said.

'I think it sounds like the right thing to do,' Martha said. 'But I'm just wondering whether this sudden freedom might be too much - for certain people ....'

'You mean Anti-Corp radicals running off?' Ben said, thrusting his chin defiantly at the screen. 'Freedom of choice is freedom of choice,' he continued. 'You can't be seriously considering the continuation of Corporation's restrictive regime? We are on the brink of individual personal freedom here.'

'I am not suggesting anything,' Martha said. 'I just think that we need to be careful. We don't want to destroy the healing that has already happened out here by tramping about all over the place.'

Kira chimed in. 'We have to respect the balance of nature and man working together.'

The men in the room digested the women's words.

'So what's your grand plan then my dear?' the Professor asked Martha.

'I think new governance should be voted for by the

public, with representatives from each echelon of our society. The best way to move forward should be discussed openly, with the public given the opportunity to have their say. This is an opportunity for City Forty-Two to create a new way of life, interacting with the environment around us for the benefit of man and nature. We could then roll out the concept to other cities.'

Agent Deveraux leant back in his chair. 'Miss Hamble has a valid point. This city is the only one we know of free from Corporation. Other cities are more than likely firmly pro-Corp, pro-Tech and probably still consuming treated water.'

'Won't the sweeps have gotten through to them?' Kira asked.

'Ha!' Ben barked. 'The sweeps are the biggest joke of all. They are held within a self contained data unit, unhackable – believe me, we've tried.'

Jed and the Chief looked at Ben who held his hands up in mock surrender.

'It's true,' Deveraux agreed. 'Whoever designed the sweeps program created a self contained media platform. We believe each city has one but they are not linked and efforts to link them so far have proved ineffective.'

'Even more reason for us to get it right the first time,' Martha declared. 'Then we can save the rest of the world.'

'You can't be serious?' Ben asked, looking around at the room at the resolute faces staring back at him. 'You honestly believe that we can affect that much change?'

'And you're the representative that claims to be fighting against the machine?' Kira said flatly.

'Hey, I'm all in. If you think we can do this.'

'We're happy to liaise at this end with our findings,' offered Max.

The Chief and Agent Deveraux glanced at each other, before they both nodded. Jed looked at the Surgeon General and the Professor. Each man looked slightly stunned but both nodded in agreement.

Deveraux spoke with authority into the holo again. 'Let the record show Steps One and Two have been actioned.' He paused the holo. 'I suggest we regroup after lunch?'

The other men agreed, and filed out of the meeting room, leaving Jed standing in front of the video screen. Max gave a wave and left the tent.

'Can we come home now?' Kira asked.

'Soon my love. Soon,' Jed said. 'Kiss Gracie for me.'

Jed waved goodbye to his wife and Martha before ending the link, then sat down heavily in an empty chair.

FORCE: We urge citizens to stay at home and avoid areas of violent activity.

C42N: Rioting continues across the city. Sweep your experience, stay safe.

Jed was sat twirling his Force ID in his hands when the others returned from lunch, and the meeting resumed.

'Welcome back Gentlemen,' Deveraux said, turning on the holo. 'Our next step is to identify and neutralise the culprits responsible for this mess.'

'I believe Force already took care of that,' Jed said.

Ben looked at his cousin, but it was the Chief who spoke.

'It's true that Detective Barnes took it upon himself to eliminate the high ranking members of Anti-Corp.' The Chief spared a sympathetic glance for Jed, who was looking down at the table in front of him. 'Detective Barnes was mortally wounded and declined medical attention. He has been dishonourably discharged from Force, and condolences have been sent out to the families of those murdered.'

Jed's hand tightened on the cup of synth-caf in front of him but he refrained from speaking or looking up at the others.

'Is there anyone else significant left that we should be aware of?' Deveraux asked Ben, who shifted in his chair.

'Not that I'm aware of. You have to understand, I didn't stand very high in the organisation. I was way below Bobby - Roberto Travelli. And he was only in charge of recruiting.'

'What about the people responsible for the bombing of Corp Tech?' the Surgeon General asked.

Jed cleared his throat, and pushed his chair back from the table. He leaned forward, his head down, hands clasped together. Ben watched him warily for a moment.

'That was a....splinter cell if you like, the 42nd Army. Radicals who felt we didn't do enough.' Ben paused, fidgeting in his chair before continuing. 'You have to understand Anti-Corp was formed as a student body twenty years ago. It has its roots in Academy, and it looks to the student ranks for new members. We aren't – and we never have been - a terrorist organisation. Frag, I didn't even know about that plan.'

Ben scrubbed a hand through his hair and shot another look at Jed.

'And the culprits responsible for killing the remaining Board members?' the Surgeon General asked, a touch of worry in his voice.

Deveraux responded a little too smoothly.

'Hamble was the unfortunate victim of an angry mob. The others were driven to their deaths by staff. Pity.'

Jed finally looked up from the table, and glared at the agent.

'Hamble's killers are in custody. The drivers are being investigated to make sure they acted alone and weren't paid off by someone in a position of power.'

The two men glared at each other.

'I want a complete list of Anti-Corp members on my desk first thing in the morning,' the Chief said, jabbing his finger at Ben. 'You can work with intelligence to provide any gaps in contact information. Everyone will be tagged and charged with a work detail.'

'What about the unruly members of the public out there?' the Professor asked.

'Everyone involved in destruction of property and disturbance of the peace will also be tagged and given a work detail accordingly,' Jed explained.

'So you're just going to give everyone a criminal record?' Ben asked in disbelief.

'No. We are going to make them work off their debt to the sensible members of society who stayed at home and refused to descend into madness.'

'Sounds like mass control if you ask me.'

'I don't remember asking your opinion.'

The cousins scowled at each other, barely flinching when the Chief slammed his fist on the desk.

'That's enough,' he bellowed. 'What's done is done. We need bodies to sort out the water crisis – this way we get bodies. Those idiots stupid enough to get themselves involved in public unrest will work off their debts, and if they don't like it they can rot in a containment cell. Now,' he said, turning his attention to Deveraux. 'What's left?'

'We need to propose interim governance. A new leadership.'

'Yes,' said the Professor. 'We can't carry on like this indefinitely.'

'I don't have time to deal with bureaucratic nonsense,' the Surgeon General said heatedly. 'I have a medical centre to run and real people to help.' He began stuttering as everyone turned to stare at him. 'I mean..not that.. it's very...'

'We know what you mean,' Jed said.

The Surgeon General smiled gratefully at Jed's rescue.

'What about a senior official from Special Investigations?' Deveraux suggested mildly.

'I think anyone with an institutional background will be unpopular with the people,' Professor Kamir countered. 'Perhaps an academic?'

'What about a member of the public voted for by the rest?' the Chief proposed. 'That way they would have the city behind them.'

'But no real idea of what to do,' Ben muttered.

'I would like to put someone forward as an interim governor,' Jed said. 'Martha Hamble.'

There were some loud mutterings from around the table. 'Hamble!' 'A woman?' 'Is he mad?' 'I say, shouldn't it be someone more distinguished?'

'Let me finish.' Jed had to shout over them. 'She has a unique viewpoint on the situation. Being the daughter of the Marketing Director of the Corporation Board in City Forty-Two, she has links with both hard line Corpers and those at the upper end of society. She is a woman affected by the pregnancy anomaly, so has the sympathy and genuine interest of the general public. She has a scientific background, so the people will trust her explanation of the water crisis and the proposed solution.'

'She certainly understands politics,' the Professor mused. 'Top of her class.'

'I have no objections,' the Surgeon General said.

Deveraux looked hard at Jed, before nodding and agreeing, followed swiftly by Ben. The Chief stroked his upper lip thoughtfully, and added his approval.

'Let the record state that Martha Hamble will be offered the position of interim Governor on her return,' Deveraux announced. 'She will be assisted by those city representatives here present, as and when appropriate.'

Deveraux looked round the room for any objections before stopping the recording and officially sealing the file. 'I believe we are done here gentlemen. Thank you for your input.'

Deveraux stood, nodded to the others and shook hands with the Chief before leaving. Once Deveraux had left, most of the men hurried back to their own personal empires – full of self importance and the desire to tell others what had happened here today. Ben was escorted to Force Intelligence by his minders. Only Jed and the Chief

216

remained. A harassed looking Force operative popped his head in the room.

'Sir? You asked for a status report on the riots.'

The Chief gestured for the operative to continue.

'It's over. Tagging the rioters stopped the escalation and we've got positive idents via Drone TV for all those involved.'

'Thank you Sergeant. That will be all.' The Chief turned to look at Jed. 'You holding up Jenkins?'

'Yes Sir.'

'Long road ahead of us.'

'Sir?'

The Chief looked at his weary detective, and held out a hand. As Jed took it in his own, the Chief shook it firmly. 'Till tomorrow Detective.'

Chapter Nineteen

A bee flew into the window, bumbling its way across the pane, trying to find a way out. Its buzzing grew ever more frantic. Jed watched as it bounced off the pane, again and again and again. Finally, he walked over to the window and opened it. The bee buzzed once round his head, and was gone.

The vidcom link chimed, it was Camp Eden. Jed accepted the link and waved a greeting to his wife.

'Oh Jed, are you okay? You look tired.'

'I'm fine,' Jed replied, and he flopped into an empty chair.

'How did the meeting go?'

Jed puffed out his cheeks, and nodded.

'That good, huh?'

'I'm sending out a unit to come pick you up, they should be there first thing in the morning.'

'Hang on, aren't you going to tell me what happened?'

'I'll get the file sent over to you. Martha needs to watch it. We'll have a sit down about it tomorrow when you get back.'

Kira sniffed as Jed paused, and looked down at his hands for a moment. 'I miss you,' he said.

'I miss you too.'

They said their goodbyes and Kira watched the screen dwindle to blackness. Martha poked her head into the tent.

'Is everything alright?'

'I don't know. Jed's sending over the file from the

rest of the meeting – he says you have to watch it.'

Martha came through into the tent. 'Me?'

Kira nodded. 'They're coming to pick us up tomorrow,' she said. 'I'd better tell the others.'

Martha watched her friend walk out of the tent, leaving her alone. Her reverie was broken by an incoming message on the com system. It was addressed to M Hamble. She pulled up a chair and began to download the file.

SIF: Interim Governor Martha Hamble appointed. City Representative's Meeting available for download.

FORCE: All citizens tagged in the recent riots will be given work duty.

ANON88: Fight the fascists! Refuse to be tagged. Blame the Corpers.

C42N: Hamble proves a popular choice but will she solve the water crisis?

The sun had set by the time Martha had finished listening to the meeting. She felt dazed as she walked out into the communal area where everyone had gathered for the evening meal. Dina beckoned her over.

'Hey Ma, come here and try some of this.'

Martha sat down, hugging her knees, refusing the proffered food.

'Are you okay?' Dina asked.

The group quietened to listen to Martha but she shook her head, struggling to find the right words. Finally, she spoke.

'The city representatives have met and decided on a course of action regarding the water issue.'

'Well that's good isn't it?' Max queried.

'They are tagging everyone involved in the riots and putting them to work duty.'

219

Ruth scowled at Martha from across the camp fire. 'Work duty? What are we – some kind of fascist state?'

Martha ignored her. 'The workers will clean and seal the old sewer system so the natural water supply can be brought into the city.'

'Solving the problem of the affected water,' Dina said in a pleased voice.

The others made congratulatory noises.

'That is not all,' Martha said, still holding her knees tight and keeping her eyes down.

'Well,' Ruth demanded. 'Spit it out.'

'They have chosen an interim Governor.'

'What poor fool has been roped into that?' Kira asked.

'Me,' Martha said, finally looking up.

There was a stunned silence as everyone processed the information. Ruth was the first to speak. She leant over to pat Martha on the knee. 'It's about time those in charge used their brains instead of their wallets,' she said.

'Oh wow Ma,' Dina's voice squeaked. 'This is so exciting. You'll be in charge of everything!'

'I'm so pleased for you Ma.' Kira squeezed Martha's arm and then looked horrified as tears began to run down Martha's face. 'Oh honey, what's wrong?'

'I can't be in charge, can I?' Martha was half sobbing the words. 'I don't have the faintest idea of what to do. I work with plants, not people.'

'It doesn't matter,' Ruth said brusquely. 'You care about what happens to the city, to the people. You have a good head on those shoulders and I'm sure you'll have advisers.'

'But what if I can't do it?'

'We believe in you,' Kira said.

The Camp Eden scientists who had been listening to the conversation added their encouragement.

'I, for one, think you'll make a great leader,' Max said. 'Listening to you the other night talking about putting the needs of the people first - you can't go far wrong thinking like that.'

Martha looked around the circle and saw the approval on everyone's face. She wiped her eyes dry and lifted her chin a little. 'I will do it. At least, I will try. For the city.' Martha looked down at her tummy. 'For my baby. And for my Father.'

'Hear, hear,' toasted the others, before falling back into their individual conversations, leaving the women to themselves.

'Will you be there to help me?' Martha asked her friends.

'Of course we will,' Kira said.

'Actually.' Dina looked sheepish. 'I've been speaking with Max, about staying here. The work they do is fascinating. There's nothing waiting for me in the city. If it's alright with you guys?'

Kira looked a little surprised, then noticed Max watching from across the fire. Realising Kira was looking at him, he turned quickly, knocking over his drink and cursing to himself.

'No, we understand,' Kira said, looking back at Dina.

Martha and Ruth echoed their acceptance, and the group fell silent for a moment.

'What about me?' Ruth asked. 'Where do I fit in?'

'With us silly,' Kira replied, but it was Martha who Ruth was asking.

'I have an idea,' Martha said. 'You would be a wonderful advisor for the interim Governor.'

'Are you sure?'

'I am.'

'This calls for another toast,' Kira said, and refilled everyone's cups. 'To us.'

'To us!'

MAHA: Proud to be chosen to lead City Forty-Two forward.
Tackling the water supply will be my first task.

C42N: Anon88 has been bound by law for inciting aggressive behaviour.

Jed watched the scenery roll past him on his way to Camp Eden. Here and there flashes of green interrupted the tangle of abandoned skimmers and ramshackle buildings. Nature was slowly creeping back but there were still massive swathes of burnt, dead land. Harsh reminders of what had come before.

Jed was looking forward to seeing his wife and baby. Although it had only been a few days since he'd seen them, it felt like weeks. The sweeps had announced the outcome of the City Rep meeting and their plan for the immediate future, which had been received well by the public. Everyone involved in the riots had been tagged for work duty, and there had even been some additional volunteers to help with the clean up of the city. The skimmer slowed down as Camp Eden came into sight.

Kira shifted from leg to leg impatiently. She wanted to see Jed, and she wanted to go home. 'Over here,' she called, waving. 'I didn't know you were coming as well.'

Jed beamed at her as he hurried over, scooping her up for a hug. 'I missed you,' he said, kissing her. 'Where's Grace?'

'It's okay, she's inside sleeping. I didn't want to wake her, she looked so peaceful.'

Jed kissed his wife again, feeling both relieved his daughter was in such good hands, and a little disappointed at not seeing her straight away.

'Are you ready to go?' Jed asked.

'Almost. Do we have to rush off now?'

Jed didn't answer, instead he checked his wristplant.

'Is Martha nearby?'

'Yeah, come through. Meet everyone.' Kira took her husband's hand and pulled him after her into the camp complex.

Jed looked around with interest. There were plants everywhere, and insects hummed in the air. He could just make out Dina, and the scientist they'd spoken to on the vid-link, over in the far corner of the camp. Kira was chatting away, telling Jed about this and that, but he was only half listening. Martha sat in the communal area, hands wrapped round a cup, looking off into the distance.

'Martha,' Kira called out.

She turned and waved at the approaching couple.

'Hi Martha. You got the file?' Jed asked.

'Yes.'

'And? Do you accept the post?' Jed held his breath in anticipation.

'I do. But I have a few stipulations.'

Jed's breath whooshed out in relief. He sat down next to her. Kira followed.

'I'm sure whatever they are it will be fine,' Jed said. 'I have to tell you some things first.'

Ruth came out of the sleeping quarters, and seeing the others in the communal area hurried over to join them. Jed smiled a greeting, as Ruth sat down.

'Well,' Martha said. 'This is my first requirement. Ruth will be my personal assistant.'

Jed looked at the two women, and then nodded. 'Makes sense. You'll have other members of the city to guide you as well.'

'Will that be the men I saw in the meeting?' Martha asked.

'I expect so, details haven't been finalised but I'll be part of that guiding team as well.'

Kira congratulated Jed softly, and he continued. 'There will be a medical rep and an academic rep, as well as someone from Special Investigations.'

'Sounds like you've got almost all bases covered,' Ruth said. 'What about a representative of the populace?'

'Public vote,' Jed replied. 'It's one of the first things

we need to organise when we get back to the city.'

'What are the others?' Martha asked.

'A Governor's parade, to begin with.'

'A parade?' Martha gasped, her hand over her mouth.

'Is that a good idea?' Kira asked.

'It's procedure. New governor – city gets a parade. That's why we have to leave...' Jed checked his wristplant, '...five minutes ago.' He got up quickly. 'Come on ladies, let's get going. We can talk about it in the skimmer.'

There was a moment of stunned silence before the three women slowly got up. A few minutes later and the camp was bustling. Bags were loaded into the skimmer, and grateful farewells were being made between the women and the scientists.

Jed found himself face to face with Dina. 'You're staying then.'

'Yes,' Dina looked down at the floor.

Jed put his finger under her chin and lifted her head. 'You can come back anytime, Dina,' he said. 'You'll always have a home with us. You know that, don't you?'

Dina flung herself at Jed, and hugged him tightly. Jed patted her on the back and looked at Kira for some help but she just grinned at him. Dina broke away and kissed him on the cheek, then went to hug Kira and say goodbye to Grace.

Finally everyone was in the skimmer, calling goodbye, and promising to stay in touch. They watched Camp Eden dwindle in the distance as the skimmer picked up speed. There was a sudden flash in the brush nearby and a flock of birds swooped into the sky following the skimmer, dancing intricate patterns in the air. Kira watched them, taking it as a good sign.

'What happens when we get back to the city?' Martha asked.

'We have another skimmer waiting for you, with armed guards, for your safety,' Jed replied.

Kira looked at her husband in alarm. 'Is that necessary?'

'I don't think we should take any chances,' Jed said. 'We will follow in this skimmer. It's armoured too, so everyone will be safe.' Jed glanced at Grace who was trying her hardest to eat the strap holding her in place in the travel cube. 'There will be a tour of the city. Sweeps went out this morning informing everyone of the route, and encouraging people to attend.'

'And what am I supposed to do?' Martha said, sounding panicked.

Jed tried to sound encouraging. 'Smile. Wave. Be Martha Hamble.'

Kira took Martha's hand and squeezed it. 'You'll do fine Ma. We'll be right behind you.'

C42N: Join us in meeting our new Governor as she returns to City Forty-Two.
Download the route and pick your spot. This is not a virtual experience.

The rest of the journey was spent in silence as each of them contemplated the changes that lay ahead. In no time at all, they arrived at the city walls. Martha hugged Kira and Ruth, then got out of the skimmer and into the bigger, grander, open topped version that awaited her.

'Back in a parse,' Jed said to Kira, and went over to the other skimmer to greet the security team. 'Everyone know what they're doing?'

'Yes Sir. The route is pre-programmed. We'll activate the shield once Miss Hamble is settled, and you'll have direct comm link.'

'Good. Carry on.'

Jed gave Martha a small nod of encouragement and rejoined the others.

The two skimmers entered the city. No-one lived on the city outskirts - this close to the wall the streets were empty. Martha shifted in her seat feeling vulnerable and exposed. No-one spoke. She reached out to touch the personal shield that extended two feet around her, reassuring herself that it existed.

'Alright Ma?'

Jed's voice sounded tinny, yet comforting.

Martha swallowed and managed to croak a yes.

As they rounded the corner it seemed to Martha that every single person in City Forty-Two had come out to line the main street. They were all standing silently, watching her skimmer move closer. Someone, somewhere, began to clap. The sound echoed loudly. Then it was joined by another. And another. And another. The crowd began chanting.

'Hamble. Hamble. Hamble.'

Martha raised a hand tentatively and waved. There was an explosion of noise as the people began cheering and shouting and waving. Martha waved more confidently and began smiling at the people, her people. Streamers flew through the air and children sat on shoulders waving enthusiastically. As if in response to the crowd, the baby moved in her stomach and Martha felt it kick for the first time. Tears of happiness began to stream down her face.

This was a new beginning.

A new beginning for them all.

I'd like to say thank you to my husband Kevin, to my Pen to Print mentor and friend Ian Ayris and to my dedicated readers/editors Donna Tyrell, Ashvin Mathora and Taron Wade for all their support and encouragement throughout this process.

I'd also like to thank Lena Smith and the team at Barking & Dagenham Library Service for all their hard work in making this whole project possible.

Check my website for latest news and other projects I'm working on:
www.cbvisions.weebly.com

Follow me on Twitter: @grasshopper2407
Like me on Facebook: www.facebook.com/busswriter/

Read my blog: www.butidontlikesalad.blogspot.com

Lightning Source UK Ltd.
Milton Keynes UK
UKOW04f2206020917
308451UK00001B/11/P